GALAXYS EDGE

STRYKER'S
WAR

ORDER OF THE CENTURION

C000285558

JOSH HAYES WITH
ANSPACH + COLE

Galaxy's Edge: STRYKER'S WAR
by Galaxy's Edge, LLC

Edited by Ellen Campbell
Published by Galaxy's Edge Press

Cover Art: Fabian Saravia
Cover Design: Beaulistic Book Services

Website: InTheLegion.com
Facebook: facebook.com/atgalaxysedge
Newsletter (get a free short story): InTheLegion.com

"The Order of the Centurion is the highest award that can be bestowed upon an individual serving in, or with, the Legion. When such an individual displays exceptional valor in action against an enemy force, and uncommon loyalty and devotion to the Legion and its legionnaires, refusing to abandon post, mission, or brothers, even unto death, the Legion dutifully recognizes such courage with this award."

98.4% of all citations are awarded posthumously.

Dear Mom and Dad,
If you're reading this, I'm not coming home.

PROLOGUE

Corporal Garo Lankin ducked as blaster bolts chewed holes out of the duracrete wall above him. Little fragments plinked off his helmet as he pushed his back against the wall and pulled the empty charge pack from his N-4.

A blast from a 74K blaster cannon slammed into the building in front of him, tearing a fist-sized hole in the duracrete. Lankin scrambled away from the falling debris, bumping into LS-34, Corporal Burga. They rolled into the dirt, coming up on their knees.

"Hey, watch it, Lankin!"

Lankin ignored him, turning to search their line for LS-12, Sergeant Talon. The squad's leader was at the far end, laying down an impressive amount of fire with an N-60. Somewhere in the back of his mind, Lankin knew that if Sarge had the 60, one of the platoon's four heavy gunners had gone down, and he didn't want to think about who that might be.

"Stryker-17 to Stryker-10," LS-15, Corporal Pax said over the squad's L-comm channel, using Talon's call sign.

As squad leader for 1st Squad, the sergeant's designation was Stryker-10 and his subordinates designated

1

11 through 19. 2nd Squad's team leader, Sergeant Jarel, was designated Stryker-20 and his subordinates were 21 through 29.

"Go Seventeen," the sergeant said, blasts from his 60 echoing through his transmission.

"If we don't get moving, Sarge, these kelhorned apes are going to pin us down and we won't have anywhere to go!"

"I'm aware of that..." He let off a burst from the 60.

Dat-dat-dat-dat-dat-dat!

"...and I'm working on getting..."

Dat-dat-dat-dat-dat-dat!

"...us out of here!"

The platoon battle channel buzzed. "Stryker-21 to Command, we're taking fire from the ridge in Grid-12-Charlie, request suppressive fire, over!"

Captain Kato, commanding officer of Stryker Company, 71st Legion, answered. "Command to Stryker-21, acknowledged. We're all taking fire, leej. Keep your head down, we're setting up artillery as we speak."

Lankin caught a glimpse of Corporal Eriston, LS-37, lying face down in the dirt, blood pooling under his body. His stomach turned at the sight of his friend. He clenched his teeth, working his jaw muscles in frustration. With Eriston down, their casualties had reached six already.

And the situation was only going to get worse.

Larkin tore his gaze away from his friend and made a silent vow. *I'll make them pay.*

The Tarax had attacked just as the platoon had reached the outskirts of the city, pinning them down in a row of one and two-story, red or brown brick houses. The blue-skinned mercenaries had kidnapped a traveling senator, en route to negotiate a trade deal with a neighboring system, and were trying to ransom him. Not the best idea in the galaxy to begin with, but what complicated their prospects even further was the Legion cruiser *Vendetta*, whose company of legionnaires just happened to be conducting training in the very same system.

From his position behind the village's protective wall, Lankin couldn't see the four-eyed, big-headed aliens, but he knew they were out there. They'd pinned his squad down in a hilltop sculpture garden featuring a collection of statues arrayed around a fountain. At any other time, the view might have been beautiful; now the only thing Lankin could see was a distinct lack of cover.

Other Tarax fire teams had taken up positions atop the buildings across the square, raining down almost constant fire on the legionnaires' position for what felt like hours, though the mission clock in Lankin's HUD told him they'd only been engaged for fifteen minutes.

We're not going to last another five if we stay here.

Lankin scanned the row of brick huts situated along the south side of the square, running between his squad and the line of buildings occupied by the enemy. As far as he could tell, the Tarax hadn't secured any fighting positions among the huts. If he could find a good vantage point...

Keeping his head down, Lankin worked his way down the squad's line, stopping beside Sergeant Talon. Blaster bolts raked the top of the brick wall, spewing fragments over the legionnaires. Talon ducked, pressing his back against the wall as Lankin took a knee beside him.

"Sarge," Lankin said. "I got an idea."

"What do you got, Garo?"

"If I can make it to those huts to the south, I might be able to flank them." Lankin pointed with a bladed hand.

"This another bid for the Gauntlet?"

Lankin shook his head. "Just tired of being a fish in a barrel, Sarge."

Talon looked over his shoulder. "Even if you make it over there, you'll never be able to make those shots."

"I can make the shots," Lankin said, sounding more confident than he felt. "If I can take out that 74 emplacement, it might give us enough time to maneuver out of this kill box we're in. I just need a little bit of suppressive fire and maybe a can of smoke."

"I knew you were stupid, Garo. Are you crazy, too?"

"I think maybe a little bit of both."

The sergeant paused, seeming to consider Lankin's request. A moment later Lankin heard Talon's voice over the company channel.

"Stryker-1, Stryker-10, we might have a way to flank the enemy to our west. Lankin will be moving to the south, repeat, Stryker elements will be advancing along the south side of the square. How copy?"

"I copy, Sergeant. Friendlies to the south." Captain Kato relayed the information to the rest of the company, ensuring everyone had the information. With the new friend-or-foe targeting system on the helmet's HUD, friendly fire wasn't much of an issue, but completely trusting Republic military equipment—even legionnaire equipment—was a recipe for disaster. Lack of battlefield communication had led to more defeats throughout history than anything else, especially in the heat of intense blaster fire.

Sergeant Talon readied his men. "Stryker company, on my command, I want suppressive fire on the buildings to the west, copy?"

As the chorus of acknowledgements came in, Lankin got to his feet, ready to spring into action.

Talon pulled a smoker from his chest harness and popped the safety. "You ready?"

Lankin nodded. "Let's do this."

"Smoke out!" Talon tossed the smoker over the wall, lifted the N-60 into position, and went back to work. "Covering fire!"

Lankin took several breaths, trying to steady his nerves. The smoke curled into the air, and he sprinted forward, leaving the cover of the wall behind. He was halfway to the huts when pockets of earth and grass erupted, blaster fire tearing the ground behind him. He cursed and pushed himself harder.

As he neared the first building, he jumped into the air, diving to cover as fire from the 74 converged on his position. He landed hard, somersaulting forward, coming to a stop on his chest. Blaster fire tore into the corner of the building, sending chunks of red brick and dust into the air.

Lankin got to his feet and tongued his L-comm. "I made it."

"Oba, you're a crazy scat-brained idiot, do you know that?" Talon told him.

"I've been told that, yes."

Lankin dusted himself off and pulled the butt of his N-4 into his shoulder. He peered around the edge of the building, scanning the alley behind the row of huts. The best vantage point would be the second to last house in the row. From there he'd have a superior line of fire to the Tarax gun emplacements. In theory.

Starting down the alley, his N-4 up, he scanned for threats. He made his way around trash bins, most of which hadn't been emptied for quite some time, their contents spilling out onto the ground. He passed what was left of a service bot, its silver frame shattered. Power cables strung between the buildings sagged, looking like they hadn't been serviced in years.

A high-pitched whistle cut through the air, followed by the smoke trail of incoming artillery fire. A second later a large boom ripped its way across the battlefield. The ground shook and the blast wave rattled the surrounding buildings.

As the dust settled, movement from a second-floor window caught his attention. He stopped short, putting his back against a brick wall and bringing his rifle around on target. Through his sights, Lankin saw a Tarax woman closing her shutters. She froze, four round eyes locked on Lankin's weapon. Her long red hair contrasted sharply against her blue skin, but concealed the prominent bulge at the back of her skull.

"Stay inside," Lankin told her, not bothering to switch on his helmet's speaker, waving a hand at the woman. She couldn't hear him, and even if she had, Lankin wasn't positive she'd have understood him. Finding a Tarax who spoke Standard was hit or miss. But she pulled the shutters closed, disappearing inside the hut.

You've got to be kidding me, Lankin thought, keying his L-comm. "LS-16 to all leej units, be advised there *are* civilians in the engagement area. Repeat, Tarax civvies in the engagement area."

Captain Kato's icon flashed on Lankin's HUD. "LS-16, are you positive about that?"

"Positive," Lankin said, eyeing the closed window. "At least one Tarax female, second floor of a house in this row to the south."

"Maybe you just didn't see the blaster rifle?" suggested Sergeant Talon.

"Possible, Sergeant. But she's a hell of an actor if she's a combatant."

Lankin pictured Captain Kato cursing the intelligence people who'd told them "with one hundred percent certainty" that the village had been evacuated of all civilians.

Kato's voice came through the L-comm a second later. "Stryker Command to all Stryker units, be advised, there are civvy targets present in your AO, check your fire."

Military intelligence, Lankin thought, shaking his head. *Riiiight.*

He checked the closed window again, making sure she really wasn't just trying to lull him into becoming a target, but it remained fastened. Lankin pushed on. He reached the rear entrance of the house he wanted and pressed himself against the wall, listening. Even with his external pickups on, he couldn't hear anything over the constant barrage of blaster fire coming from the east. Which, he decided, would probably work in his favor. If it was too loud for him, it was surely too loud for any Tarax waiting inside.

"Moving inside," Lankin reported in through his L-comm, keeping Sergeant Talon informed of his progress.

"Copy."

The door was locked, but a hard kick snapped the wood from its hinges, sending it tumbling inside. Lankin charged in, sweeping his N-4 across the small living space. One room—a table and chairs to his right and a small cooking space on the other side of that. He crossed to a set of stairs partially hidden behind a brick wall.

Lankin rounded the wall and barely caught a flash of movement before something slammed into him. The legionnaire went down hard, landing on his back, helmet smacking against the tile floor. The N-4 flew from his grip, clattering to the tiles.

On instinct, Lankin scrambled back, away from the hooded figure that had knocked him over.

"*Tam booya see nassa!*" his attacker screamed.

He rolled to his hands and knees, reaching toward his rifle, then aimed a powerful backward kick into the Taraxian. The alien grunted, stumbling back, regained his footing and charged again. Lankin made it to his feet just as the Taraxian reached him, screaming and throwing wild punches, all four eyes wide with rage. Lankin let his armored forearms and sides absorb the blows. He waited for an opportune swing and used the shrieking Taraxian's momentum against him, tossing him aside.

The alien crashed through the table, snapping the old wood. Picking himself up again, the blue warrior drew a long, curved blade from his black robes. Lankin drew his pistol and fired twice. The shots slammed into the alien's chest, dropping him back into the ruined table.

"Idiot," Lankin said, holstering his pistol and retrieving his rifle.

He pushed up to the second floor, finding several cots and trunks full of clothes, but no other hostiles. Lankin kept his distance from the windows looking out over the town square, staying in the back of the room where a ladder led to a hinged panel in the ceiling.

"Building clear. Heading to the roof."

"Copy, LS-16. We do not see anything on your roof, but there's a low wall obscuring vision. Proceed with caution."

"Copy."

He slung his N-4 over his shoulder and climbed up one-handed, keeping his pistol ready. He let his helmet hit the panel, and then slowly pushed up a few inches. Sunlight spilled into the space—his HUD darkened almost instantly to protect his eyes from the sudden change from dark to light. Lankin quickly scanned the roof, relying more on his eyes than the bucket's passive bioscan sensors to tell him if anyone else was on the roof with him.

He was alone. A thigh-high retaining wall bordered the roof, blocking his view of the surrounding buildings, but also providing some cover from enemy fire teams. He pulled himself through the hatch, slithered across the roof, and nestled against a wall. He craned his head back, looking over the edge of the wall, searching for his targets.

Ten brick houses—most two or three stories tall—made up the northern edge of the square, eighty meters to Lankin's right. Two Tarax fire teams hunkered down on the last two houses, firing on his fellow legionnaires. His bucket's computer put the distance to the nearest three-man team, working a crew-served 74K blaster, at one hundred seventeen meters.

Lankin lined up the shot and fired. His first bolt slammed into the gunner, a short, stocky Tarax whose lips were curled into a snarl as he squeezed the dual butterfly triggers on the weapon. His blue head snapped back and the long-barreled blaster swung up as the alien fell, firing wildly into the air. The two others instinctively dropped to the roof, not realizing the shot hadn't come from the ground or that Lankin still had eyes on them.

Sergeant Talon spoke softly to Lankin over the comm. "Nice shot, Garo."

He grunted an acknowledgement and drew a bead on one of the prone Tarax. It was shouting warnings—drawing the attention of the fire team on the next building. Lankin shot both and turned his attention to the second building.

"Rooftop one clear," he reported, his tone calm and matter of fact.

"Copy. Nice work."

Four Tarax scattered for cover. Two ducked behind a large condenser unit, another scrambled to a hatch and disappeared inside the building, and the last cowered behind a small dish antenna. It was clear that this crew had figured out that the incoming fire was from the surrounding roofs.

Lankin's first shot took out the Tarax behind the antenna dish, who was busily searching in the wrong direction. The blaster bolt knocked him forward—sending him stumbling over the retaining wall.

The two behind the condenser spotted Lankin and sent a barrage of answering fire, forcing the legionnaire down. Bits of brick exploded, raining fragments down around him. A chorus of alien shouting filtered in through his bucket's audio receptors. The third Tarax returned and added his fire to his companions'.

Lankin went to his right, pressing himself against the north wall and keyed his L-comm, switching from his direct link with Sergeant Talon to the company comm frequency. "Stryker-19 to Stryker-10, one fire team down. The second is focused on me for the time being, I'd suggest you move out."

"Roger that, 19, good work! Stryker-10 to command, 1st platoon is moving to the south, copy?"

Captain Kato replied, "Copy that, Stryker-10."

The incoming blaster fire abated enough for Lankin to risk a peek over the wall. The three Tarax fighters split their attention between popping off random shots at him and the moving 1st platoon. He snapped off two quick volleys, forcing the Tarax to duck for cover. The one by the hatch returned fire at Lankin. The air around him sizzled as he dropped behind the wall again, counting silently and visualizing the enemy's positions in his mind.

When the barrage ceased, he pushed up to a knee, stabilizing his N-4 on the wall. He leveled his optics, held his breath and squeezed the trigger. The Tarax's head vanished in a mist of red. Lankin searched for his next target, not bothering to watch the dead Tarax fall. Behind the condenser, one of the aliens was bringing his blaster to bear on Lankin's position. Lankin fired first.

He held his optics there, waiting for the last Tarax to pop his head up, when movement in the alley caught his attention. Four Tarax trotted between the houses to the west—escorting a hooded figure, practically dragging him down the street.

Oh, crap, Lankin thought, keying his L-comm. "LS-19, I've got an eyeball on the Primary! I count four indigs escorting him through an alley to the west."

Lankin tagged the party through his HUD, allowing the rest of his legionnaires to see on the map grid where the aliens were and what direction they were traveling in. The helmet's software system would plot likely courses and update in real time.

A blaster bolt zipped a few inches from Lankin's head, sending up more chips of brick and dust into the air. He'd kept his head up too long. *Stupid*. But hopefully getting eyes on their objective would prove worth it. Lankin ducked and crawled through the roof hatch. He half-fell, half-slid down the ladder, then sprinted for the street. Pausing, he checked for targets, then turned left and headed west.

"Stryker-19, Command, repeat! Do you have eyes on the senator?"

"That's affirmative, sir," Lankin said. "Four hostiles. Still moving to the west. I'm in pursuit."

"Lankin, confirm your position," Talon ordered. "I show you moving parallel to the objective."

Lankin puffed, "Affirmative. I'm heading west behind the huts on the south side of the village. The senator is approximately two hundred meters from my position, I'm going to try and flank them."

"Okay, stand by," Talon said. "I'm bringing 1st platoon up behind you, hold position until we can link up."

A service bot floated through the alley, air shimmering underneath from its repulsor pad. It beeped annoyance at Lankin as he swerved to avoid it, seemingly unaware of the fierce battle going on around it.

"Sarge, if I wait, we'll lose them again. This might be our only chance to get him back."

Talon sighed. "Copy that. Stay with them, but don't get in over your head, leej. First is inbound."

"Roger." Lankin slowed, coming to a wide intersection. Peering around the corner, he saw a few Tarax several blocks down to his left. They were charging west, obviously trying to catch their companions, ignoring the legionnaires behind them. *Playing catch up too, eh?*

He took aim at the last alien and fired. The blast slammed into the Tarax's shoulder, spinning him like a top, sending him staggering behind a brick hut.

Lankin sprinted across the street dodging answering fire from the aliens. They were wild, shooting more for effect than anything else. He pressed on through the tight alleys to the music of echoing blaster fire. After several minutes he managed to catch up to the fleeing Tarax and their hostage.

They were crossing another courtyard, this one more like a graveyard than a shrine, with small stone tablets and pillars scattered randomly. A small shuttle sat on the far side of the courtyard, atmo-wings folded in, cargo ramp lowered.

"I've got them," Lankin reported through the L-comm. "They've got a shuttle at the far end of the square. Probably counting on us not blowing up the senator."

"Copy that, 19, we'll be at your position in three minutes. Do not engage until we arrive."

Lankin shook his head, clicked off his L-comm and muttered, "They're not going to be here in three minutes."

He took a knee, checking the distance to his targets. One hundred seventy-eight meters. Not terribly far for the N-4, but on moving targets holding a friendly? He would have to be sure of his shots. The senator's captors were in tight formation around their prisoner—two in front and two in back. He didn't have a shot on the lead element, but he felt reasonably confidently he could drop the two rear guards...

Lankin went prone to steady his aim. He sighted a shorter Tarax wearing purple robes and carrying an old projectile rifle. The alien wasn't moving fast. Because of their prisoner, they could only manage a brisk walk. He lined the crosshairs up and took a long breath, trying to slow his heart rate. In that space between breaths, the space of complete stillness, where he'd learned all those years ago to live, Lankin pulled the trigger.

His N-4 gave its miniscule buck and the blast hit home, sending the alien tumbling to the ground. Without waiting to see if the Tarax was dead, Lankin lined up his next shot.

Breathe. Hold. Squeeze.

The second alien fell with a cry of pain, caught in the middle of a surprised turn at the spectacle of his fallen comrade.

The two forward guards turned out of the column, exposing themselves and giving Lankin a clear shot. They'd barely registered what was happening before Lankin's blaster shots dropped them as well.

Without the Tarax forcing him along, the prisoner stopped, hooded and bewildered, obviously trying to figure out what was happening.

"Hello?" the prisoner said, his voice muffled by the hood.

Pushing himself to his feet, Lankin activated his external comm. "It's okay, Senator Hyskern, the Legion is—!"

Blaster fire rang out and something punched Lankin's chest armor, knocking him down. He landed on his back, gasping for air. Alarm bells clamored as he rolled to his side, struggling to gather his senses. A distant part of his brain told him if he didn't react and return fire, he was dead and so was the senator. Four Tarax attackers came into the open from between a pair of houses sixty meters away.

Ignoring the burning in his chest, Lankin rolled to his stomach, brought his N-4 up and fired. He didn't bother with precision shots, there wasn't any time for that. He simply pointed the weapon in the right direction and filled the air with deadly bolts of energy.

Two Tarax fell as he emptied his rifle's charge pack. The other two ducked back between the houses. Lankin rolled from the middle of the alley, behind the edge of the nearest house. He hastily swapped out charge packs, slapping in a fresh one with one hand before peering back around the building.

Out of the corner of his eye Lankin saw the senator hunched over in the middle of the street, trying to pull the hood off. He struggled and managed to pull it free, his human face written in fear and confusion. He flinched at blaster fire snapping around him, unsure which direction to turn.

"Stay down!" Lankin yelled over the external comms. "Just stay down."

He adjusted his position behind his N-4, grimacing at the pain in his chest. The Tarax were nowhere to be seen. Lankin took several agonizing breaths, wondering just how badly he was injured. The legionnaire armor provided some protection against small arms, but that protection was a bit more limited than their Republic overseers might want them—and the rest of the galaxy—to believe.

A barrage of blaster fire sounded in the distance, followed by a short burst from projectile weapons, then more blasters. A moment later a Tarax stumbled into the courtyard. Lankin leveled his sights, but the alien collapsed before he got a shot off. It shuddered, then lay still.

"Stryker-10, Stryker-19, are you all right? Confirm your position."

"HUD marker confirmed. I'm on the far west side of the houses. I've got the senator in sight and several enemy targets down."

"Copy that, we're almost to you. Your bio-report says you've been hit."

"I'll be all right."

"Copy," Sergeant Talon said. "Kessler! Get your butt over to Stryker-19. Blue squad secure the senator. Green squad take care of the shuttle. I want the rest of you setting up a perimeter. No more surprises from the alleys, Legionnaires."

Lankin's fellow legionnaires arrived, his HUD's display filled with green dots setting up.

Corporal Kessler, the squad's medic, knelt beside Lankin and put a hand on his shoulder. "You okay, Lankin?"

"I feel like I got hit by a truck," Lankin said. "But I'm okay, I think."

Kessler helped Lankin to his feet. Sergeant Talon came over, his N-4 draped across his chest, barrel down.

"That's some crazy shooting, Leej," Talon said. He nodded at Kessler. "Go check on the senator. Make sure he's all right."

"Roger, Sarge." Kessler took off, passing a pair of Tarax pilots being frog-marched away from the idled down shuttle by green squad.

Lankin grimaced at the pain in his chest. "Just point and shoot, Sarge."

"Yeah, but there's maybe three other guys in the unit I'd trust to make those shots consistently, including Pax. And charging out here by yourself the way you did..." Talon shook his head. "You should've waited."

Lankin looked over his shoulder, making sure there wasn't anyone else around to hear. "I had to do something, Sarge. I couldn't let them get away, not when I was close enough to do something about it."

"I know. I would have done the same thing in your shoes. But that's how legionnaires get themselves killed."

"Yes, sir. Platoon okay?"

Talon nodded. "Lieutenant Friedo was hit by indirect fire, and—" the sergeant straightened as another legionnaire approached. "Captain Kato, sir."

The legionnaire captain slung his N-4 over one shoulder. His bucket was off, something most officers frowned upon, but then, Kato wasn't most officers. His beard was trimmed short and even after years of wearing the bucket, his complexion was dark-tanned.

"Sergeant Talon. Corporal Lankin."

Both legionnaires snapped to attention, saluting sharply, saying in unison, "Sir."

A group of legionnaires escorted the senator, Kessler still scanning him for internal injuries. He looked fine on the outside, a little banged up, but nothing critical.

"Senator Hyskern, I'm Captain Kato, 71st Legionnaires, Stryker Company. We're here to get you home, sir."

The senator looked shaken, maybe from physical abuse he'd endured or just the mental strain of being taken prisoner by aliens. Either way, he was obviously not accustomed to the horrors of war. He didn't much look like a senator now. His expensive clothes were ripped and dirty. The skin around his swollen right eye was turning shades of black and purple. He could barely keep it open. His face was cut and scraped and blood dribbled from one ear.

"Thank you, Captain. You saved my life. Oba knows what those kelhorned scum would have done had they gotten off-world."

Two shuttles zoomed by overhead, wings folding into landing position as they banked on approach. Three Republic tri-fighters screamed through the air behind the shuttles, splitting up to patrol.

"Thank you, Senator. I'll have men from First Platoon escort you to the shuttle and back to the destroyer."

"I appreciate that, Captain, thank you."

Captain Kato turned back to Lankin and Talon as the senator was led away. "I'm not going to say I'm entirely pleased with your actions, Corporal Lankin, but there's no doubt they were instrumental in the success of this mission."

"Thank you, sir."

"If I remember correctly, you've been turned down twice for sniper school, is that correct?"

"Yes, sir."

"If you're still interested, consider yourself enrolled. I'll make it happen," Kato said.

Lankin couldn't stop the smile that broke across his face. He was thankful he was still wearing his bucket so that no one could see him grinning like a goof. He fought back the urge to laugh and, gathering himself, said, "I am, sir. Thank you, sir."

"It's a tough school, Corporal. I won't lie to you, the Gauntlet's washout rate is ninety percent. But if you graduate, I'll be sure to push the paper to have an extra rocker waiting for you when you get back to the company."

"I... I don't know what to say, sir. Thank you."

"Don't say anything until you've passed the Gauntlet. You might not be so thankful after that week. Trust me. Get with Pax, he'll get you spun up on what you need."

"Yes, sir. Thank you, sir. I won't let you down."

Captain Kato nodded. "We'll get the paperwork started as soon as we're off planet. In the meantime, let's get that looked at." He motioned to Lankin's chest. "And we have some houses to clear, Sergeant Talon. You have the duty."

"Roger that, sir." Talon clapped Lankin on the shoulder. "Nice work."

I'm sorry about that. I love you very much and I miss you already.

01

Six Months Later

Sergeant Garo Lankin cursed, grabbing the yellow safety bar above him as the shuttle bounced. He steadied himself with one hand, keeping his N-18 balanced, holding the barrel in the other. "Is it too much to ask to have a steady flight? I don't think that's too much to ask."

The shuttle's bay rattled and clanged from legionnaire gear. Each of the twenty leejes was strapped into their own drop seat, weapon clamped to the wall beside them, bucket secured in cubbies overhead. On any other drop, the seats would have been filled, but thanks to a combination of inept leadership and lack of actual tactical experience, only half of the available seats were full.

Sergeant Talon, sitting across from Lankin, laughed. "Got used to those civilian transports! Welcome back to the suck. You should be glad your seat has a cushion on it."

Lankin glared at his friend. Sergeant Chase Talon lounged in his drop seat, absently twirling a braided cord around one finger. A small pendant twinkled in the light of the shuttle bay.

Lankin couldn't keep the smile from his face. Talon was the only man he knew who managed to be so nonchalant about a Silver Sword, the Legion's fourth highest citation. "You know, for a minute there I thought I'd actually missed you."

His friend's observation was accurate, however. Lankin had gotten used to the creature comforts of non-Legion life, even if the majority of his twenty-week sniper course had been spent cooped up in a classroom for ten hours a day. The school hadn't taught him much more than he already knew about the fundamentals of long-distance shooting. Most of his time was spent debating the legal and moral—which he thought was more than a little ironic—implications of killing enemy targets.

Their current situation notwithstanding, Lankin was glad to be back with his unit and friends. Though his return had brought with it more than one surprise.

Talon caught the pendant and sat up, face covered in mock indignation. "Missed me? Says the guy who turned cloak and moved to 2nd Squad." Talon shook his head. "I guess the standards for squad leaders are a bit more lax than they used to be."

Lankin laughed. "Now, you know I had nothing to do with that."

"Oh, sure, sure! It's fine, you don't hurt my feelings none." Talon clutched at his chest and grimaced. "And after everything we've shared together."

"And everyone," Corporal Joshua "Sweets" Sipin said from the end of the bay.

Laughter rippled through the bay.

Jerking a thumb toward him, Talon said, "Secret's out, man."

Lankin shook his head. "The rumors never cease."

"You talking about that Putari girl last year, Sweets?" Corporal Burga asked.

"That was never confirmed, Burga."

"Oh yeah, sure. Deny, deny, deny."

"Who's denying?" Talon asked. "But if you're going to tell the story, tell it right."

Burga held his hands up. "I'm just telling it like I heard it."

"That's enough," Lieutenant Duval said from near the front of the bay, rocking back and forth with the shuttle's movements. From the strained look on his face, he was having a hard time keeping his calm and collected façade intact.

1st Platoon's new lieutenant looked like he was barely out of his teens—his angled jaw and pale skin didn't look like it had ever been touched by a razor. He'd been appointed by a senator Lankin had never heard of and had graduated from an accelerated officer training class three days prior to joining the company.

"We are legionnaires," the lieutenant said. "We are not a company of ruffians like the army or marine grunts. I don't know what kind of leadership you men have experienced in the past, but I intend our platoon to be beyond reproach at all times. This kind of talk will not be tolerated, understood?"

Silence fell over the bay, as if some magical force had just sucked all the life from the men inside. A couple of the legionnaires gave Lankin and Talon questioning glances, looking to their sergeants for confirmation of the lieutenant's order.

Lankin saw Talon was about to retort and spoke up before he could put his boot in his mouth. "Yes, sir. Strykers are the storm, sir."

On cue, the legionnaires bellowed, "Feel the thunder!"

Their battle cry was accompanied by a resounding thud as the men of Stryker Company hammered fists against the unit crest emblazoned on their chest plates, an armored hand holding a lightning bolt against a red shield.

Lankin held Duval's gaze, absorbing the feeling of being loathed as the lieutenant's eyes bored into his. The hatch behind the lieutenant opened and Captain Kato leaned through the opening. "Lieutenant Duval, would you assist me, please? We're approaching the coast and I'd like your opinion on close approach vectors."

Duval kept his eyes locked on Lankin for another second, then turned away. "Certainly, sir. Always glad to be of assistance. I understand. Aerial reconnaissance wasn't your specialty in OCS."

Kato shook his head, mouth twisting in a sardonic smile. "Couldn't ever pick up the knack for it."

The lieutenant slipped past Kato, who gave Lankin a knowing look. Lankin grinned and shrugged. Kato pointed, shaking his head, then pulled the hatch shut, leaving the enlisted men to their rituals.

Lankin chuckled, returning his attention to his sniper rifle, finishing some adjustments to one of the retention knobs on his optical scope. "She was Rugarian, not Putari."

The platoon erupted in laughter.

Talon threw his hands up in surrender. "Now you've done it. Already got the new point on our butts."

To Talon's left, Private Bishto leaned forward, eyes wide with curiosity. It was his first operation with Stryker Platoon and Lankin could see the kid was plenty green. It seemed like the warfighters coming out of Legion training were getting younger and younger.

"You had two Rugarians at the same time?" Private Bishto asked.

"No," Talon pointed a finger at the legionnaire. "You don't get to ask about that, you're too young. And don't get any ideas, either. There isn't going to be any funny business on this op, I can tell you that for sure."

Bishto frowned. "Why not?"

"Because, Boot," Talon said, "This isn't some core world with money to spend on beautiful women. If it was, they wouldn't be having the kinds of problems that need leejes like us to solve. Gestor's a backwater, nowhere world no one cares about, and no one's ever heard of before. But some politician somewhere got their feelings hurt, so they sent us in to educate."

Lankin felt a twinge of sympathy for the private as his confusion deepened, but he'd been a boot too, it was all part of the game.

"I don't understand," Bishto said.

Garo slipped his N-18 back into its retention clamps. "It's a babysitting mission."

Talon leaned back, crossing his arms. "Damn basics couldn't protect a tarpple from a pupatar. Honestly, how hard is it to protect a town full of miners? And look," he motioned at the twenty legionnaires in the shuttle bay, "this drop doesn't even rate a full company."

"Sorry to burst your bubble, kid," Lankin said. "We're the kinder, gentler Legion now. The days of dropping in, smashing everything, and going home are long gone. We're glorified police."

"Not even," Talon said. "Hell, the major didn't even see fit to join the rest of us leejes on the ground."

Major Kuala Wyeire, Commander of Bravo Platoon, 71st Legion, had been appointed in much the same way Lieutenant Duval had been, by virtue of his political connections. Wyeire's lack of prowess as a military commander was a well-known fact throughout the Legion, even if it was only talked about in the deepest, darkest depths of the enlisted corps. Lankin had met the major only once, at a regional Legion ball two years before. He'd been a captain then, but no less arrogant.

Since Wyeire assumed command of the 71st, Lankin hadn't seen or heard from the man. The only thing he'd done was abolish the use of nicknames, calling them an unprofessional and useless tradition that reduced company cohesion and only led to confusion during combat situations.

"I, for one, am glad he's not coming with us," Lankin said.

Talon nodded toward the hatch to the cockpit. "No, we're stuck with Duval. That's even worse."

"One point's better than two," chimed in a leej from somewhere down the shuttle.

"Lieutenant Duval's a point?" Private Bishto asked. "But I thought—"

"You thought?" Talon said, cutting the boot off. "What did I tell you about thinking? Until you earn your stripes, you don't get to think."

Lankin eyed the young man, trying to decide if he'd truly ever been that green.

You've got a lot to learn, kid.

There were far too many companies in the Legion unfortunate enough to have an appointed commander; it was something you got used to. You worked around it, planned for the foul up that would eventually happen, and tried your hardest to mitigate the fallout. It seemed to Lankin that even those in Legion High Command were aware of the complications inherent in such commanders and worked diligently to ensure any negative repercussions due to appointed commanders wasn't traced to them, or at least kept to a minimum. Having two points in the same chain of command? That was virtually unheard of, a grim reminder of the House of Reason and Senate's growing influence on what was supposed to be a supported but independent military. How First Platoon had been unlucky enough to draw a second point—and a brand-new lieutenant at that—Lankin would never know.

We're the storm all right, Lankin thought. *A kelhorned hurricane.*

"At least Captain Kato is coming," Talon said. "Maybe the mission won't be a retantor cluster after all."

"Maybe," Lankin said, not entirely sharing his friend's optimism.

The lights flickered from white to orange and the shuttle's internal comms buzzed to life. Captain Kato's voice boomed through the speakers. "Okay, men, heads up. We'll be wheels down in five. I want buckets on and linked in thirty seconds."

Without getting up, Talon reached into the cubby and pulled his bucket free of the retaining strap. "Finally."

Lankin pulled his own helmet loose. "Do me a favor will ya?"

Talon hesitated, his bucket almost covering his eyes. "Yeah?"

"Don't get me in front of the CO this time, deal?"

Talon smiled. "Hey, it's me!" He pulled the bucket down. His next words came through the helmet's external speakers, distorted and mechanical. "Have I ever steered you wrong?"

I want you to know it isn't anyone's fault.
We all fought hard, I guess it was just my
time to go.

Sergeant Chase Talon stepped off the ramp to allow his squad to file past. He mentally checked off every leej, visually inspecting equipment and weapons. Legionnaires were the best of the best, but that didn't mean they didn't sometimes forget things.

Lankin's squad was next out and the new sniper, and even newer squad leader, joined Talon, his N-18 cradled in the crook of his arm. Talon admired the weapon—new and shiny, only fired in training, and Talon could guess how much his friend was itching to use it in combat. But before that happened, they had to survive the real horror of mission deployments: managing the troops.

"Not such a dump after all," Lankin said, scanning their surroundings.

Talon grunted at four combat sleds pulling up to the edge of the landing pad. They boasted turret-mounted, twin-barreled N-50 medium blasters manned by Republic marines in jungle camouflage and helmets.

The Gangeers Spaceport was bustling with activity. At the far end, a large transport barge lifted off the tarmac, repulsor drives kicking up a cloud of dust. Several heavy lift bots carried unmarked containers from delivery trucks to collection points around the complex. Two shuttles sat in the southeast corner. One looked like it was in the middle of a complete refit.

Guard towers marked all four corners of the port and the midpoints between, all manned by full marine squads. The towers had been reinforced with old shipping containers and plasma-hardened fencing. The perimeter was a no man's land, open space enclosed between four-meter fences.

The main gates at the north end of the complex were massive. Four additional towers provided overwatch for a pair of side-by-side entrances into the spaceport, one for regular ground traffic, the other for rail transport from the mines.

The spaceport was surrounded by lush green jungle. Wide emerald and gold leaves formed a canopy that stretched for kilometers to the east, north, and west. To the south, tall cliffs plunged into the coastline of Gestor's largest ocean.

They'd received a bare-bones pre-op briefing package from Legion Intelligence, but words on a tablet did little justice to the sights they were taking in now.

Talon used his bucket's optics and zoomed in on one of the taller trees to the north. Several small birds circled above it, though a few dove into the leaves then climbed back up through the canopy. Even with the shuttle's engines still spinning down behind him, he could hear the birds screeching and cawing to each other.

"It's beautiful," Talon said.

Lankin slapped him on the shoulder. "Come on, you ol' softy, we're warfighters, not tourists."

Talon killed his optical zoom. The squads had formed up, all twenty legionnaires standing at attention, awaiting orders. His men were disciplined and, judging from what he'd observed of the point's attitude, that would probably be their only saving grace during the mission.

"What's this?" Lankin asked, nodding at four trucks pulling up beside the sleds. Marines jumped from the beds, taking a defensive formation around the edge of the landing pad.

Talon frowned. "What the hell are they doing in those things?"

Captain Kato came down the shuttle's ramp, followed closely by Lieutenant Duval. As the point passed them, Talon's L-comm chimed with an incoming call. "Go for Talon."

Duval's voice came through with a slight tinny sound. "Sergeant, your men's formation is sloppy. See to it before the captain notices."

The connection terminated before Talon could reply.

It's not a parade, you kelhorned idiot, Talon thought, looking over his men. They all stood perfectly straight, their gear in presentable condition. Talon couldn't find any fault. Even so, he made a show of adjusting Bishto's shoulder armor.

A marine captain stepped to the front of their formation and saluted Captain Kato.

The legionnaire returned the gesture with crisp precision. "Captain Campbell."

"Captain Kato."

"Have your men stand down, Captain Campbell. This isn't a parade."

"Of course, sir." He ordered his men to stand easy, then motioned to the sleds. "I apologize for the condition of the sleds, Captain Kato. I've been asking for additional vehicle support through Command, but my requests have gone unanswered."

The sleds were older models but appeared operational. Talon had seen worse. The trucks the marines had arrived in bothered him more than the sleds. Not only were they local, which meant not built or serviced to Legion standard, it meant that they were most likely without armor. Driving around in unarmored vehicles in a combat zone was a recipe for disaster.

The red paint on the trucks had long ago faded in the Gestor sun, and many places were splotched in gray primer or simply rusting away. The tires—the rigs weren't repulsor equipped—looked like they might blow at any moment and one of the trucks was completely missing a windshield. Squad automatic blasters were mounted in the beds of two of the trucks, their charge packs strapped to the base of the turret.

"Well," Captain Kato said. "Maybe, with a little help from the Legion, we can work on improving your situation here. Why the extra security?"

"A few weeks ago, a Republic envoy team and some replacement workers were attacked as they departed the port. Insurgents destroyed the vehicles and killed all fifteen people, then disappeared into the city before we could get a team out here."

Kato nodded. "Sergeant Talon, Sergeant Lankin, would you accompany the Lieutenant and me?"

"Yes, sir," they answered in unison.

"Corporal Burga," Talon said, stepping to his squad. "Get the men loaded up."

"Yes, sir."

As the squads filed into the three combat sleds, Talon and Lankin followed Captain Kato, Lieutenant Duval, and Captain Campbell into the command sled. Legion transport sleds typically appeared in three configurations: combat, command, and medical. The command sled housed combat and control systems required for battle.

Talon and Lankin took seats at the rear, giving the officers room to work. As a staff sergeant, Talon was generally privy to command briefings, but he'd learned quickly, that being privy to and having a say in were two completely different things.

The ramp on the back of the sled folded up and Talon swayed as it started off. Large screens displayed images from exterior cameras.

On screen, the convoy formed up: two of the local trucks at the front, then the combat sleds, followed by the command sled with the two remaining trucks bringing up the rear.

Outside the port, the convoy tightened up—the road was barely wide enough for a pair of sleds. It was barely a road. Almost immediately they were plunged into a tunnel hacked out of the jungle winding back and forth through the trees. Some sunlight filtered through the dense canopy, revealing multicolored foliage on the jungle floor.

"It's about five klicks to Gangeers," the marine captain told them. "The mag-lev track runs more or less parallel to the east side of the main road."

"The track isn't visible from the road?" Captain Kato asked.

"Occasionally it is, sir," Captain Campbell explained. "At several points they butt up to each other. They also cross at three points, but yes, it's hidden by the trees for most of the route."

Talon pinged Lankin on a private channel.

"Go for Lankin."

"This terrain is a tactical nightmare."

Lankin nodded. "You're telling me. I wonder why they haven't pushed back the jungle? At least give it a few meters on either side. This whole road screams ambush."

"If the rest of the place is like this, no wonder they've been getting their butts kicked."

The sled slowed to pass two trucks filled with Gestori heading to the spaceport. The natives were about a head shorter than humans with mottled, almost reptilian skin. Two golden eyes separated by a flat nub just above their lipless mouths. They ignored the sleds, their expressions cold and dispassionate.

"They look horrible," Lieutenant Duval said.

"They're temporary workers from the mainland. The company flies them in to bolster the main workforce. They work for about a week, get a paycheck, and go home.

Besides the residents in Gangeers, not a lot of natives like being so isolated from the rest of the world. The only way in and out of here is the spaceport and the old docks to the west, but those are only used for logistical traffic."

"How often do you patrol this road?" Captain Kato asked.

The marine hesitated, as if not wanting to answer, then said, "At least daily."

You've got to be kidding, Talon thought.

Kato cleared his throat. "And that seems adequate for the mission?"

"No, sir, it's what we have the manpower for. As it stands, my company has been on continuous rotation for two months, with no down days. Headquarters assured me a relief force would be on station three weeks ago, but it has yet to arrive. I have to say, I'm slightly disappointed at the number of men you've brought with you."

"Unfortunately, Captain, we all have mission parameters, and orders from our superior officers."

"Orders which were approved very high up the chain of command," Duval put in.

Talon wished he could see Kato's expression underneath his bucket. He was sure the captain was boring blaster holes into the lieutenant with his eyes.

"Here's where the envoy team was attacked," Campbell said, pointing to the screens.

Outside, three charred vehicles—frames, really—had been pushed to the side of the road. The driver's side of the lead vehicle had been imploded by something.

"And the enemy?" Kato asked, turning away from the display. "Any local knowledge you can share?"

Captain Campbell shook his head. "We don't know a lot. According to the reports provided by Duracore—that's the local company that runs the operations—when the attacks started, they were few and far between, mostly relatively minor sabotage. But after an explosion at the mining complex, the Republic sent in the marines to help. Apart from knowing they're sneaky, we've been able to uncover nothing else about them. We're not even sure what they want."

Duval coughed. "How can you know *nothing* about your enemy, Captain? That's the first rule of any conflict. If you don't know who they are, how can you defeat them?"

"We've tried a number of times to capture one of the insurgents, but they're well equipped and know the jungles better than we do."

"Don't the locals have any information?" Captain Kato asked.

"Doesn't that seem a little odd to you?" Lankin asked Talon through their secure channel.

"*Extremely*," Talon answered.

"The locals..." The marine captain rubbed his chin, looking sheepish. "How to put this... The Gestori take their privacy very seriously. And it's like pulling teeth to get anything from Duracore. They don't interact with us much, the marines or Republic representatives stationed here. Hard to blame them really."

Duval stiffened. "Hard to blame them? Sounds like they're a bunch of ungrateful swine. They should be singing the Republic's praises for everything we've done for them. We are providing them protection at the risk of Republic lives and resources. This is why the House of Reason ought to move to take control of this entire operation. Refresh my memory, Captain. What is actually at stake here?"

"The terms of the treaty... *negotiated* by the Republic offer certain tariff reductions in exchange for forty percent of the gross revenue of the mine and its subsidiaries."

Talon barely managed to hold back his surprise. He was no financial genius, but he had a little money invested in the market, and forty percent of the planetwide take was an astronomical amount. Billions and billions of credits. *No wonder the Republic doesn't want to lose control of this operation.*

But why the lack of security? One would think with that large a financial stake in the success of the mining operation, the Republic would at least invest in adequate security forces.

Then again, Talon thought, *it is the Republic.*

"Forty percent is a lot of money," Captain Kato said.

"Yes, sir," Campbell said. "And as you can imagine, the company shares your sentiments. Which, I think, is the main reason they're reluctant to share anything else with us. They feel as though they're already paying the Republic a fortune; they expect us to do the rest without any further help from them."

"Have you explained to them that assisting us benefits them in the long run?"

"Captain Kato, as I said, my company and I have been on station for a little over two months. With the shortfall of manpower, I've precious little time to foster any kind of meaningful relationships with the Gestori people. Though I doubt I'd have any luck with them anyway."

"Meaningful relationships." Duval practically spat the words. "They are subjects of the Republic, in practice if not by name, and they should present themselves accordingly."

Captain Campbell nodded. "Of course, Lieutenant."

The sled's internal speaker buzzed. "We're reaching Checkpoint Alpha, Captain Campbell."

"Thank you, Corporal."

Images from the exterior cameras showed a break in the trees ahead—the road opened up into a field. Sunlight glared against the screens as they drove out from below the canopy. The field was filled with stumps of felled trees and piles of brush and logs. Worker bots chopped and carried wood, while others loaded the wood into waiting trucks.

A few Gestori were gathered near one of the flatbed trucks, these better dressed than the Gestori they'd seen just a few minutes before, but by a small margin. They stopped their discussion and stood stock-still, only their heads moving, following the Republic vehicles.

"I was able to convince the local executive board to clear some area around the city, something they should have done a long time ago," Captain Campbell said. "It was a close vote and was nearly shot down. Most of the people aren't happy about it."

The outskirts of Gangeers lay on the other side of the clearing. The road heading into the city was flanked by two small guard posts manned by marines..

As the convoy approached the black and yellow vehicle barriers, a marine next to the road pushed a switch causing the barriers to fold back vertically on either side of the road. The marine saluted as the command sled passed.

The marine captain touched a button on his command station and a light flashed on the screen. "Wolf Base, Wolf Actual, Checkpoint Alpha clear."

"Copy that, Wolf Actual, you're clear for Route Bravo-2, repeat, Bravo-2."

"Roger, Bravo-2, on station in five. Wolf Actual out."

Campbell killed the connection, then grabbed the overhead bar to keep from falling over as the skid made a sharp turn. "Gangeers was built almost fifty years ago," he explained. "The streets weren't designed for repulsor sleds, so there's only so many ways for us to navigate the city. We take random pre-mapped routes for every trip."

"How many routes are there?" Kato asked.

"Eight completely separate routes, but we can combine some of them to change it up more."

The buildings grew progressively taller the farther into the city they went. Some of the taller ones held clusters of antennas and satellite dishes on top. At the center of town stood the tallest—about ten stories and surrounded by a large, open square filled with small shops and vendors pushing repulsor carts.

Tiny icons appeared in Talon's bucket, identifying possible threats. Gestori crossing the footbridges, standing by open windows, or watching the convoy from rooftop vantage points.

"This just keeps getting better and better," Lankin said through the secure L-comm link.

Talon kept his eyes locked on the display screens, forcing himself to be calm. There was barely enough room for the sleds to drive single file through the streets, and they were doing it with hordes of Gestori on either side of them. The two forward escort trucks sped ahead, blaring warning horns and shouting for people to get out of the way.

They reached the wide town square. The street cut right down the center, separating large crowds of shoppers and rows of makeshift storefronts. Salesmen shouted, vying for the crowd's attention.

Tall service bots walked among the throng, lanky, metal giants, most carrying items for their masters, some pulling repulsor carts filled with goods. One Gestori, dressed in a purple tunic and trousers, sat on the shoulders of a squat bluish bot with irregularly long arms. The bot held a robotic hand against his master's back, stabilizing him, and sliced through the crowd like a torshark through a school of fish.

Gestori leaned from open windows, sometimes shouting at passersby, others simply watching with an air of disconnected interest. Most of the window-sitters stared as they passed by, looking down at the vehicles with very obvious disdain.

"You see that, Garo?" Talon asked, nodding to the screens. "Look at those vantage points, there're thousands of them."

Lankin nodded. "If anyone wanted to ambush us, they'd have an almost limitless number of attack—"

The sled lurched, rocking on its repulsor pads, almost throwing Talon and Lankin from their seats. Curses from the driver echoed back, joining those of the three Republic officers.

"What the hell is going on up there?" the Lieutenant shouted, pulling himself back to his feet.

A group of Gestori had walked directly in front of the sled, forcing the driver to slam on the brakes. Warning horns blared as the driver punched the accelerator again. Two aliens near the back of the party had to jump out of the way to avoid being hit. One turned and kicked the sled's armored side.

The driver's voice echoed back on the sled's comm. "Kelhorned lizard walked right in front of us, sir! Never even slowed down."

Another blast from the sled's horn hastened a few stragglers out of the way. Several onlookers threw up gestures Talon didn't recognize.

He keyed his secure link to Lankin. "So much for a warm welcome."

When Oba calls you home, you don't get to
ignore him. If you get nothing else from this
letter, know this: I died for a reason.

Lankin adjusted his position for a better look at the display screens as the convoy approached Camp Wolf. The forward operating base was positioned just outside the city's western edge, in a clearing a hundred meters from the jungle. The perimeter of the base consisted of two rows of gabion walls, filled with rock and earth, topped with plasma-reinforced razor wire. The slightly shorter outer wall was reinforced with a concrete T-wall along the outside, the inverted "T" shaped barricade painted with various Repub marine signs and graffiti from the locals.

The entry control point faced the city, fortified with more T-walls, impervisteel gates, and squat watchtowers on either side. Two N-60 repeating blaster emplacements, manned by three-man teams of marines, provided overwatch from the towers. Four Repub marines stood guard on the ground in the exclusion zone from inside two fortified bunkers at the entrance. Any non-military transport would be detained and searched in this area prior to entry.

The outer, then inner gates rose, allowing them unimpeded entry. Inside, the compound was separated into several partitioned areas, creating a disorienting maze effect for any opposition force that managed to breach the ECP or exterior walls. The partitions were a mixture of T-wall and gabion wall, sometimes both.

The sleds took them to the southwest corner of the base, to a semi-enclosed barracks, and parked. Lankin and Talon filed out of the back of the command sled and waited for the officers to exit.

"Sergeant Talon," Captain Kato said.

"Yes, sir?"

"Have the men secure, rack, and unload. I assume we've been provided with adequate space?" he said to marine captain.

Captain Campbell nodded. "Yes, sir. Building one-bravo has been assigned to your troops, sir."

"When you're satisfied, meet us in the command hut," Kato said.

Talon saluted. "Roger that, sir." He moved off to manage the chaos.

Camp Wolf's headquarters was little more than two large premanufactured huts pushed together and covered with a large tent. Captain Campbell led the legionnaires inside, returning the salute of the marine standing guard at the entrance.

Captain Kato lifted his bucket as he stepped inside. Lankin followed suit and waited for his eyes to adjust to the dark interior.

Recessed combat lighting cast a red hue over display screens and communications equipment, all manned by marine intelligence technicians. A large holo-table occupying the center of the room was projecting a top-down view of Gangeers and the surrounding terrain. The three-dimensional image flickered occasionally, remarkably steady for marine equipment.

Holding his bucket under one arm, Captain Kato looked over the map, shaking his head. "It's a tactical nightmare."

A lone road cut through the jungle to the west away from the FOB, then turned north to the mining complex in the foothills of the Gangeers Mountains.

"Yes, sir," Captain Campbell agreed.

Lankin didn't like what he saw. They could've brought three times the number of legionnaires, and still been unable to provide adequate security. Not without completely strip-clearing hundreds of kilometers of jungle.

"How many patrols do you run?" Kato asked.

"We try to have a constant rover outside the compounds, but one of our sleds broke down last week and that's significantly reduced our mobility options."

"What about observation bots?" Lieutenant Duval asked, stepping around the captain to get closer to the table.

Lankin forced himself not to roll his eyes. Was it a requirement that you had to come out of OCS with an IQ of zero?

Kato spoke before Campbell could answer. "The TT-16s are great for keeping an eye on close battlefield engagements, but they don't have the range for any serious recon."

"And the jungle canopy reduces their effectiveness to nothing, sir," Campbell added.

Lankin canted his head at the captain. Even though he was higher ranking, the Repub marine deferred to the legionnaire lieutenant as he would a senior officer. Lankin wasn't sure if that was out of respect for the Legion or just an innate grasp of how things worked in the Republic. He'd seen it before, senior officers in the other services treating points as seniors in an effort to gain favor—not that a legionnaire lieutenant had much influence, but given enough time, that lieutenant would work his way up into a position that afforded him the power to reward his friends and relentlessly punish his enemies.

Duval ignored the marine and continued to study the map.

Captain Campbell broke the silence. "I'm sure you and your people will want to get settled in and unpacked, I can arrange for the kitchen—"

"That won't be necessary, Captain, thank you," Captain Kato said, holding up a hand. "How many patrols do you have out right now?"

Campbell frowned. "None, sir, I recalled them when the Vendetta entered orbit."

Lankin shook his head. He wanted to like the marine, but from everything he'd seen, he couldn't help but think the captain was completely inept. Recalling troops from an active combat zone was borderline incompetent.

Daylight spilled into the dark room when Talon ducked inside. "Men are squared away, Captain."

"Right then." Kato nodded, then asked Campbell, "You said you don't know a lot about the enemy. Take us through what we do know about them."

"As I said, almost nothing. We've only actually been engaged six times. They break contact almost immediately and disappear back into the jungle where it's impossible for us to track them with any level of confidence."

"What about your shuttles?"

"We haven't flown air support missions for several weeks. I suspended them after a shuttle took insurgent fire from the hills, killing their door gunner and damaging one of the repulsor pads. By the time we got a ground patrol into the area, the attackers were long gone."

"And jungle patrols?"

Campbell sighed. "I know it must sound like our operational tempo is substandard, but our support from Sector Headquarters has been extremely limited. Not to mention, patrolling through the Gestor jungles is extremely difficult and the chances of locating anything or anyone are slim to none."

Captain Kato let a disapproval darken his face. "But the opportunity for the chance is nonexistent if your men are not out there. Failing to do so sends a clear message to the enemy—that they have the power and they are in control. You have allowed them to operate with impunity, Captain."

For the first time since meeting Captain Campbell on the tarmac, Lankin saw the marine's frustration.

"If Sector leadership had responded to my requests for personnel and logistical support, perhaps we could've avoided this situation," Campbell insisted. "We've done what we can with a single company of marines, though I doubt our efforts would have been successful with another company or two. There is just too much ground to cover. As it is, my people are stretched to the breaking point."

Captain Kato regarded the Repub marine captain for a long moment. To Lankin's surprise, Campbell held the legionnaire's eyes without flinching. Lankin doubted even Duval would've been able to stand up against that glare.

Finally, Kato turned away from the marine, back to the holomap. "I understand your frustrations, Captain, truly I do, but the Legion is here now, and we'll have the situation under control in short order."

"Yes, sir," Campbell said. "Thank you, sir."

"Sergeant Talon, will the barracks provided suffice?"

"Yes, sir. The men are settling in as we speak."

"Good. I want your squad to make a security assessment of the base and identify any deficiencies. I want the report ready by the time Bravo squad and I return from patrol."

"Roger that, sir."

Captain Campbell frowned. "Are you not going to get settled in first?"

Kato shook his head. "Legionnaires do not require *settling in*. We are here to perform a mission and we will do just that. Lieutenant Duval, you will oversee the security assessment with Sergeant Talon and work with Captain Campbell to find solutions."

The lieutenant looked like he was on the verge of protesting the orders, but stopped himself. "Yes, sir."

"Sergeant Lankin, gather your men. Repulsors on in five."

"Yes, sir."

"And Sergeant," Lieutenant Duval said, "please try and remember we're here on a peacekeeping operation. Shooting any weapon is an extreme last resort, understand?"

Lankin fought the urge to jump clean across the table and punch the smug point square in the mouth. "Of course, sir. I will refrain from defending myself until you deem it necessary, sir."

Duval opened his mouth, but paused, trying to decide whether the sergeant had insulted him or not.

Before he could figure it out, the captain said, "All right, we're burning daylight. Let's move out."

*I died fighting alongside my brothers and I
wouldn't have wanted it any other way.*

04

The road connecting Gangeers to the mining complex to the northwest and the old docks to the west was little more than a two-lane dirt path, worn down by years of constant driving, flanked by trees and dense foliage, not to mention the hills. The foothills of the Gangeers Mountains stretched for kilometers and were the major reason the mines were so remote.

Lankin sat near the front, rocking with the motion of the sled. "You'd think they'd do something about this road."

"The Republic doesn't want to invest in this project any more than it already has," Captain Campbell said from his seat across the sled. "Trust me, I've asked."

"And this road," Captain Kato pointed at the route map on the screen. "It's ten klicks exactly?"

"Ten-point-two from Gangeers to Dirty."

"Dirty?"

"It's what the locals call the mining complex. It's impossible to leave that place without being covered in ore dust. Stuff gets everywhere. After about a week of trying to clean our uniforms every day, I finally gave up. Daily showers are a must. Probably the only real luxury we have out here."

"And no checkpoints for ten klicks?"

Campbell shook his head. "Like I said, we don't have the manpower. The security checkpoint on the east side of Gangeers and Checkpoint Bravo are the only checkpoints. Bravo is where we run all the inspections on Gestori goods coming in from the mainland."

"By boat?" Lankin asked. "Isn't that a little—?"

Campbell finished for him. "Old-fashioned? Extremely. Gestor is probably a good fifty to a hundred years behind the rest of the Republic in technology, but in some areas, like transportation, even more. Generally speaking, the only thing they fly into Gangeers is workers, everything else is brought in by boat. A local customs team goes through the boats, but nothing like what we would see on a Republic world."

"And your people search everything that comes up from the port?"

"Not everything," Campbell said, again shaking his head. "We have scanners set up to cover the road, looking for easily identifiable contraband, and we perform random physical searches on vehicles coming through, but it'd be impractical to search everything coming up from the docks."

"Impractical?" Captain Kato said. "When you're talking about operational security, nothing is impractical, Captain. Especially with the problems we're facing here now. How many transports a day run between the docks and Gangeers?"

"On average? Probably forty to fifty."

"And how many are randomly checked?"

"I guess it depends. Maybe half."

Kato coughed. "Captain Campbell, all due respect, but manpower issues aside, there's no excuse for this kind of lax security. If we don't have accurate knowledge of what's being transported, how can we be sure of our security? From now on, every transport will be searched. I don't care if it causes delays or not."

"Yes, sir."

The convoy drove through a set of metal pylons supporting the mag-lev track above the road. Four-meter fencing topped with plasma-wire enclosed each pylon. The track crossed the road and curved north around a tall hill and disappeared into the trees.

Several minutes later they came to a crossroads and followed the road west.

"From the fork here, it's another ten minutes north to Dirty," Captain Campbell explained.

"I want to get a good look at the docks before we return to Wolf," Captain Kato said.

The Old Cliff road emerged from the jungle and traced the edge of the tall cliffs overlooking the Gestor Ocean. Ahead, the road descended through a draw and switched back to the coastline and the docks.

Checkpoint Bravo was situated at the base of the hills, nothing more than an overwatch tower and a fold-down barricade blocking the road. Five marines manned the security station, working the scanners and operating the barricade.

The convoy paused briefly so Captain Campbell could relay Kato's orders to check every incoming shipment, then continued into the port. A barrel-chested marine sneered at the lead sled, and Lankin thought he was about to do something ill-advised, but the marine seemed to reconsider himself and turned back to his men.

Lankin's private L-comm beeped, Kato's name appeared on his HUD, and he tongued the switch. "Yes, sir?"

"They're too complacent."

"Yes, sir."

That might be the understatement of the year, sir, Lankin thought.

"We will assume primary supervision of the checkpoint tomorrow," Kato said to the marine commander. "Your men will continue to search; we will provide overwatch. Work out a rotation."

"Yes, sir," Campbell said. "Though you might get some pushback from the Duracore people."

"Pushback does not concern me."

The Port of Gangeers stretched for almost a kilometer along the coast, most of it built on reinforced impervisteel platforms just above the water. Maintenance buildings and warehouses lined the cliffside, and long, raised docks stretched out into the water almost a hundred meters. Workers and sailors milled around, some driving loaders, some sorting goods, others simply lounging on crates, soaking up the sun.

Five ocean haulers sat at dock in various stages of unloading. Lankin wouldn't have thought a city of twenty-five thousand would need so much. Hundreds of shipping containers stacked up in rows off the main docking platforms.

Lankin keyed his secure link to Captain Kato. "That's going to be a nightmare."

"Yes, Sergeant," Kato replied, sounding none too pleased. "It is."

*You may not want to believe that now, but I
hope someday you will.*

05

"They really weren't kidding," Corporal Burga said, wiping off his armor yet again. "This dust gets all over."

Sergeant Talon stopped to let one of the mining carts pass. The Duracore emblem painted on the side—the letters DML below two mountains—had faded over time and it rocked along on ancient wheels that looked on the verge of falling off. With the amount of money the Republic was pulling out of this place, he was surprised they hadn't at least updated the equipment.

After several days of correcting mistakes that should have never been, it was nice to be out on patrol. Nicer still to be on patrol without having to babysit any of the Repub marines. They were competent, just didn't have the level of skill and battlefield instinct a legionnaire did.

Talon had heard tales of marine battalions on the edge who really knew how to fight, but these weren't them.

The mining complex was, for all intents and purposes, a small suburb of Gangeers, complete with apartments, stores, maintenance and fabrication workshops, and huge warehouses for storing the mined ore. On the northern edge of the complex a massive processing station stripped base rock and other impurities from the precious ore.

The buildings didn't seem to be arranged in any particular order. Apartment buildings stood in between warehouses, adjacent workshops, and sorting stations. Dirty was home to about a thousand people at any given time, twice that on changeover days when the workforce swapped out.

A mining cart pulled away, its native driver staring down the squad of legionnaires as he passed. It rocked down the road, wheels creaking.

"Keep looking, skethole," Talon muttered under his breath. A part of him wished the driver would do something, give him a chance to show the self-righteous prick that legionnaires weren't a force you wanted to mess with.

The marines have been too easygoing here, Talon thought, watching the Gestori drive off. Then again, rude looks and gestures were something he and the rest of his men were used to. When the Legion showed up somewhere, it wasn't to bring kind words and flowers.

The constant *clank-clank-clank* of the ore processing station to the north echoed through the streets of Dirty like some ominous giant out for a stroll. Pillars of black smoke billowed from stacks, adding a distinctly dreary pall.

Five different shafts arrayed along a three kilometer stretch of mountain produced the ore brought in on the rattling carts to the processor. Talon didn't know how the processor worked, but the valuable ore was separated and stored in secure containers near the loading docks. Teams of marines provided overwatch at the processing station and the loading platforms, making sure the ore made it safely onto the waiting train.

Talon had heard several of the marines complain about the increase in operational tempo, but Captain Kato wasn't going to put up with the lax security measures.

Corporal Burga's ID appeared on Talon's HUD. "Eyeballs, ten o'clock high," he said.

Talon's HUD highlighted four figures pointing and talking together on the roof of a five-story tenement.

"What do you think they're talking about?" Private Bishto asked.

"Well, I doubt they're sizing us up for Unity Day sweaters," Talon said. "Probably never seen legionnaires before."

Talon's HUD identified three different comm sources and at least one firearm. *Not just a worker then*, Talon thought. "Heads up, one of them is packing."

The Gestori working out of Gangeers and Dirty weren't supposed to be armed. The local magistrate was supposed to enforce this with help from the Repub marines, though like everything else in this Oba-forsaken place, that edict wasn't strictly enforced. The marine intel section, for what it was worth, estimated that one in four Gestori was armed or had access to firearms. Operationally, that knowledge didn't change the legionnaires' approach to the mission. Armed or not, legionnaires treated anyone that wasn't one of them as a hostile until proven otherwise.

"Let's get a scan of the lizard on the right," Talon said. "Anyone who's packing out here, I want to get in a database—"

An emergency klaxon sliced through the air, cutting him off. Several Gestori ran across the street, heading west, shouting something Talon couldn't make out.

"Report," Talon said across the squad channel. He jogged to the end of the street and peered around the corner. More workers had joined in a hurried procession. "What's going on?"

Before anyone had an answer, Talon saw orange smoke billowing above a row of warehouses several blocks away. The klaxon shrieked again. Gestori converged on the burning buildings.

"First Platoon, on me," Talon said, then started toward the fire.

The fire had consumed one whole side of a storehouse before they'd been able to slow the progression with retardant sprayers. Acrid smoke filled the air. The fire snapped and popped inside the building. Fire control teams surrounded it and poured on the water. Evidently, basic internal fire prevention systems were also something the Republic and Duracore scrimped on.

The fire spread to the surrounding grass and bushes, the vegetation bursting into flames almost immediately. Orange smoke curled into the air, mixing with black.

"Pretty," Private Bishto said over the squad comm.

Clouds of the orange smoke rolled down the street, blowing past the legionnaires. Talon's HUD flickered slightly as the smoke grew thicker and then switched to infrared. He backed out of the smoke and his HUD cleared.

"I don't like that," Corporal Pax said over the L-comm. "My bucket just went all funky."

"Same," Private Noshey said.

"Yeah," Talon said. "Mine too. Burga, remind me to ask Captain Campbell for intel on the local vegetation. If the smoke is fouling our buckets' electronics, we could have a major problem."

"Roger that, Sarge. At least the filters kept the smoke out of our lungs."

Talon rounded a building and watched the workers fight the fire spreading across the grass, away from the warehouse. Half of the warehouse had been reduced to steel support columns—whatever had been inside, now just ash and debris.

Ten minutes later they contained the fire. A company supervisor showed up and started shouting. Workers cowered and backed away from the tan-skinned lizard, his blue Duracore robes whipping around him as he ranted.

"He's not happy," Burga said.

"No," Talon said. "No, he's not."

*The Legion is a calling, and the day I signed up,
I gave my life to that calling.*

06

Lankin adjusted himself behind his N-18, rolling his neck, attempting to work out the stiffness. He took a long breath, easing the urge to stand up and move around, then settled behind the rifle's optic again.

He'd found an ideal overwatch position on a hill two hundred meters to the east of Checkpoint Alpha with an excellent view of traffic waiting for the leejes to clear them at the docks. He was well inside his maximum effective range—he could shoot accurately at fifteen hundred meters without even breaking a sweat. The HUDs and linked weapon optics reduced human error, though Lankin could make ninety-nine percent of his shots anyway.

The Duracore people hadn't been too happy about the new security measures, but aside from grumbling, there wasn't much they could do about it. Captain Kato made clear his authority over everything related to the security of the mining operations and that anyone attempting to undermine said security would be subject to Republic law, and the Duracore people backed off.

"This one's good," Corporal Joshua "Sweets" Sipin said through the L-comm.

The leej waved a flatbed repulsor transport through the checkpoint. The driver answered with a gesture showing the gathered legionnaires what he thought about their security checkpoint. Lankin was glad he didn't have to deal with the local drivers, but lying behind the scope of his rifle for hours on end was starting to wear on him.

It had taken a couple days for the legionnaires to find a routine, but now they were pushing almost thirty transports a day through the checkpoint with minimal delays.

The next transport rolled into position and Sweets motioned for the driver to step out. The driver waved an angry hand toward the bed of his truck, shouting. Lankin couldn't make out what the Gestori was saying, but had a pretty good idea anyway. It was the same story with every driver to come through the checkpoint. His shipment was going to be late, or the Legion ruined their cargo and they wanted compensation. They all got told to file a complaint with the local Republic office. Complaints that would be filed away on some computer somewhere and never see the light of day again.

Sweets again motioned for the driver to step out, but the alien shook his head and waved his arms even more.

Are they ever going to stop complaining? Lankin thought as two more legionnaires stepped up to assist the corporal. If the drivers would just comply with their instructions, everything would flow smoothly.

One of the leejes, Private Corse—LS-07, according to Lankin's HUD—slapped a palm against the driver's door and motioned for him to step out. The driver continued shouting.

Lankin keyed his comm. "Are we having a problem, Sweets?"

Sweets replied, "The lizard won't dismount."

"Did you ask him nicely?"

"I said please."

"Ask, tell, make, Corporal."

"You got it, Sarge."

Three legionnaires opened the driver's door and helped the driver out. The Gestori pulled away from the legionnaires, then shoved Sweets hard in the chest, still shouting obscenities.

Private Corse pulled him away from Sweets. The corporal pointed a gloved finger in the alien's face.

The only thing Lankin didn't like about his position was not being privy to the conversations on the ground. "Sweets?" he asked through the L-comm.

"Just making his situation a little clearer, Sarge."

Lankin shifted the optic view down the road to the line of vehicles still waiting. A few drivers were standing outside their transports, watching the scene play out. They pointed and talked and shook their heads, obviously not happy at all. The longer they spent arguing the more agitated the aliens would get.

"Let's get the truck cleared and move on."

"Roger."

Sweets left the Gestori, who was still cursing and complaining, and climbed into the cab. As the leej went through the driver's compartment, Corse and Saretti were having an increasingly difficult time keeping the driver from following Sweets to the cab.

"What's he saying?" Lankin asked.

Private Corse came over the L-comm. "He just keeps going on and on about how we don't have the right to search his belongings and that we're ruining his shipment and blah blah blah."

"I'm gonna patch into your bucket's audio feed."

"Roger."

A second later the Gestori's angry voice came through Lankin's helmet speakers. "You Republic criminals! That's all you are! Criminals! You shouldn't be here in my home, telling us how to live our lives! Who are you to come here and steal from us?"

Sweets finished his search of the driver's compartment, ignoring the alien's complaints. The cargo hatch was secured.

"It's locked," Sweets said. "Open this."

"I don't recognize your authority here, Republic scum! Kelhorned thief is all you are. You won't steal from me! I have a family to feed."

"Look, you don't have a choice here," Sweets said. "You're going to open this hatch, or I'm going to open it for you, and then I just might confiscate everything you've got. No? Okay."

Sweets grabbed the handle. The Gestori screamed and jumped onto Sweets's back, wrapping his arms around the legionnaire's neck. Sweets spun around with the Gestori pounding on his bucket, legs kicking wildly. Corse and Saretti couldn't get close enough to get hands on the alien. In any other situation, the scene would've been hilarious, and Lankin found himself grinning despite himself.

Sweets finally managed to get a hold of one of the Gestori's arms and pulled him off, flipping the alien over his shoulder. The alien landed on his back, the impact knocking him silent.

"Stay down!" Sweets shouted. "You're under arrest."

The alien scrambled to his feet and spat in Sweets's face. Sweets lunged and caught the Gestori by the throat, shoving him back against the truck and getting right in his face.

"You'd better just calm the hell down right now," Sweets told him. "I could kill you for that."

"Sweets," Lankin said, wanting to end this before something really bad happened.

The legionnaire ignored him. The Gestori clawed at Sweets's gloves, coughing and gasping for air.

"All I have to do is squeeze just a little harder and you're done, you know that? I don't want to be on this Oba-forsaken planet any more than you want me to be here, but neither of us have a choice."

Lankin cringed when his L-comm's command channel buzzed and Lieutenant Duval's ID tag appeared on his HUD. A quick glance found Duval's TT-16 circling above. "What is going on out there, Sergeant Lankin?"

Hell-spawned big brother, Lankin thought. "Nothing, sir. We have it under control."

"Under control? It doesn't appear as though you have anything under control, Sergeant. You need to get hold of your man and stop him from escalating the situation any more than he already has. I want to see his name on a report by the end of the day."

"Sir, the Gestori—"

"Sergeant, we are the elite are we not?"

Lankin ground his teeth. "Yes, sir."

"That's right, and as such, we will not let our emotions or actions be decided for us by the people we are here to protect. Now, order your man to release that driver or I will have reprimands ready for both of you to sign when you return to base."

Angry shouts from the crowd of onlookers drew Lankin's attention. There were twenty of them shouting and pointing and waving fists, with more coming up from further down the line.

This is going to get bad.

"Sweets, stand down."

The legionnaire didn't immediately release the Gestori, holding him for another few seconds before allowing the alien to drop to the ground. The driver kicked his legs to scoot away, holding his throat and coughing dramatically.

Sweets paid no attention the gasping indig. "Bring me a cutting torch."

The alien muttered a string of raspy, local curses, but didn't reengage. Instead, he backed farther away from the legionnaire, eyes filled with hatred and rage.

A second later, Sweets had the torch lit and was stepping toward the hatch.

Through his optical scope, Lankin saw what he interpreted as cold determination on the alien's face. Something had changed about the driver's demeanor, something that made the hair on the back of Lankin's neck stand up.

Whether he got the same feeling or had his own reasons, Lieutenant Duval likewise didn't care for what he saw. "Sergeant, have the corporal stand down. We aren't going to be destroying any property today."

"Stand by, sir." He changed comm channels with a flick of his tongue. "Sweets, eyes up, your driver is—"

Lieutenant Duval cut him off, breaking into the squad comm. "Sergeant Lankin, my orders are to stand down. We are not destroying any property."

"Cross, Saretti, keep an eye on that guy," Lankin said, following the Gestori with his optics. The alien took a last look at the legionnaires and ducked between two vehicles.

The two men broke off from the team, each taking one side of the road, jogging back along the column of vehicles. Saretti, on the near side, kept his N-4 close to his chest, barrel pointing at the ground, bucket turning back and forth, searching.

"I don't see him, Sarge," Saretti said.

"He's two vehicles up on your left," Lankin told him.

The Gestori crouched down, vanishing briefly behind a group of bystanders, then reappearing again a moment later, still watching the legionnaires.

"He's definitely worried about something," Lankin said. "Right there—he's just past those drivers."

Saretti worked his way through the small crowd. A couple individuals backed off, shouting alien curses at the leejes. One tried to shove Saretti, but the leej sidestepped the push, brushing the alien's hand aside.

Good restraint, Lankin thought.

The Gestori turned and broke into a jog, moving down the line of parked vehicles, weaving between other aliens and vehicles. Every few meters he checked over his shoulder, obviously watching for pursuers.

His hands disappeared inside his loose tunic.

Oh no. "Eyes up, he's reaching for something." Lankin keyed his rifle, locking the man's target signature into the optics link with his HUD.

Saretti slowed, lifting his N-4 to his shoulder. "What is it?"

"I don't know." Blood pounded in Lankin's ears when he realized he might actually have to take the shot. Two hundred and seven meters. Child's play. Still, this wasn't a computerized target on the range. This was an actual flesh and blood being.

The Gestori ducked behind a flatbed, the truck's repulsor pads making the air shimmer and kicking up dust. He took a knee and pulled something from his tunic. It gleamed in the sunlight and Lankin's heart skipped a beat.

"Saretti, watch out he's got a—" Lankin didn't have enough time to finish, the Gestori was already moving. The alien slid between two onlookers and raised an old-fashioned slug-thrower in his green, scaled hands.

Lankin didn't think twice.

Krak-bdew!

The rifle recoiled at almost the same instant the bolt slammed into the Gestori's chest, leaving a gaping entry wound. The alien landed hard on his back and lay still.

The Gestori scattered. Legionnaires jumped from their overwatch stations, taking up defensive positions around the target vehicle, N-4s leveled at the crowd.

"Dammit! Cease fire!" Lieutenant Duval screamed through the L-comm, his voice cracking. "Cease fire!"

When there were no more shots fired, the crowd re-formed, angrier now. They shouted at the leejes, shaking fists. One picked up a rock and hurled it at Sweets. It bounced harmlessly off the legionnaire's armor. Sweets pointed his N-4 at the alien, shouting for him to get back.

Lankin ignored his lieutenant's screaming for a cease fire that had already happened. He'd only needed one shot anyway. "Sweets, enemy down, secure the target."

Sweets shouted orders for the crowd to disperse, but that only enraged them further. They pressed closer, their courage growing when the legionnaires held their fire. Two more rocks sailed through the air, one striking a leej square in the bucket's visor. The second leej twisted away just in time, the rock glanced off his shoulder and dropped to the ground.

Lankin panned his scope across the crowd, looking for more weapons, but aside from a few rocks, the aliens weren't armed.

"Disperse!" Sweets shouted again. "By the order of the Legion!"

"Sergeant, get ahold of your people now!" Duval shouted.

Captain Kato came over the L-comm. "Sergeant Lankin, what's your status?"

"One hostile down, sir," Lankin said, feeling helpless behind his N-18, so far away from the impending riot. It was the only downside to the weapon—if legal action wasn't called for, it was nothing more than a highly advanced optical scope.

"I've got a lot of angry indigs out here, sir. They're pretty pissed off. You might want to send some marines down here ASAP."

"Hold what you've got. I'm sending a squad to reinforce your position, they'll be there in five."

"Roger that, sir."

Chaos erupted and spread down the transport inspection line. The crowd was growing by the second. Some Gestori had found pipes and were brandishing them at the edge of the mob. The new weapons and swelling crowds fueled the aliens' rage.

"Sarge?" Cross asked, from the guard shack, his N-4 at low ready. "KTF, right?"

"No," Lankin said. "None of them are armed, Private. You wanting to shoot unarmed civilians?"

"Don't look unarmed to me," Cross replied.

Cross and Saretti had fallen back with the rest of the squad, forming up around the truck they'd been inspecting when this started. Sweets shouted warnings at the crowd edging closer to the legionnaires' position.

A Gestori at the front lobbed a rock at Private Saretti. Saretti caught it in one hand and threw it back, hitting the alien in the shoulder.

"Saretti, stand down!" Lankin shouted.

The private threw his hands up, shaking his head. "What are we supposed to do, Sarge, just stand here?"

The telltale hum of sleds coming in at high speed stopped him from responding. Two combat sleds appeared through the trees, rocketing down the road toward the gatehouse. Each sled had a marine behind the turret gun, holding the weapons as steady as they could.

"Stryker-10 to marine sleds, let them know you're here," Lankin said.

"Aye, sir."

The lead sled's turret gun opened up, sending a trail of blaster fire through the trees several dozen meters away from the mob of Gestori. The amount of fire the turret guns put out still impressed Lankin, and the Gestori agreed. They ran for cover, the crowd scurrying like pelcorse roaches under a flashlight.

"Yeah, that's right, you scat-brained skets," Cross shouted.

"Hold formation," Lankin ordered, panning over the fleeing crowd with his optics. Here and there a Gestori stopped, turning to glare and shout alien curses, but most realized they'd lost the advantage and fled, dropping rocks and pipes and making their way back to their own vehicles.

"Sergeant Lankin, report status," Captain Kato said.

Lankin blew out a long breath. "Situation under control, sir. They've dispersed."

Lieutenant Duval's voice came over the L-comm next. "Report to Command, Sergeant. And I mean, right now!"

*I want you to know just how important both of
you are to me.*

07

Lankin yanked on the door of the office without waiting for Lieutenant Duval to answer his knock. Duval looked up from behind his desk, his face turning red with anger. He slammed down a palm, spilling his tea across a collection of data pads.

"Dammit, what in the hell is wrong with you, Sergeant! You don't come barging your way into my office unless you want to get busted down to private real quick!"

"Sir, I need to speak with you immediately."

"The hell you do! You and your men are out of control! We are here as peacekeepers, not kelhorned assassins!"

Lankin was taken aback. "Assassins? Sir, that Gestori was going to—"

"You don't have any idea what he was going to do or not do!"

Lankin fought hard to keep his outrage from boiling over. "He had a weapon, sir! He was a threat, plain and simple!"

"No, Sergeant," Duval said, holding out a datapad. "It's not plain and simple."

Lankin took the pad. As what he was seeing on the screen registered, he knew exactly where the point was going.

An infrared video feed of the checkpoint from Duval's TT-16 aerial surveillance bot, looking down on the first few vehicles stopped at the checkpoint. Lankin's legionnaires and the marines were pushing back the wildly gesticulating mob. There was no audio, but Lankin could still hear the cursing in his mind.

It took several seconds for the squad to secure the scene, and as they surrounded the dead Gestori, Lieutenant Duval paused the feed.

"If this man was such a threat, care to explain why no weapon was found on the body?"

"Someone in the crowd must have picked it up, sir," Lankin said, struggling to control his voice. "He had a weapon. A pistol of some kind."

Duval snatched the pad back. "Of some kind? Of some kind! That's not an acceptable answer, Sergeant. I know your relatively uneducated mind doesn't have any concept of thought outside of marching and shooting, but the Legion does have regulations and rules of engagement we must adhere to. We're not a company of gunfighters that can go and do whatever we want."

"I'm well aware of the rules of engagement, sir. 71st Legion Regulations, Section 3, paragraph a.1: Force deemed necessary to stop a threat shall be permissible, even if such force is applied before such threat has taken overt action."

"Did you just quote regulations to me, Sergeant?"

"He had a weapon, sir! He was threatening my men, I took action."

Duval sneered. "And yet no one else saw this threat. No one else fired. And no weapon was recovered."

"It was there," Lankin said, enunciating each word.

"What is it about you meatheads that you can't get it through those thick skulls of yours? We are here to protect life and property of the Republic. Not to take lives. Not to kill." Duval stood up and snatched the datapad back from Lankin's hands. "Killing is not protecting! If the House of Reason wanted these people dead, they'd have sent more than twenty of you kelhorns, now wouldn't they? The days of mindless warfare and destruction are behind us, Sergeant. You missed the Savage Wars and you have my apologies for that, but we are peacekeepers here. That is our role."

"No, sir," Lankin said. "We're warfighters. That's what the Legion trained us for. That's what they pay us for, to fight the wars no one else wants to. And I'm telling you, that Gestori had a weapon, I saw it as clear as I see you right now. I took action to protect the lives of my men."

"You took a bad shot!" Duval screamed. "Why can't you just admit it! You're wrong, Sergeant, and you're testing my patience!"

The door behind Lankin slammed open and Captain Kato strode in. He stepped between the two men, eyeing them both in turn. "What's going on here?"

"Captain Kato," Duval blurted out before Lankin had a chance to speak, "I'm just in the middle of dealing with a critical situation, sir. But I have it under control."

"Control? It doesn't sound like there's much control in here."

Duval cleared his throat. "Yes, sir. Apologies." He straightened his uniform. For the first time since entering the office, Lankin noticed the lieutenant wasn't wearing battle armor, he was wearing battalion greens, the Legion's office uniform. It wasn't *quite* a regulation, but standard operating procedure called for the wearing of armor at all times while in theater unless sleeping or bathing.

Of course he'd go against SOP, Lankin thought.

Kato turned to Lankin. "Sergeant?"

"Yes, sir. Everything is under control."

The captain regarded him for a moment, then nodded.

"Very well," Duval said, trying to reassert some authority into the conversation. "Until this investigation is over, you're off overwatch duty, Sergeant Lankin."

"You can't take me off overwatch!"

"Are you telling me what I can and can't do, Sergeant? This is my platoon!"

"Easy, Sergeant Lankin," Captain Kato warned.

Lankin opened his mouth then closed it, clenching his jaw.

The lieutenant continued, "You're also to turn over your weapon. You will join the rest of the platoon on the ground. A more fitting place for a sergeant is with his men, don't you think, Captain?"

Lankin saw red. A cold determination washed over him. "You're not taking my weapon, sir."

"You'll hand over your rifle, Sergeant Lankin. That's an order."

"No, sir. I won't."

"Enough," Captain Kato said. "Both of you stand down."

Duval's eyes widened in shock. "Captain Kato, I'm well within my—"

"I said stand down, Lieutenant." He pointed at Lankin. "You're off overwatch for now, but you'll keep your rifle. Store it in your barracks and keep it unloaded. Requisition an N-4 from the armory."

Lankin was on the verge of protesting but a look from the captain told him now was not the time. "Yes, sir."

Kato nodded. "Very good. We'll all continue our discussion at a later time, roger that, Sergeant?"

"Roger that."

"You're dismissed."

*I could not ask for a more caring set
of parents.*

Talon knelt in the tall grass, inspecting the jagged hole in the security fence around Pillar 13B. They were off the main road and, once again, the insurgent forces had disappeared without a trace.

"I'm really getting tired of this," Talon muttered, running gloved fingers over the smooth line a cutting torch burned into the fence.

"What is that, four this week?" Burga asked.

Talon nodded, searching the ground for any evidence. The insurgents had definitely stepped up their attacks on the fencing, but so far it had only been probing missions, testing response times. The constant alarms were starting to wear on him.

Even more frustrating was the fact that they'd yet to see a single enemy target. The jungle made their TT-16 aerial surveillance bots all but useless; the canopy was just too dense. Talon guessed that even if the peepers could track through the foliage, by the time they managed to get into position after an attack, there wouldn't be anyone to track anyway. These locals had proved themselves to be a wily bunch.

"Unpack the replacement," Talon said, standing.

He checked the time on his HUD. Patching the fence would take another thirty minutes and they still needed to get their load of additional security barriers to Dirty, before the next shift of marines came on duty.

The two trucks they'd commandeered to transport cargo containers appropriated from the docks sat parked behind their combat sled. Duracore had provided drivers, though Talon would've preferred to have his own people operate the vehicles. The company drivers stood around, watching the legionnaires work.

One of them, a tall, slender Gestori male in Duracore overalls, tossed his smoke aside and asked Talon, "How long is that going to take, eh? We need to be back before sunset, I've got stuff to do tonight."

"Keep your pants on," Talon called back. "You'll be home in plenty of time to take 'em off later tonight."

Burga lit his cutting torch, making a popping sound. "It should only take another four hours to get this thing fixed up."

"Four hours?" the alien screeched.

"Relax," Talon told the driver. "It won't be four hours. Go back to your vehicle so we can roll out when we're ready."

The driver spat out a string of native curses Talon didn't understand and stalked to his truck.

"Was it something I said?" Burga asked with amusement.

"You know, if I didn't know any better, I'd think you were intentionally trying to set me up for failure."

"Not me, Sarge. No way! I'm here for you."

Talon shook his head and jabbed a thumb at the damaged fence. "Get to work, Corporal."

Burga saluted. "Yes, sir, Sergeant Talon, sir. By your command!"

Talon grinned and stepped out of the way to let the marine repair team pass. The patch job would only take another ten minutes, then they'd be on their—

A two-tone alarm chimed in his helmet, a secure L-comm request from the command post.

"Go for Stryker-10."

"Stryker-10, Stryker-1," Captain Kato said. "We've had another alarm triggered on Pillar 29-bravo. That's about a klick south of your current position. I need you to respond immediately and assess the situation."

Talon cursed silently. "What about the transports, sir? I can't leave them unprotected."

"Leave two sentries and proceed at best speed to the alarm site, Sergeant. You're the closest team."

Talon again cursed to himself, trying to picture the road back down to 29. "Roger that, sir. Stryker-10 out." He switched to his external speaker. "Sergeant VanZant."

"Yes, sir?" The Repub marine looked up from instructing a group of marines on installation procedures. Talon waved him over.

"Hey now, Marine, we both still work for a living."

The marine grinned. "Roger that."

"We've had another alarm. CP wants us to check it out. You good with your team here?"

"Yes, sir, it'll take another ten minutes or so to get that fence unpacked and installed. We'll be fine."

Talon nodded. "Good. I'm going to leave two legionnaires here, and once we're done checking it out, we'll link back up at your location."

The marine nodded. "Roger that, Sergeant."

Burga fell into step behind Talon as he called for his team. "What do you know, Sarge?"

Talon shook his head. "Probably just another false alarm. One of those orange and white critters bumped the fence again or something."

Burga stopped beside the sled's ramp, propping his N-4 over his shoulder. "We really need to set up holocams."

Talon gestured for him to get on board. "Yeah. You got any?"

***

Talon watched the external feeds as they made their way through the thick jungle. Burga was absolutely right. If the Republic would've ponied up the credits for cameras out here, most of these assessment missions would be unnecessary. But asking the Republic for more credits for anything that might help the Legion was like asking a mother to give up her firstborn.

What is this now, six false alarms in two days? Talon thought.

Next to the live feeds, the sector map marked their squad's position as a green triangle moving through a satellite view of Gangeers' jungle. A flashing red dot indicated the pillar, directly southeast of their current position.

Pylon 29 was in a small valley, about a hundred meters across. The area immediately around the two-meter wide impervisteel columns had been cleared at some time in the past to facilitate construction of the mag-lev track, and more recently the protective fencing around the complex. Now though, the area had regrown considerably.

The sled crested the northern hill and slowed as they neared the twenty-meter access road connecting the main road to the pillar complex. The lane was barely wide enough to get the sled through and—

A high-pitched whine cut through the air. Talon had just enough time to process what the sound was before the rocket slammed home.

The explosion rocked the sled, knocking the unsus-pecting legionnaires from their seats, sending weapons flying. Talon hit the floor hard, bucket knocking against the opposite bench. Fortunately, his bucket's sound damp-eners kicked on.

Someone started shouting over the L-comm and Talon heard the *dat-dat-dat-dat-dat* of the sled's twin guns. He grabbed his N-4 and shouted for his team to bail.

Another rocket streaked through the air, trailing smoke. Talon sprinted down the ramp as the missile slammed into something behind the sled and exploded.

"Eyes up!" Talon shouted, taking cover behind the sled, hoping it would stand up to additional punishment. A hail of weapons fire shredded the nearby trees, filling the air with sprays of bark and leaves. Plumes of earth marked blaster bolts pounding the ground.

Bishto took a bolt to the shoulder, the impact spinning him around, knocking him off his feet. He fell in the middle of the access road and lay still.

Burga darted from behind the sled to help the fallen leej. "You okay, buddy?"

Bishto groaned. His armor was charred where the bolt had caught him. Burga knelt to examine the wound. A blaster bolt sizzled through the air above them, then a second glanced off Bishto's helmet, knocking it slightly askew.

"Son of—" Burga grabbed Bishto with one hand, adjusted his bucket with the other and hauled the injured leej back to cover. "It's going to be all right, Bish. Medic!"

"Open up!" Talon shouted, leaning around the bumper and releasing a barrage of blaster fire. "Get some fire on 'em!"

His HUD identified nine hostile targets and immediately forwarded the data to the squad's battlenet. His optics zoomed in, giving him a clear view of the insurgents. Five of the tall, bipedal attack force scrambled for cover behind a six-wheeled, all-terrain transport. Thick orange fur stuck out of gaps in their black, leather clothes and tactical gear. A few wore masks, but Talon could see the faces of the others clearly enough. Their tiny red eyes and orange and black mottled skin was all he needed to see.

Talusar, Talon thought. *What the hell are they doing all the way out here?*

The other four insurgents made it through the fence around the pylon, took cover behind one of the pillars, and fired bolts of energy toward the legionnaires.

Blaster fire slammed into the sled's turret, forcing Private Mazine to duck for cover.

Another high-pitched whine cut through the air.

Talon shouted, "Mazine, look—"

But Mazine was gone before Talon finished his warning, diving out of the turret and launching himself into the air before the rocket slammed home. The blast wave caught him mid-flight, turning his dive into a cartwheel, and he hit the ground hard, rolling to a stop face down in the grass.

The sled rocked violently on its repulsors, the impact pushing it several meters back. The back collided with a fleeing leej, knocking him to the ground. Flames engulfed the front of the sled and Talon's heart sank at sight of the destroyed driver's compartment, now a burning coffin for two marines.

Talon found cover behind the trees, checking the enemy positions on his HUD. Burga threw Bishto over his shoulder and followed. Mazine picked himself up and scrambled after them.

Fifteen meters in, Burga laid Bishto down behind a tree and pulled his helmet off. Lancil dropped to a knee, shrugging his medkit from his back.

"You're supposed to dodge those things," Lancil told him, pulling a skinpack from his bag and pressing it against the wound. Bishto grimaced, pulling away from the pressure. Lancil used his free hand to push the leej down. "Hold still."

"He going to be okay?" Burga asked.

"He'll be outta commission for a couple days, but he'll be fine."

Bishto pushed himself up on his elbows, gritting his teeth, face contorted in pain. "I can fight."

"You need to let this stuff work," Lancil said.

"Fix me later," he growled.

Lancil appealed to Talon, "Sarge, help me out here."

A blaster bolt snapped overhead. "Stay put, Bishto, that's an order," Talon said.

"But, Sarge—"

"No arguments. Stay down and stay still."

Talon needed to get control before the situation deteriorated any further. The Talusar were going to pin them down if they didn't get moving.

"Burga, Ginn, flank right; Lancil, Mazine left. Pax, find a perch and do some work with that N-18. The rest of you, with me."

Staying low, Talon made his way through the thick jungle, away from the sled. Another rocket found it and this time punched through rear armor. The explosion ripped the transport in half, sending debris and flames into the air.

"Where in the hell did they get A-P rockets?" Burga asked over the L-comm.

"See if you can keep them busy," Talon said. "I'm going to try to work my way around to the north and come up behind them."

"Roger that, Sarge."

Talon ducked blaster bolts zipping past his bucket. "Come on!"

He led his small group through the trees, praying that the enemy's equipment couldn't see through the thick foliage. The random fire tearing up the jungle around him suggested they couldn't, but it was impossible to know for sure.

As they got farther away from the sled, the fire became sporadic and the battle noise faded into the jungle background.

Talon took a knee when they reached a spot due north of the pillars, taking a breather and allowing his bucket's computer to map out the enemy positions again. From here, he could see where they cut through the fence. They were working on something next to one of the pylons.

Talon zoomed in with his bucket's optics.

It's a bomb.

"Stryker elements, heads up, they've got explosives, they're trying to demo a pylon, check your fire. Those things don't react well to blasters."

"We don't react well to blasters, Sarge," Burga said, over blaster fire in the background.

"Okay, Pax, move right; Singh, you're left; Ginn, on my six. We can't let them detonate those explosives. Burga, let them know where you are!"

"Roger that, sir."

Leej fire erupted from the south, battle cries projected at max volume through external speakers announcing Burga's team engaging. Two tangos ducked behind a truck in the center of the clearing. Three more took off at a sprint to the northeast, heading for the tree line.

"Go!"

Talon brought his N-4 up and advanced.

One of the aliens hiding behind the truck turned, somehow aware of Talon's movement, and fired in his team's direction. Talon dropped to a knee. Blaster fire tore through the jungle around him. He kicked his N-4 to full power, aimed and fired at the truck, just missing the insurgent standing next to it. The enemies fled farther behind the truck, taking themselves out of Talon's sights.

"Ginn! Get that A-P launcher up—take out their cover."

"On it, Sarge!"

Talon heard the lock-on beep of the anti-vehicle launcher and then felt the air blossom from the pressure of the missile streaking toward the vehicle. The back of the truck exploded in a brilliant fireball, sending it flipping. The blast blew both insurgents back, flailing like rag dolls. The one that had been shooting at Talon lost his weapon on impact. The other smacked into a tree, his body snapping at an awkward angle.

Out of the corner of his eye, Talon saw the other three disappear into the jungle.

"They're disengaging to the northeast," Pax advised.

"On it," Burga replied.

"Watch those two," Talon said, pointing. He kept to the edge of the tree line, seeking a better position to watch the remaining enemies.

One had dropped to a prone position, firing in the direction of Burga's team, covering his companions. The other two leaned out from their cover behind one of the pylons, firing on Talon's position.

Talon ducked as the tree beside him erupted in blaster fire, sending bark and dust spraying into the air, adding to the already thick haze. He dove and rolled behind another tree, avoiding the super-heated bolts tearing up the jungle around him.

Singh and Ginn opened up. Talon felt the concussions from their fire as he low-crawled forward, debris clinking off his helmet.

"One down!" Ginn advised over the squad channel.

Talon rolled right, behind a fallen tree. He peered over the trunk and saw the proned out tango trying to reload a charge pack. The Talusar was one of the few with a mask on, which seemed pointless. Talon doubted if any human, let alone his squad could identify a particular Talusar in a lineup. They all looked the same to him.

Not fast enough, Talon thought. He used the tree to steady his shot, then put a bolt through his Talusar's mask. The alien's head jerked back, bounced forward, and face-planted, as dead as his charge pack.

Another insurgent, holding his rifle at waist height, fired wildly, shouting curses at the legionnaires. Talon lined up his shot and fired. The alien's rifle went spinning out of his hands. He landed hard on his back and didn't move.

The last Talusar stumbled over his companion's body and bolted for the jungle.

"I got him," Pax said over the L-comm.

The bolt took the insurgent in the back, sending him sprawling forward, as dead as the rest.

"Boom," Pax said, lowering his rifle to admire his shot. "Ya dead."

Talon stayed where he was, waiting. None of the downed saboteurs moved and the ones who'd fled weren't engaging. They'd disappeared into the thick jungle.

"Move up," Talon said, getting to his feet.

The legionnaires came carefully out of the jungle, into the clear.

Talon ignored the burning vehicle, making straight for the pylons. He ducked through the fence, stopping next to the small bundle the insurgents had been working on.

"How's it look, Sarge?" Burga asked.

Talon didn't respond, instead holding up a hand for silence. He was no explosives expert and part of him screamed to get away, but he crouched down and inspected it, trying to determine whether the device was active or not. It only took a second to figure out.

"It's not armed," Talon said and got to his feet. "But let's clear out until we can get a team here, just in case."

"Hey, Sarge," Burga said. "You might want to come check this out, too."

Burga was holding one of the corpses' black helmets. The alien's head was covered in orange and black scales, its blood-red eyes staring lifelessly into the sky. Its mouth hung open, blood seeping between jagged teeth. Curly orange fur stuck out from the collar of its green and brown camouflage shirt.

Talon stopped next to the corporal, inspecting the alien corpse. "Talusar?"

"You ever heard of them operating outside the Neburai Cluster before?" Burga asked.

Talon shook his head. "Never. And they're typically freighter pirates, so what the hell are they doing here?"

Take heart in the knowledge that you raised a smart, caring, and courageous young man, and everything I am today, I am because of you two.

09

"These legionnaires were meant to protect us, not kill us!" Sharn Lun, a representative of the Gestori Workers League shouted, pointing at Lankin and Captain Kato.

The two legionnaires stood at the back of the room, watching the locals argue and shout back and forth at each other. As Lankin understood it, the captain had been invited to take part in the discussion about recent events, but it quickly dissolved into a shouting match, with the two legionnaires as targets rather than participants.

Lankin had spent the last few days attached to the captain's hip, following him around during his mandatory cooling off period, something he'd repeatedly tried to explain was unnecessary, but the captain wasn't having it. The event he'd thought was the highlight of a new sniper's career had turned into a huge mess.

In sniper school, earning your Death Angel wings was laudable—a special occasion, something to remember for your entire career. The Death Angels didn't have a scoreboard per se, but some snipers were more accomplished than others. They didn't share their exploits with anyone who didn't wear the wings, and usually only the newest members actually talked about their kills. But what else could you talk about? A sniper's job was to kill.

The investigation was ongoing and Lankin had no doubt it would continue for weeks after this crap mission was over. He'd never been the focus of a wrongful death investigation, but he'd seen them and knew they weren't quickly dealt with.

The captain had pulled him from regular patrol and assigned him to a personal security detail. With the increased attacks, Kato had found an alternative to kitchen duty, which neither Lankin or Duval could complain about. Lankin would've preferred to be with his men, but he couldn't deny that garrison duty wasn't a bad gig, especially working directly for the captain.

Major Wyeire wanted Lankin recalled to the *Vendetta* after the checkpoint incident, but Captain Kato had somehow managed to keep that from happening. No one knew for sure, but rumor was Kato leveraged some connections in higher Republic leadership. But Lankin never heard any specific names and wasn't sure he believed it. Kato certainly wasn't a point and he didn't seem the type of man to use personal connections for professional gain—unlike appointed officers. The truth of how it happened was something Lankin would probably never know, but the major had relented and allowed him to stay with his platoon.

Lankin didn't enjoy the townhall meetings taking place on an almost nightly basis. Company representatives, along with civilian representatives for the workers, were not only at odds with each other, but with the Legion as well. The captain attempted to get both sides to see reason but had failed miserably. The only thing they could do now was listen to the ruckus and hope it didn't get too out of hand.

"That is not what happened," Gabriel Fartush said, wagging a finger at the worker's representative.

Fartush was a low-level Republic diplomatic envoy flown in two days after the incident at Checkpoint Bravo, "To ensure a fair and impartial investigation." Lankin had trouble not rolling his eyes when the envoy had presented himself to the captain, but Fartush had done just what he said he was going to do. Not to mention trying everything in his power to shift blame for the incident with the insurgents.

Fartush continued, "We have shown you the evidence from the transport. You are all well aware of what that driver was trying to bring into the city. I can't believe any one of you would be so blind as to believe he was not the real enemy. Your enemy is certainly not these legionnaires."

Forgot about the rockets, did ya? Lankin thought.

The saving grace for Lankin was when they were finally able to inspect the transport at the checkpoint, they found fourteen rocket propelled grenade launchers stashed in a hidden compartment in the back. They hadn't been able to recover any documentation about the origin or destination of the weapons, but they'd traced them back to the ship that delivered them and now the hauler was impounded off the coast, unable to leave until the investigation was complete.

That should have been enough to show Lankin was justified—the driver clearly knew what he was doing. But for some reason, the townsfolk always conveniently forgot about the weapons being smuggled and focused on the Gestori Lankin shot. The weapon he tried to use against Lankin's team had yet to be found and Lankin was under no illusion that it would magically turn up some day. The evidence was gone and the HUD recording from Lankin's bucket was deemed inconclusive.

After some bickering over semantics, Sharn said, "You expect us to just believe something is true because the Republic says it's true? You people have not only been lying to us the entire time you've been on our planet, but long before as well. The Gestori Workers League sees no reason to trust blindly. That man was a father and a husband and had no criminal record or history of violence in his entire life. He'd been a schoolteacher, for Oba's sake!"

A schoolteacher with a crapload of high explosives.

As the meeting dragged on, Lankin found it harder and harder to keep his mouth shut. He managed it, knowing the fallout wouldn't be worth whatever cathartic release came with putting these kelhorns in their place.

"Schoolteacher or not," Kato said. "Our investigation is ongoing. And any pressure on us to presume the guilt of a legionnaire is futile."

Lankin was impressed with the captain's control, holding his temper so well under the circumstances. He'd felt the urge to pummel everyone in this room like an Acabar cougar.

"Oh, I'm sure your investigation will be fair and balanced," Sharn said, his voice dripping with sarcasm. "It's insulting that you have this killer—" he pointed at Lankin "—anywhere other than in prison! And why is it you all-powerful legionnaires haven't been able to find one shred of evidence as to the origin of these insurgents? With all the resources available to you, I find it hard to believe you haven't discovered any useful information."

"We will root out the insurgents," Kato said, ignoring the comment about Lankin beyond a fractional headshake at the sergeant that suggested he not react. "Make no mistake about that."

"And in the meantime," Sharn continued, crossing his arms and addressing Pentu Solusar, the highest ranking Duracore manager in the room, "how are we going to guarantee the safety of the workers during this crisis? Surely you can't expect my people to continue to work under these conditions—the threat of murder from terrorists *and* those supposedly protecting them—for the pitiful stipend Duracore provides?"

And there it is, Lankin thought. *It always comes back to credits.*

The Duracore manager, himself a Gestori, stood, his long purple robes pulling tight across his ample stomach as he pushed himself out of his seat. His gray skin was spotted with patches of black and white, some kind of skin disease according to the marine doctors.

When he spoke, his jowls bounced and his neck jiggled. "Now, you hold on there just a minute, Sharn. Duracore pays all our employees a fair wage. A wage, I might add, that all parties agreed to when the contracts were signed."

"Bah," Sharn brushed it off. "*Fair wage.* It's a pittance, nowhere near what we should be earning for the work. I know of several other off-world operations where laborers are compensated at ten times what my people are for similar work. Not to mention, they don't have to be in constant fear."

"Then perhaps your people should seek employment on those planets," Solusar said. "As for protection, we have provided security and will provide additional services as the need arises."

"Services! Whatever you want to call them, they're not enough to keep us safe, obviously! Our people are here to provide for their families, not to die for your ore. I have half a mind to encourage them to—"

Solusar's face turned darker shades of gray. "I would choose your words carefully, Sharn. Anything that might be considered a breach of contract will be dealt with accordingly."

Sharn narrowed his eyes. "Encourage our people to start taking precautions for their own safety. I don't think we're at the point where striking would be necessary."

"Nor lawful under the terms of the agreement!" the Duracore lackey growled back.

Fartush took the reins. "It may be a prudent time to remind everyone present that while this is a Duracore project, the Republic is spending exorbitant amounts of money to fund and operate this endeavor. Any worker or representative that is found to be actively obstructing or hindering the operation will face legal action and be responsible for restitution of costs incurred by such legal action or interruption of mining operations."

Lankin smiled behind his helmet as both the Duracore manager and workers' representative gaped at Fartush. The envoy just revealed himself to be an attorney. And while Lankin had no love for lawyers—in his opinion, they weren't worth the oxygen they used and should all be served up to hungry retantors—but in this situation, he didn't mind hearing the man's legal opinion on the case.

"Now," Fartush said. "It's getting late. I think we can adjourn our meeting tonight and set a date next week for 3rd Day."

The representatives hastened to agree and the crowd began to disperse.

Captain Kato motioned for Lankin to meet at the door. Outside, Kato opened a private L-comm channel. "Aren't you glad you never got into politics?"

"Yes, sir," Lankin agreed. They climbed into the back of the waiting command sled. "Maybe next time they'll actually let you speak at the briefing you were asked to give."

"Doubtful."

Lankin took a seat across from the captain. "My father wanted me to go into politics. He'd been a planetary rep for fifty years before retiring to the wind farm."

Kato pulled his bucket off and ran a hand over his short-cropped hair. "Why didn't you?"

Lankin laughed, pulling off his own helmet. The air inside the sled was cool and dry. "I didn't want to sell my soul to the devil, I guess. Shooting people is a whole lot easier than trying to get them to work together. Well, most of the time."

"What do you mean by that?"

Lankin hesitated.

Kato nodded at him. "Speak freely, Sergeant."

Lankin sniffed. "Well, sir, part of me agrees with that Sharn character—we do need more support down here. I think we've seen that the situation is more unstable than was originally anticipated. At the very least, we should bring 2nd Platoon down. Even using the marines like we are, we don't have the numbers to act as security *and* launch an effective offensive against these insurgents."

The captain considered Lankin's words and said, "You surprise me, Sergeant."

"How's that, sir?"

"You see the entire picture, not just your small area of responsibility. A lot of legionnaires, while extremely effective killing machines, can't see past the muzzle of their own blaster."

"Thank you, sir."

"And, as it happens, I agree with you. I've already broached this with command, and they don't agree. The need to prevent this situation from getting out of control was expressly addressed, reinforced by the suggestion that personnel files would reflect the success or failure of the mission."

Lankin opened his mouth, but no words came. He was surprised the captain would entrust such information to one of his NCOs—typically complaints flowed up the chain, not down. Then again, Captain Kato wasn't a typical

Legion officer. The fact that Major Wyeire had all but said *succeed and further your career, or fail at the expense of it*, spoke a lot about the importance of their mission here.

"We've got to hold what we've got, Sergeant Lankin. That's as simple as it gets. As it stands now, we're not going to get any help down here, so we're going to have to make do with what we have."

"I understand, sir."

"Good. Because tomorrow we start pushing back."

Although it might seem like my life was cut short, I believe I have lived a life that most can only dream of.

10

The jungle air was hot and despite the temperature regulators inside Lankin's armor, he was feeling it. After the first hour of hiking, he'd stopped fidgeting with the controls and resigned himself to the knowledge that it was just going to be hot, and there wasn't any way around it. Fortunately, the synthprene base layer he wore underneath the armor was doing its job and wicking most of his sweat away.

"Are you as good with that N-4 as you are with your N-18?" Corporal Kessler asked over the squad's L-comm.

From the front of the formation, Lankin said, "I've been known to hit a few targets with it from time to time."

Not having his N-18 with him gave Lankin a weird, naked feeling. He'd had that rifle with him nonstop for months, but here, progressing deeper into the jungle, Lankin found he much preferred having the N-4 in his hands than the bulky sniper rifle. Visibility was limited to say the least, not to mention their engagement range was significantly reduced. Unless he climbed to the top of a tree to find a perch, a long-barreled rifle was more a liability than help. And even then, he still wouldn't be able to see what was in front of him beyond a few dozen meters.

Their HUDs helped somewhat. Lankin's was set to a cross section of infrared and true vision. The left half of the bucket's display was a mixture of grays and whites, the right showing the full color foliage around him.

Bugs chirping and birds singing filtered through his bucket's external pickups. He'd switched off the odor filter to smell the fresh jungle air, which probably had something to do with how hot he was under the shell. It was really a nice place, somewhere he'd voluntarily spend time, exploring and enjoying the rainforest. Minus the bloodthirsty Talusar, of course.

Lankin led the squad through the undergrowth. According to the mission map, they had another two kilometers in their search grid. Despite Lieutenant Duval's objections—something the point seemed to be more comfortable doing—Captain Kato had spent the past few days laying down specific search patterns and sharing coordinates and schedules with his squad leaders only.

If the attack at Pylon 29 had shown them anything, it was that the insurgents were well informed of the Republic's movements, and they needed to work harder to conceal the operations. That there were spies in Gangeers actively feeding information to them was a foregone conclusion. Rooting out those spies was another story altogether. Kato put people to work on the intelligence leak. Maintaining random but comprehensive patrolling of the surrounding jungle would produce results.

Lankin squeezed between two flowering purple bushes, enjoying their aroma. Red, purple, and yellow leaves splashed against the verdant greens, a riot of color. After living in cities for almost his entire life, the sweet smells and lush landscape were something Lankin felt he definitely needed more of.

Another, more acrid smell reached him.

Smoke, he thought, frowning.

He twisted around, bringing his N-4 to low ready. "Hold up," he sent on the L-comm. "Do you guys smell that?"

"You got your scrubbers turned off? I can't stand the smell out here," Sweets answered. After a moment, he asked, "Is that smoke?"

Lankin panned his gaze back and forth, waiting for his HUD to tag potential targets. The IR feed detected elevated heat levels from a point seventy-five meters ahead.

"Smells a little like it," Lankin told his team. "Not enough PPMs for the buckets to say either way, but it's possible. Keep your eyes open, I'm going to scout it out."

Keeping low, Lankin pressed through the underbrush, taking care to keep his footsteps light. The heat signature on his IR got more defined as he made his way through the jungle. By the time he reached the base of a small hill, the column of heat rising was clearly visible on his IR spectrum, and through his unfiltered view, he could see a thin line of smoke curling into the air.

"Yeah, something's burning up this way," he announced into the L-comm. "Maybe a campfire or something. Hang back. I'm going for a closer look."

He climbed the hill, dropping a third of the way up and crawling the rest of the way to the peak. He pulled himself up next to a tree and peered around the trunk.

You've got to be kidding me.

The unmistakable remnants of a camp. It had been abandoned recently and hastily, the fire in the center carelessly doused. Smoldering embers were the source of the smoke. Logs had been dragged on either side of the fire for benches. Three tents, large enough for two, maybe three full-grown human males, and crates of supplies piled next to them.

He made a quick scan of the surrounding jungle but detected no enemy signals or movements.

"Heads up, leejes," Lankin said through the L-comm. "Insurgent camp, at the heat signature. It's been recently abandoned."

He gave them the details and marked a spot south of the camp with his HUD. "Sweets, take Kessler and move to this position. I'm not seeing any—wait, no, I am picking up some possible targets inside the middle tent on the west side of the camp."

Lankin held his position, waiting for any sign of hostile targets. The heat signature in the tent hadn't moved since he'd picked it up, which meant whoever was inside was either sleeping or killed recently.

"I'm moving up," Lankin said, getting to his feet. He kept low, creeping slowly, keeping his N-4 trained on the tent and scanning the entire camp.

"On your six, Sarge," Private Corse said over the L-comm.

"Roger."

Sweets reported in. "All right, I'm in position at the south end of camp."

The corporal's silhouette was just visible behind a thick cluster of red and purple fronds.

The heat source inside the tent moved. Lankin froze, finger tensing ever so slightly on the trigger, ready to blast whatever was inside to bits. The tent fabric rustled but nothing emerged through the flap.

His N-4 trained, Lankin inched forward, hyperaware, looking for anything left in the camp that might be a boo-bytrap. There was a tuft of orange fur caught in the hinge of one of the supply crates. On the ground next to it, a tipped over cup.

The tent moved again as Lankin passed the smolder-ing firepit.

Lankin stopped a few feet away from the tent. "Sweets?"

"In position. I've got a clear shot right through the front of the tent but no idea who's in there."

"Private Corse, be ready."

The legionnaire came up behind Lankin. "Roger."

Lankin activated his external speakers. "This is the Republic Legion. We have you surrounded, come out with your hands up and surrender."

The tent rustled again. Someone was definitely moving around in there. Through his IR feed, Lankin could make out what looked like a humanoid near the back of the tent.

"Sweets, you have him on IR?"

"Locked on, Sarge."

"If he comes up looking like he wants to play…"

"Roger that."

Lankin knew the best-case scenario was to take the tent's occupant alive and bring him in for interrogation. There were some in the Republic that frowned upon legionnaire interrogation techniques, but Lankin knew, for the most part, they produced results. The opportunity to acquire actionable intel about their adversaries, their capabilities and agenda would be priceless.

Lankin decided to try another tack. "Listen, we know you're in the tent. You're the only one here. All your buddies left you. Looks like they cared more about themselves than they did you. Come on out and we'll protect you, even give you a meal that's better than whatever you were eating. We're not going anywhere."

"Maybe he doesn't speak Standard," Corse said.

Lankin increased his external volume and repeated his order to come out peacefully. On the IR the figure moved, pressing itself into the far corner.

He shook his head and cursed. "The hard way it is. Corse, grab the flap."

"Roger."

The private stepped up to the front corner of the tent, trying not to give away his position. With his N-4 in one hand, he bent down and grabbed the tent flap with the other.

Lankin let his rifle hang, pushing it around behind him and drew his blaster pistol from its holster on his thigh.

Corse pulled the flap back and Lankin ducked in, frowning at the mass of blankets and—

A blood-chilling screech ripped through the tent and a creature the size of a large dog lunged. All Lankin saw was skeletal limbs and a gaping maw with rows of razor-sharp teeth before it clamped down on him.

He screamed as pain shot through his gun hand. Knifelike teeth tore through armored glove, flesh, tendon, and bone. Lankin fell back, instinctively pulling the trigger, but the blaster pistol didn't fire. He pulled again and again as he fell to the ground. The weapon wasn't firing.

"Oh, sket!" shouted Corse, and Lankin heard the private push his way into the tent.

The creature landed on top of him, adding confusion to the pain clouding his mind. The half-light gave it a devilish look, like a demon from the gates of Hell itself. Four jagged horns stretched out like bony claws behind the eyes. And its mouth…

Blood sprayed from its jaws and Lankin screamed as it wrenched its head back and forth, jerking Lankin with him. The creature's mouth was as wide as its head, almost the width of a legionnaire bucket, but half the height. It made high-pitched guttural sounds, still shaking Lankin like a rat.

Lankin slammed his left fist repeatedly into the side of its head, every blow eliciting a snarl.

Why wouldn't his pistol fire?

"Sarge!" someone shouted over the L-comm.

"Shoot it!" Lankin yelled. "Shoot it! Shoot it!"

One of the rows of eyes locked onto Private Corse. It snarled again, wrenching its head around for a better look at the leej.

Pain like Lankin had never experienced before: he could actually feel the tendons in his hand rip as the thing jerked its head around. The legionnaire kicked out, trying to knock the creature off of him, but six finger-like claws at the end of its spindly legs dug into his armor.

A single shot.

The impact knocked the creature sideways, but not completely off Lankin—its exoskeleton deflected the bolt. It screamed and worked its jaws furiously, redoubling its attack.

Several more shots and the creature howled louder and this time it fell, but the thing still refused to let go.

It backed away from the legionnaires, snarling as it dragged Lankin, teeth digging deeper, determined to keep its prey.

Time lost all meaning for Lankin as he desperately scrambled with the monster trying to keep the pressure off his mutilated hand. The thing had to be some kind of apex predator. The king of the jungle. Lankin could hear himself screaming in pain. The screams gave way to desperate prayers for the pain to stop.

A third barrage of blaster fire slammed into the beast. The creature shrieked again, its furious cry loud enough to cause his bucket's sound-dampeners to kick in. It snapped its jaws several times, glaring at Lankin with both sets of eyes, and in that instant, Lankin's hand was free. His pulled it in close against his chest and rolled away, blood spraying.

It seemed to be considering how badly it wanted to make a meal of the leej. More rounds slammed into it, and it decided. With a final screech of contempt, it turned and disappeared into the jungle.

Lankin rolled onto his back and gritted his teeth, trying not to think about the pulsing pain in his hand. He uncovered his injured hand and saw a mass of mangled flesh.

"Hold on, Sarge, I got you," Sweets said, kneeling beside him. He pulled his medical kit free and rolled it open.

"Holy hell," Corse said. "I've never seen something that could stand up to blaster fire like that before."

Lankin groaned and clutched his hand tighter.

Sweets pulled out a tube of sealant. "Okay, Sarge, let me see."

Lankin heard the words, and on some level even understood them, but he couldn't make his hand move. He cursed through gritted teeth.

Sweets pushed down on his shoulder, forcing him to stay on his back. "Someone help me hold him down."

Lankin felt hands grab him, hold him down. The predator's mouth gaped from his memory and he began to shake. The weight of its body pinned him to the ground as rows of teeth tore through him. The snarling, its ear-splitting screams, rang in his ears.

His leejes held him down even as he tried to wiggle away. He had to escape from the pain. He was convinced the burning agony in his hand would consume the rest of his body if he didn't get away.

Something stung his shoulder and coldness flowed down his arm, washing away the fire.

"Sergeant Lankin, can you hear me?"

Lankin didn't know how to respond, as though he'd forgotten how to speak. He felt his bucket being pulled off.

No, it's still out there, Lankin tried to say, but the words stuck in his mind. He reached up with his good hand and tried to pull his bucket back down, but it was no use. He could only paw feebly at it.

Tears blurred his vision. All he could make out were dark, unfocused figures looming around him. And they spoke to him as if from some distant plane of existence.

"Dude, he's jacked up."

"Maybe that thing had some venom in those fangs?"

One of the figures leaned close. "Sarge? Talk to me, Garo."

He managed a groan through the hazy fog and closed his eyes again, trying to block the swirling world around him.

"Come on," the voice said. "We need to get him back to Wolf."

*Dad, my friend, my teacher, my idol. You taught
me to be brave.*

#

Sergeant Talon stepped up to the small desk just inside the front door to Gangeers' hospital, which was little more than a clinic. "I'm looking for a patient. Garo Lankin?"

"Yes, sir," the reception droid answered. "He is currently under the care of—"

"Thanks, I'll find him." Talon stalked off, leaving it chattering about needing an escort and having to sign in.

Several medbots scurried between rooms, carrying trays and towels, assisting their Gestori minders. Talon cradled his bucket under one arm and weaved through the controlled chaos. The clinic smelled like any other clinic he'd ever been in: sterile, mixed with sweat and blood. An almost constant chorus of coughs echoed through the place. As Talon passed one of the rooms, a medbot pushed aside the curtain on its way out.

Talon stole a glance and saw a Gestori worker lying under several blankets, face covered by a breathing mask.

"Oh, excuse me, sir," the medbot said, pulling the curtain back into place.

Talon ignored the bot, continuing down the line. He'd heard some rumors about the miners getting sick after prolonged exposure to the ore dust, but now he wondered just how many of them had occupied these beds, sick or dying since the operation started up. And whether they were contagious.

He covered his mouth with his free hand.

His buddy Lankin had been in a rough place. The bite was nasty enough in itself, but things went freaky once the docs on base realized that the legionnaire wasn't respond-ing to digit regeneratives—he'd lost three fingers and they weren't growing back in spite of treatment. Compounding the problem was the skinpacks seemed to be fighting to contain some sort of venom or infection the antibodies and multi-vens couldn't bring under control. Reluctantly, Captain Kato made the call to transfer Lankin to this lo-cal clinic after a Gestori working on base said they would know how to fix the legionnaire up. They'd dealt with bites from these creatures before.

Today was the first day Lankin was lucid enough to have visitors, and Talon wasn't going to wait any longer to see his friend. Given the rumors he'd heard, it might be the last chance he'd have while on-planet.

A Gestori woman standing in the aisle asked, "Can I help you?"

"Yes, I'm looking for Sergeant Lankin," Talon said through his gloved hand. The woman's eyes flicked to the hand, which he dropped to his side, feeling silly.

She didn't respond right away, looking him up and down as if she was determining if she would allow him ac-cess to his friend. Finally, she turned and said, "This way."

She led him to the last room and pulled back the curtain.

Lankin looked up from a datapad and grinned. "Well, well, well, finally decided to come see the little people, eh?"

Talon edged around the Gestori woman with a nod of thanks. His friend wore a light blue hospital gown, tied on the sides. His wounded hand was encased in a metal cylinder attached by wires and tubes to a large square machine beside his bed. Two pumps on the top of the device moved up and down, pumping green liquid through the tubes connected to the gauntlet. Another display showed his vitals and toxin levels.

"So, I hear you're going to make it," Talon said, grinning.

"He's stable," the Gestori woman said, without a hint of humor. "His injuries were not life-threatening. Fortunately, I had the supplies on hand for the operation, despite a distinct lack of Republic assistance."

Lankin rolled his eyes, sighing.

Talon snapped, "You mean our efforts to keep you safe? Would you rather we let those Talusar skets blow up your town?"

The woman sniffed. "I'm not worried about being blown up."

"Doc," Lankin said. "Can you give us a minute?"

The Gestori regarded both legionnaires for a long moment. "Five minutes. That's it." She turned and left without another word, pulling the curtain closed behind her.

Talon leaned forward and whispered, "She seems like a barrel of fun."

Lankin closed the datapad he'd been reading and set it on the bed next to him. "You have no idea. And the food in this place..." He made a face.

"Word is, Sweets has been hooking you up with chow."

"Shhh." Lankin raised a finger to his lips. "Keep that on the down low."

"I have a feeling if Doctor No-Fun catches Sweets, he'll end up in a bed right next to you."

"You're right about that. Doc Pendisa has the personality of a bot with faulty emotive software."

"So what's the prognosis?" Talon nodded at Lankin's encased hand.

"Lost three fingers. And the toxins from that damn hellhound are still fighting off the regeneratives. Sounds like the best option is cybernetic replacement—in the short term anyway."

"You know what that means, right?"

Lankin nodded. "Marine docs think they'll be able to reverse the process once we're done here. It's weird; I know my fingers are gone, but I can still feel them."

Talon chuckled, hiding the unease he felt. A sniper losing fingers meant he would be pulled from the field and reassigned. There was a whole slew of evaluations to get through before the Legion decided whether you were functional enough without cybernetics to successfully operate on the battlefield. Most guys weren't.

Talon set his bucket on Lankin's legs, then pulled the chair close, spinning it around to sit backward. "Didn't your parents ever teach you not to pet strange animals?"

"Kelhorned thing can burn in hell."

"Well, rest easy," Talon said. "We caught the thing for ya, strung it up outside the barracks." He crossed his arms. "Not sure how long LT will let it slide, but we'll see. I guess the locals call them kuruprats, not sure what that translates to. They're kind of a menace."

"You don't say."

"That's what I hear," Talon said with a grin. "Near blaster-proof exoskeleton, sharp teeth, venomous saliva... nightmare fuel. Even dead—nightmare fuel."

"I'm surprised Duval let you keep it this long."

Talon sniffed. "Well, technically, he hasn't seen it yet. Hasn't come out of the CP since the Pylon attack. Probably still washing his pants. I hear he was crapping himself during the battle, such as it was."

Lankin arched an eyebrow. "Way I hear it, it was barely that."

"It was a good little gunfight," Talon said. "Talusar are just like Hools, all brawn, no brains. We sent them running for the hills."

"You let them get away, eh? You're slipping in your old age, Chase."

"Ha! Run after them and end up like you? No thanks," Talon said.

"And they haven't shown back up?"

"I think we scared the fight out of them," Talon said. "We've had teams riding with the cargo train ever since, without encountering so much as a probe. Been almost a week. Kato's still asking for reinforcements, but the major keeps shutting him down. Said this small insurgent group shouldn't be causing this many problems and all but blamed Captain Kato for the pylon attack. Said his security measures were inadequate and poorly thought out."

"Coming from the guy who refuses to step foot on the battlefield."

"Hell, I heard the major wants to investigate you for that," Talon said, nodding at Lankin's bandaged hand.

"You've got to be kidding me."

Talon chuckled. "Claims you must have been negligent and that you knowingly put yourself in danger and therefore intentionally damaged Republic property. Next time throw a fragger in the tent first and KTF, huh?"

"You know," Lankin said, shaking his head. "That doesn't surprise me at all if what you're saying is true. Not one bit."

"Doesn't make any sense to me, man."

"Hell, this whole thing doesn't make any sense," Lankin agreed. "The insurgents, the attacks, I mean it's not like they can just sneak the stuff off-planet. So what are they doing here? And don't you think it's weird that the locals don't have any idea who could be behind these attacks? I mean this is an orchestrated thing, you know it is."

"I know," Talon said, even though he wasn't entirely sure it was. "But proving it, that's the issue."

"We need to just crush the bastards. Wyeire needs to bring the rest of the company down and overwhelm the enemy."

"Ha! If you think the major is going to leave the comfort of his cruiser, I think you're going to need your head examined too."

"I thought success here was a career maker."

"It is," nodded Talon, "but you gotta look at it from the big picture. Tossing twenty leejes into a problem and then fixing it makes your star shine a whole lot brighter than sending in a company with air support. I don't think you'd see him come down here even if the entire mission went to hell. He'd just pull anchor, blame the failure on the ineptitude of his ground commands and run back to the Republic. Hell, the House of Reason would probably give him a medal."

"Wonderful leadership we've got," Lankin muttered. "How's Kato handling it?"

Talon shrugged. "About as well as you'd expect. Yesterday we had some Duracore reps at the gate, demanding to speak with him. Practically blaming the Legion for the increased attacks, like us being here antagonized the insurgents."

"Hell, we should just leave then. Let them deal with their own problems."

"Right there with you, brother. But you know the Republic isn't going to just up and leave a valuable resource to some backwater nobodies."

"You're right about that," Lankin said.

"Lucky you though, right?"

Lankin frowned up at his friend. "What are you talking about?"

"You've got a mandatory medical," Talon said. "Your transfer papers came through this morning. That poison the thing pumped into you did a number, brother. No chance for regeneratives, remember? I guess you were pretty out of it…"

Lankin jerked up, almost pulling the monitor cables free of their machines. "What do you mean my transfer papers? I'm not going anywhere!"

"Not sure you have much of a choice, brother."

"I'll refuse the orders," Lankin said, prying the medical gauntlet off his arm. "I'm not going to leave my men behind when I can still fight."

Lankin groaned when the leads pulled free of his skin. His metal fingers twitched open and shut after he pulled the gauntlet free. His thumb and first two fingers had been replaced by cybernetic implants.

"See," Lankin said, holding the fingers and miming a firing motion with his index finger. "I can still pull a trigger."

The digits were jerky and Talon could tell his friend was concentrating hard on hiding his unsteadiness. "*I* see that. But you know regs. Legion don't have room for cyborgs most times."

Lankin frowned. "Come on, man, you remember that old-timer... what was his name? The guy from Fratis II? You know, the one that lost both legs and an arm and still managed to beat back an advanced Savage horde? Took a rocket in his sled... sket, what was his name?"

"Winters? Wickers? It's been a while since I took leej history."

Lankin flipped his half-hand. "Doesn't matter, the point is, as long as I can physically fight, I'm not going anywhere. Besides, one of my instructors in marksmanship school was a mechy, didn't seem to slow him down that much. Just need practice is all. KTF, right?"

"KTF," Talon agreed.

You taught me to not ever take sket
from anyone.

12

Lankin's mechanical fingers twitched and he dropped the canteen he was holding. It bounced across the floor, rolling under the next bunk. He squeezed the fingers tight, listening to the whine of the internal motors, watching the joints turn.

He could still feel his last two fingers, and despite having motor control over the other three, he couldn't actually feel them, like he could his natural ones. There were more sophisticated cybernetics in the galaxy, ones that connected to existing nerves and felt no different—but the Republic didn't pay for those in the field. And rarely approved upgrades to the veterans trying to navigate the criminally apathetic bureaucracy in charge of their after-war care. Learning how to judge without tactile sensation was difficult and knowing exactly how much pressure to exert was even harder.

"Ha, three of a kind!" Lieutenant Valpasi slapped his cards down on the table in the bunkhouse to a chorus of groans and jeers. The four legionnaires at the table with him threw down their cards in disgust, causing the holographic faces to shimmer and distort.

"What is that, five hands in a row?" Cross asked.

"Six," Kessler said.

Lankin stood, ready to leave the canteen. "I told you guys, pilots are shady."

Valpasi held his arms out. "Hey, I resemble that remark."

Cross tapped a finger on his small stack of chips. "All right, I got this. All-in blind."

Kessler dealt cards and triggered their faces to shuffle. "You sure?"

"No way he can pull out seven hands in a row. No way."

Valpasi shook his head as he pulled in his winnings. "I keep this up I might never have to fly again. I'll just retire to some tropical planet near the core and drink all of Cross's credits away. Maybe start up a tour charter or something. Beats flying those old Republic tin-cans, that's for sure."

"Not a chance," Cross said.

"So, spill the beans," Markyle said, inspecting the cards Kessler had dealt. "Who'd you piss off to get this sket assignment?"

"What do you mean?" the pilot asked. "I check, by the way."

Markyle tapped the table, also checking. "I mean, you seem like a squared away guy. Most of the competent featherheads I know are off on some destroyer somewhere, flying tri-fighters. How'd you manage to get shafted all the way out here, flying transport shuttles?"

Kessler and Cross both checked and Kessler dealt the Flop.

"I flew tri-fighters when I first joined," Valpasi said. "But the damn things are like flying an impervisteel coffin that's way too small, if you ask me. Bet one hundred."

"I'm out," Markyle said, tossing his cards down.

"Call," Kessler said, then dealt the turn.

"Besides," Valpasi continued. "I'd much rather be flying in atmo than void. At least if your ride gets hit down here, you have a chance. Up there, you're just done. Raise."

"Thought you featherheads had protective suits?"

"Sure. And those never get breached when your cockpit is blown apart, right?" The pilot tossed in another handful of chips.

Kessler called, "Here we go." He laid down the River card and sat back.

Valpasi considered his hand again, eyed Kessler for a moment, then said, "Three hundred."

Lankin couldn't see what the legionnaire medic was holding, but the expression Kessler tried to hide told him everything he needed to know.

He set his cards down on the table. "I'm out."

Valpasi looked at Cross. "What you got, brother?"

The private glared at the pilot and then looked back at Kessler. "This is unbelievable." He flipped over his cards. "Two stinking pair."

"Not bad. But..." Valpasi flipped over one of his cards. "Three of a kind."

Cross jumped up. "You've got to be kidding me! You have some cards shoved up your sleeves or something?"

The pilot held up his hands, fingers spread, laughing. "Not a thing."

"That's got to be some kind of record or something," Markyle said.

"It's kelhorned ridiculous is what it is," Cross replied.

But Lankin's mind was elsewhere. Beyond the card table. "Don't you even miss the thrill?"

"Of what, battle?" asked Valpasi.

"Yeah."

"You'd be surprised how much action shuttle jocks get. More than the fighter pilots."

"C'mon..." Cross protested.

The pilot shook his head. "No. It's true. No one has a fleet that can go up against the Republic. All the fighting happens in atmo. Hell, one time I was dropping off some executive types on this trade mission on Fernaris, when we were ambushed by these zhee pirates. Had the entire port side of my bird riddled by blaster fire before I could get off the pad. Managed to save the execs by dropping my repulsor pads right onto those donks, roasted and crushed them as they tried to run."

"Impressive."

Valpasi shrugged. "Fernaris government didn't think so, got the whole team banished from the planet before they'd even started negotiations. That's part of the reason I got shipped out here."

"Out of sight, out of mind," Lankin said.

"Exactly."

The barracks door opened and Talon came in, his helmet held under one arm. He took one look at the table, eyed Cross, and grinned. "How much did he lose this time?"

"Sarge, that's hurtful," Cross said.

"Too much," Lankin said. "Might have to put him on a Hold 'Em restriction."

Pax came in behind Talon, his N-18 slung across his chest. He'd been raised on a farm and his father had taught him how to shoot from the time he'd been able to hold a weapon. The corporal had gone through the Gauntlet right out of basic.

Lankin's chest tightened at the sight of the rifle. He hadn't touched his own N-18 since he'd been attacked. It rested in clips above his bed, above his newly acquired N-4. The urge to take it out to the range and dust it off was almost overwhelming.

Talon stopped next to Lankin, noticing his friend's distress. He put a hand on Lankin's shoulder. "You okay?"

"Yeah, fine. How was the patrol?"

Talon slid his N-4 into the rack above his bunk. "Uneventful. Checkpoint traffic has been really reduced since your deal. And haven't heard a peep from the insurgents. Maybe they finally got the hint."

"I doubt it," Lankin said.

"Captain told me he submitted your paperwork for your pin," Pax said, joining them and nodding at Lankin's N-18. He slapped a stencil of a skull with wings and a crosshair on Lankin's chest. "How's it feel getting your Death Angel wings on your first mission?"

Lankin shook his head. "I told him not to."

"Well, he's doing it anyway," Pax said.

Talon frowned. "You don't want your pin?"

"It's not that," Lankin said. "It's just that I don't feel like I've actually earned it. A sniper's first kill is supposed to be in combat, not during some crummy security mission."

"Hey, a kill's a kill," Pax said. "And I've seen the recordings, it was a damn good shot."

"The guy wasn't even a combatant, though. Not really. He was just some lackey the Talusar paid to bring in their equipment."

"He wasn't just some lackey," Talon said. "He was armed and he was bringing in weapons that would've been used against us eventually. You saved lives with that shot, Garo. Don't ever think any different."

"Maybe. I hope so."

"I know so," Talon said. "And show a little gratitude, pal. Kato did you a favor keeping your crippled ass on-base while you recover instead of sending you up to the ship. He's trying to do you another one with this."

Lankin nodded. "No, you're right."

"Only favor I want," Cross said, slinging his N-4 over his shoulder, "is for these kelhorned insurgents to stop playing hide and tease games. They won't stand a chance in a straight up gunfight. What do you say, Kess, you want to see if we can find some today?"

Kessler grabbed his bucket off his bunk and shook his head. "Hell no, man. You still have credits I need."

I remember what you told me when I signed up: you'll come home a hero, or you'll come home in a box.

"That's the last one," Burga said, coming up behind Talon as Gestori workers loaded transport bins behind them.

Talon checked the time readout on his HUD. "It's about time. Chow's gonna be cold by the time we get back to Wolf."

"If it's even still there."

Two weeks had passed since the attack on Pylon 29, and with them, the only sign of insurgents. Major Wyeire was satisfied that they were gone, on the run, terrified of the Legion's might and ferocity. He was making plans to withdraw the Legion, leaving the pacified planet in the Repub marines' care.

Sergeant Chase Talon knew better.

He stood on top of the train, watching workers. Clouds of black dust filled the air as tons of ore poured into the open top cargo bins. The workers glared at the legion-naires, occasionally cursing them. They may have been re-signed to the fact that the Legion wasn't going anywhere, but they made no qualms about showing their displeasure at the situation.

Don't you know we're here to protect you? Talon thought.

He'd given up repeating the imaginary argument he wished he could've had with the locals several days before, knowing whatever he said would make no difference in their opinion of him or his men. Things seemed to have deteriorated to an all-time low, even with the insurgents' apparent disappearance. Even the Gestori that had seemed genuinely appreciative of their protection when the Legion first arrived now seemed to despise them.

Protests at the gates of FOB Wolf had become a daily routine. The crowds had grown from a handful of poorly organized protestors to over a hundred disciplined demonstrators. Fortunately, there were enough marines to rotate through the guard posts that no one had to endure the hate being spewed for more than a few hours.

To Captain Kato's credit, he'd kept up the regular patrols and maintained their security presence on the train during shipments. He'd even managed to convince Major Wyeire to rotate the company, giving the men on-planet a much deserved break, even though that rotation wouldn't happen for two weeks.

The ore hauler's back-up alarm brought Talon out of his reverie. The oversized six-wheeled vehicle turned and rolled down the ramp, disappearing into a field of stacked storage containers.

His bucket's HUD identified over a hundred workers, logging their locations for his squad's battlenet. There'd been rumors of sympathizers amongst the workers, and with the hostility on display at the gate, Kato didn't want his men taking any chances. Everyone, everywhere, was tagged, logged, and tracked. But without having a full complement of TT-16s, the tracking was extremely limited.

A worker near the base of the loading ramp barked a Gestori curse, holding forefinger and pinky up in what Talon had come to know as the Gestori equivalent of flipping someone the bird.

"I'm never going to get this stench out of this suit," Burga said.

"You're telling me. I think my skin has a permanent film on it. Every time we put the armor back on—there it is. I'm counting the days until we get back to *Vendetta* and can spend a few days out of the suits while they're decontaminated."

"I hear that."

On the platform below, Corporal Lancil jogged up and waved to get the sergeant's attention. "All sealed up, Sarge. We're ready to go."

"Roger that," Talon said. "Try to keep up with us this time, would ya?"

Lancil protested, "I told you, I wasn't driving last time, that was Pax. He drives slower than your grandma."

A panel flashed on Talon's HUD, route information forwarded from the train's conductor.

"Looks like we're going all the way to Able," Talon said, using the platoon's code designation for the spaceport. Occasionally, the trains would divert briefly in Gangeers to unload ore samples or pick up new workers.

"Roger," Lancil said. "See ya there."

***

Ten minutes later, Talon and half of his team—Burga, Pax, Stoma, and Noshey—found seats in one of the passenger cars. Bishto took point, joining the conductor in the engine. Occasionally, Talon caught sight of Lancil's team in the combat sled, the rest of the time his bucket's HUD tracked it through the trees and foliage.

"You know," Talon said, "in any other situation, this might be a nice, relaxing, scenic ride."

"Bah, can't stand all the green," Burga said. "Give me a concrete jungle any day. Where I can walk to any street corner and get a burger and a beer in less than five minutes and the only thing I have to worry about is whether or not I'll get food poisoning."

"You're from Teema, right? I'm sure that's more often than not."

Burga shrugged. "Eh, it's better than having your hand chomped off."

Talon laughed. "Can't disagree with you there. But you're telling me you don't appreciate that view?"

In the distance, mountains stretched into the sky, their snowcapped peaks disappearing into a layer of clouds. A flock of birds erupted from a tree taller than any other around it, branches stretched wide over the surrounding jungle.

Burga laughed. "All right, I'll give it to you. It beats smog."

"You're damn right it do—"

The train lurched. Talon braced himself on a seat back and opened his squad's L-comm. "Bishto, what's your status?"

The private said, "Looks like something on the tracks about a quarter klick ahead."

"And we can't just knock it off?"

"Conductor doesn't want to take the chance. Whatever it is, he says it's big and I don't have a code to override the bot. Gestori are gonna need to remove whatever it is before we can pass."

Talon pressed his bucket against the window, trying to see ahead of the train. "For Oba's sake, roger that. Tell the lizards to hurry up, would you?"

Bishto chuckled. "Roger that, Sarge."

"Lancil, you up?" Talon asked.

"Roger, I copy, Sarge. I'm bringing my sled in to check it out."

"There's always something," Burga said, pulling himself out of his seat.

Talon keyed the Command channel. "Stryker-10 to Command Post, be advised, we've encountered some kind of track hazard just south of Pylon 64. The conductor says it's gotta be moved before we can continue south, how copy?"

"Roger that, Stryker-10."

A cold feeling of dread descended on Talon. The track bisected two large, tree-covered hills. The trees provided excellent positions for snipers to set up, offering cover for any troops looking to advance on their position on the ground.

The perfect ambush, he thought. "Eyes up, team. I don't like this at all. Bishto, tell—"

A sharp whistle cut through the cabin just before Talon saw the trail of smoke from a rocket rising out of the trees.

"Incoming!" Talon shouted.

The rocket slammed into the rear of the train, sending a ball of fire from the impact point. The train shook around them. A second rocket burst from the canopy, streaking through the air and slamming into the engine at the front of the train.

"Contact right! Contact right! Enemy troops engaging," Talon yelled over the L-comm.

He opened up with his N-4, blasting out a window, spraying glass everywhere. Burga added his own fire to Talon's barrage, tearing through leaves and branches, raking blaster fire across the tree line. To Talon's left, Noshey braced his SAB on a seat back and unleashed a volley.

The sound dampeners in Talon's bucket activated as his team began shooting. Incoming blaster fire sparked off the train's impervisteel frame and shattered windows.

"I don't have anything on battlenet," Burga said.

"I'll see if I can get a bead on them," Pax said, pushing past Talon.

Another rocket screamed in, slamming into the train. The impact shook their car, tossing the legionnaires to one side.

"We need to get off this train!" Talon yelled, trying to steady himself. "All Stryker elements, get to ground, now!"

The door at the end of the car slid open and five Gestori workers burst into the car, shouting for help.

Stoma pushed the first one back a step. "Stop! Back up!"

They bunched up in front of him, pleading for help.

"Sergeant?" Stoma called, looking over his shoulder.

Talon ducked again as blaster fire raked the outside of the train. Bolts slammed into the light strip above the aliens, sending out a shower of sparks. The Gestori screamed and cowered, covering their heads.

Burga took a knee when his N-4 went dry. "Changing packs! We're getting tore up here, Sarge."

"I know!"

"What about the Gestori?" Stoma said, still trying to calm them down. "We can't leave them here."

"Understood, Private," Talon said. "Bishto, what's your status?"

No response.

"Stryker-13, Stryker-10, do you copy?"

Still nothing. Bishto's readings on Talon's HUD had flatlined.

Sket, Talon thought.

Blaster fire shattered windows on the opposite side of the car, spraying the interior with glass.

"I think I've got them, Sarge," Pax said over the squad L-comm. "Thirty or so hostile targets, two hundred meters to the west and closing."

Clusters of red dots popped up on Talon's HUD as Pax's bucket AI relayed the information over the battlenet. The enemy was moving to surround them, hoping to keep them pinned down on the train and trap them.

"Stryker-10 to Command, be advised, we are under attack! I repeat, we are engaging a significant enemy force moving in from the west."

"Affirmative, Stryker-10, we have you on battlenet. Are you in control of your position and accountable?"

"Losing control is more like it!" Another burst of sparks from the ceiling, raining down on Talon's bucket. "We need a QRF now!"

There was no immediate response, the communication tech probably calling for someone with more brass on their collar. Meanwhile Talon's men sent out a steady stream of return fire, dropping a number of the advancing insurgents, their threat dots blinking off in the HUDs.

"Stryker-10, this is Captain Campbell. Be advised, QRF is mobilizing, over."

Another rocket screamed in, closer this time. The impact knocked Talon forward onto a seat. Stoma was picking himself up off the floor, trying to get the SAB back into position.

Talon switched to the squad comm. "Alpha elements, we are getting off the kelhorned train! Stoma, clear the exit."

"Roger," the leej replied, holding the SAB up and jogging down the aisle to the door.

Talon slapped Burga on the shoulder. "Let's move, Leej!"

"Roger!" replied Burga. "We're bringing the indigs out with us?"

Talon agonized. Fighting off a larger force was hard enough but doing it while trying to protect civilians was a whole different ball game. "Bring them. They'll get blown to pieces by the time the insurgents realize we're off the train if we leave 'em here."

The team spilled out onto the metal platform adjacent to the rails. The gantry was only about a meter wide, limiting them to a single file line. Having the train between Talon's team and the attackers gave them a brief respite from the constant blaster fire.

"Pax, we're dismounting this kill box," Talon snapped. "Confirm position."

"HUD location accurate. Almost to the ground, Sarge," the sniper replied. "I'm going to find a position to the north, see if I can catch their flank open."

"Roger."

Talon leaned over the railing, looking for a way down. "There, that next pylon. There's a maintenance ladder. Move!"

Talon shoved the Gestori workers ahead of him as Burga and Stoma sprinted down the walkway to the pylon. Blaster fire echoed through the jungle, punctuated by sharp bangs as blaster bolts slammed into the train on the other side.

Another high-pitched whistle tore the air and a second later an ore car exploded, sending smoke, mineral dust, and ore spraying skyward. The container car rocked on the track and the gantry shook underneath the legionnaires' feet.

Private Stoma reached the pylon first. He slung his SAB over his shoulder and pulled on the hatch. "It's locked, Sarge!"

"I got it, move!" Burga said, pushing him out of the way. He put the barrel of his N-4 against the lock and fired.

Sparks flew as the metal spread apart and the corporal yanked the hatch open.

"Go! Go! Go!" Talon shouted.

Burga scrambled through the opening, then, using his boots as pressure brakes, slid down the ladder without touching the rungs. As he passed the halfway point, Stoma started down after him.

"Bishto," Talon said, hoping his HUD readings were malfunctioning. "Stryker-13, do you copy?"

Sket.

The first Gestori climbed through the hatch.

Talon leaned out and saw hungry flames and black smoke billowing out of the engine.

A barrage of blaster fire slammed into the train car behind him, showering him with sparks. "Contact left!"

Keeping low, he pushed the last two Gestori toward the hatch, ducking as blaster bolts stitched across the train. "Move! Come on! Go!"

The second Gestori scrambled through the hatch and, unable to slide, went hand over hand, rung by rung. The last Gestori froze at the hatch, shaking his head, back pressed against the impervisteel mag-lev track. "I can't... I can't do it."

Talon put a gloved hand on the alien's shoulder. "Yes, you can. Just focus on the next rung and don't look—"

The Gestori's body jerked and he cried out. Another blaster bolt sent him stumbling into the waist-high rail. Talon lunged, trying to stop him from flipping over, but missed. The Gestori landed in a broken heap next to the pylon's base and didn't move.

Burga and Stoma reached him before the other workers reached the ground.

"He's gone," Burga said.

"Leave him," Talon said, dropping through the hatch.

Lancil's name appeared on Talon's HUD. "Stryker-6 to Stryker-10, be advised we're engaging multiple enemy contacts half a klick east of your position."

Talon could hear the blaster bolts zip past. He prayed his armor would hold up if he took one in the back... and that his grip would keep him from falling like that poor Gestori. "Roger that. We've dismounted the train and are moving to the west, how copy?"

"Copy that, moving west. I've got you on net."

"Sarge, I've got a fix on the insurgents," Pax said over L-comm. "Looks like they're setting up a 74k heavy blaster a hundred meters to your northeast. I don't have a shot yet."

"Roger," Talon said. He pressed his boots against the rails and squeezed hard, slowing his descent. He let go two meters from the ground and dropped, rolling as he landed.

Burga and Noshey were cutting a hole in the fence around the pylon. The two remaining Gestori huddled together, seemingly oblivious to their fallen companion. They shouted in terror for the legionnaires to hurry. A second later the fence was breached and they were running toward a large earth berm. The rails cut straight through a hill, leaving walls of earth in their wake.

Talon joined his team and took a knee. "Anyone hit?"

"It's a good thing those kelhorned bastards are horrible shots!" Burga said. A blaster round tore through the edge of the berm above him, dislodging a shower of dirt.

"Anyone get a fix on the gun emplacement?" Talon asked.

"Sounded like it was coming from there, Sarge," Noshey said, pointing.

"Frag out!" Burga shouted, tossing a fist-sized grenade over the top of the berm.

They all went low, pressing themselves against the soil. Talon counted down in his head, and at eight seconds the grenade detonated with a muted *whoomp whoomp*.

Talon looked up and down the length of their twenty-meter-long impromptu fighting position. "Spread out, we need eyes on that gun. Weapons free, let these insurgents know they picked the wrong squad of leejes!"

"Ooah!" the team bellowed, spreading out.

Talon switched to the command net. "Stryker-10 to Command, we are under heavy assault. The enemy force has us pinned down from the east and west, how copy?"

Lieutenant Duval's voice came over the L-comm. He was calm, almost disinterested. "Styker-10, pinned down how, Sergeant?"

Talon bit back a curse. "Sir, we've encountered heavily armed insurgents and we are under attack. The train has been disabled and we are pinned down in terrain. We have two Gestori workers in tow."

"You dismounted the train?" Duval sounded surprised. "No one gave you permission to get off that train, Sergeant. The train is your priority, nothing else."

Another barrage of blaster fire tore through the berm. To Talon's right, his legionnaires were blindly returning fire, hoping to force the enemy's hand.

"The train was taking rocket fire from the ground, sir!" Talon shouted, frustrated at having to explain his actions. "Request artillery fire on enemy position, I'm sending the data now."

"Negative on arty fire, it's too close to the mag-lev tracks. We can't risk damaging the supply route. You're better equipped than those primitives, Sergeant. Flank and engage. Oba's beard, a squadron of legionnaires should have no difficulty putting down the twenty or so hostiles I'm seeing on the net."

Talon slammed a fist against the berm.

"What's up, Sarge?" Burga asked, dropping down from his fighting position.

Talon shook his head. "Stryker-10, request contact with Stryker-1."

"Captain Kato is presently otherwise engaged, Stryker-10. I repeat my order, *flank and engage.* I will re-task our TT-16 to your location to assist."

"Sir, we are pinned down! Request mobilization of Bravo Squad to assist!"

"Denied," Duval said. "The marines are sending a relief element and I cannot commit my entire force to one engagement. The enemy could be counting on that, waiting to attack another target as soon as we depart."

Another rocket whistled through the air. A second ore car exploded, filling the air with black dust and debris. Chunks of ore rained down around them, cutting through the trees ahead of them and digging holes in the clearing behind him.

"Sir, I don't think this is another probe," Talon said. "This is something major. I think—"

Duval cut him off. "You have your orders, Sergeant. I will inform the captain of the situation. Get to work. KTF. Duval, out."

"You've got to be kidding me!" Talon shouted.

Burga could tell something was wrong. "Sarge?"

"We're not getting any backup until the marines get here."

"What about arty?"

Talon shook his head.

"That's just great." The corporal climbed back up to the lip of the berm and sent a barrage of blaster fire into the jungle.

"We need to move," Talon said. "If we stay here, we're going to get overrun. Lancil, what's your status?"

"We've managed to take out two rocket teams but can't get close to the main force. Looks like they have several trucks with mounted medium blasters."

"Forget it, we need to get clear of here." Talon checked his terrain map on his HUD, then sent coordinates to Lancil. "Rendezvous here, we'll fall back to the Dirty and regroup with the marine detachment there."

"Roger that, Sarge, moving."

"Styker-10 to all Stryker elements, we are disengaging! Fall back to position Delta. Repeat, fall back to position Delta, check battlenet for coordin—"

Three rockets screamed overhead, smoke trails cutting across the blue sky, and slammed into back of the train. They exploded in sequence, enveloping container cars in flames. The blasts rocked the train, shoving the cars sideways. A metallic groan drowned out the sound of blasters as the cars leaned over, dislodging themselves from the mag-lev track underneath.

"Heads up!" Talon shouted, pushing himself into the berm.

When the first two cars cleared the track, the rest of the train followed. Cars buckled and snapped free of each other, rolling and twisting in the air. The ground shook under the heavy cars crashing down, tearing monster divots out of the soil. Metal banged and crashed in a cacophony of destruction, accompanied by groaning frames and snapping couplings. Within seconds the entire train was a heap of twisted impervisteel.

"Smoke! Pop smoke!" Talon shouted, getting to his feet. He pulled a fist-sized canister from his harness, yanked the safety catch free, and lobbed it over the berm. "Let's get the hell out of here!"

Guess I figured the hero part was pretty much locked up.

14

"You hand looks a lot better," Doctor Pendisa said, turning Lankin's palm over delicately, inspecting the bio-mechanical connectors. Her fingers were softer than the rough, almost leathery gray skin suggested. "Not as good as if you'd left the bandages on for the duration of the healing period, but better. Flex them."

Lankin worked his implanted fingers. "Yeah, well, sorry about that. I've got work to do."

"Indeed. Make a fist." She leaned close, examining the three knuckles of his index, middle, and thumb, where they were grafted onto his true bones and wired into his nervous system.

The skin around the implants was inflamed, red and swollen, still sutured around the impervisteel base. It looked like his skin had been ripped off, exposing his actual metal body underneath.

"The conjoined skin is healing nicely." She probed it with a finger. "Give it another week and the inflammation should go away. Another month, and I doubt if you'll even feel a difference."

Lankin chuckled. "Yeah, I'll believe that when I see it. It still feels like I have my real fingers and these things are just three weird additional digits. The old ones still hurt. Is that normal?"

Pendisa nodded. "It happens when technology is as limited as it is in your case."

"When will that go away?"

"I would say within the next month or so." She picked up her datapad off the bed. "Though, in some cases I've heard the sensation doesn't go away. I can prescribe some medicine if you—"

"No," Lankin said, cutting her off. "That's okay. I don't need any more meds. Just as long as I can get back in the field soon."

The Gestori doctor regarded him with her distinctly lizard-like eyes for a moment. "Are fighting and killing the only things you think of? Deploying throughout the galaxy's edge, destroying lives, and crushing those who don't agree with you?"

Lankin searched for a response. "I, uh, no. We don't destroy anything. The Legion protects."

"Protects," Pendisa repeated, closing up a medical case. "I think you are confusing the concepts of protecting and conquering."

"The Republic is a bastion for all. It's—"

"Oh, come now, don't give me that recruiting spiel. That might be true for the core worlds, where ninety-nine percent of all Republic funds are invested, but out here on the edge, your pretty little fairy tale gets a little more slanted."

Lankin frowned at her.

"Take your hand, for example," she said, pointing. "Do you think in the core you'd be fitted with such a primitive prosthetic? Don't get me wrong, I stand behind my work, but compared to the advances being made in the core worlds, this is substandard. I'm sure the Legion doctors will tell you the same when you get back there."

"I'm not leaving," Lankin said.

"So I've heard, though I'm not sure that decision is entirely yours to make."

"They can't force me to leave if I don't want to."

Pendisa gave him a doubtful look. "You serve the Republic. You are a legionnaire. You go where they send you and do what they tell you to do. You are only a number to the Legion, and much less than that to the Republic. You think those people back in the core are concerned about you or your team? They *use* you, just like they use everyone else. They come and they take; that's all they've ever done. That's all they'll ever do."

"The Senate and House of Reason serve the people," Lankin said, and even before the words left his mouth, he felt foolish for saying them.

"The people?" Pendisa laughed. "The House of Reason is nothing more than a bunch of elitists who care only for their own bank accounts. And the Senate is there to rubber-stamp everything under the guise of planetary approval. *Our* senator hasn't stepped foot on this planet since he was elected. And won't unless he's defeated."

Lankin gaped, speechless.

The doctor was not. "I doubt they spare a single thought for the plight of some underdeveloped race on a backwater world. We wouldn't know any better. And of course, it's all about the greater good. The Gestori have something that others desperately need, so the wonderful Republic is going to take it from them—since they don't really know what they're doing with it anyway—and they give it to people who really need it: themselves. Because they're the House of Reason and they know best."

Lankin hadn't seen her speak with a fraction of this passion during the weeks of treatment.

He opened his mouth, only to close it again, still not knowing what to say. His brain told him she was wrong, that she just didn't understand. How could she know what the Republic's ultimate plans were? The House of Reason saw the big picture, she only saw just a tiny portion of that—she was obviously mistaken. But another, smaller part of his brain suggested, she might be right. Told him that he couldn't respond because all he had was cognitive dissonance. He had no argument. He was right and she was wrong because... that's the way it had to be.

Right?

Lankin looked down at his cybernetic prosthetics, flexing his fake fingers. In the end, this whole thing was way above his pay grade and really didn't matter anyway. He didn't fight for the House of Reason, or the Republic, or even for the Legion. He fought for the men standing beside him and knew there wasn't any way he could make this outsider understand that.

He let out a long sigh. "Well, thanks for your work, Doc. Am I good to return to duty now?"

She nodded. "I'm going to recommend they keep you restricted to noncombat related duty, at least for another two weeks and—"

"Two weeks? Doc, I'm fine, I don't—"

"Yes, two weeks," Pendisa said, ignoring his displeasure. "You have to give the implant time to heal and integrate. Otherwise, the entire thing is a waste. Your duty over the next couple of weeks is to work on refining your motor control."

A Gestori hand appeared around the curtain. "Pendisa, may I talk to you for a moment?"

"Father, I'm right in the middle of an examination," the doctor said, taking a half step back. She hurried to the curtain and spoke in hushed tones.

Lankin leaned over, craning to see around the curtain. One of the representatives from the townhall meetings was whispering into the doctor's ear. The legionnaire frowned, trying to remember the name... Sharn? Yes. That was him all right. The rep for the Workers Union.

After a minute, Pendisa nodded and waved the older Gestori away. He lingered, glaring at Lankin with disdainful, yellow eyes. It was clear the man still held Lankin responsible for a wrongful death.

Pendisa waved her father away again, giving him a gentle shove. The Gestori relented and left.

She turned back to Lankin. "Apologies for the interruption."

Lankin pulled on his leej camouflage fatigues. It felt weird not being in his battle armor. Generally, while on station legionnaires were required to be in their armor

anytime they left their barracks, unless there were exten-
uating circumstances. Getting your hand bitten off fell into
that category. "It's fine. Are we done here?"

"I want to see you back in a week to check your
progress."

"Sure, Doc," Lankin said, brushing aside the curtain. "Thanks."

He caught sight of Sharn leaving from the back of the
clinic. They held each other's gaze for a moment, then the
alien departed.

Outside the clinic, Sweets waited in one of the trucks
the marines had commandeered. He sat behind the
wheel, grinning, dressed in jungle-camouflage battle armor, his bucket resting on the seat next to him. "How was
your date?"

Lankin pulled open the passenger door and climbed
into the cab. "Well, she wasn't exactly a half-naked, sex-
starved Rugarian, but…"

"Too bad." Sweets started up the rig, then jerked a
thumb at the bed behind them. "But I do come bear-
ing gifts."

Lankin looked over his shoulder and laughed. "Now,
that's a sight for sore eyes." He reached over the seat and
put a hand on the barrel of his N-18 sniper rifle. "It's been
too long, ol' buddy."

Sweets put the truck in gear and turned onto the
street. "Back to Wolf?"

"Yeah," Lankin said, peering down the alley as they
rolled past. "Wait. Stop."

"What's up?" Sweets asked as the truck rocked to a halt.

Halfway down the alley, Sharn got into the passenger side of a small, blue sled parked just outside the clinic's rear entrance. A moment later, the sled started down the alley, away from the legionnaires.

"Let's see what they're up to."

Sweets turned the truck into the alley, keeping a half-block between the two vehicles. "What's on your mind?"

Lankin shook his head as the sled turned left, heading south on one of the main roads. "I'm not sure. I just... have a feeling."

Sweets laughed. "You and your feelings, Sarge. Lieutenant Duval finds out we're out here chasing one of your feelings, he's going to be pissed."

It only took a moment to reacquire the blue sled on the main road. It was stopped in traffic four vehicles ahead, waiting on a slow-moving flatbed repulsor cart.

"Duval's an idiot."

"Can't argue with you there. Although I'm pretty sure that's not what a sergeant is supposed to say about a senior officer to an impressionable young soldier such as myself."

"So what gives?" Lankin said.

"Duval is worried about local L-comm traffic being intercepted by the insurgency, so he's having everyone's buckets switched to a different operations band."

"Kind of hard to paint the lieutenant as anything but an idiot if he knows so little about the L-comm. Not even the Republic can crack it."

Sweets shrugged and held up a small insert taken from a spare leej bucket. "Luckily we had some spares."

"Oh, sket, look out!"

The pothole came out of nowhere and Sweets didn't have time to miss it. The driver's side tire fell into the small crater. Lankin slammed his hand against the dash to steady himself. The truck lurched again as Sweets accelerated out of the pothole, swerving hard to keep the back tires on the road.

Sweets slowed to a stop.

"I guess bad roads are an intergalactic issue outside the core." Lankin grinned at the medic, then frowned at the leej's expression. "What's up?"

Lankin followed the medic's gaze to the dash, the dark blue plastic marred by jagged gashes where his cybernetic fingers dug in.

Chuckling, Lankin held up his prosthetic fingers. "Guess I need to get used to these things."

Sweets shook his head. "I guess. Remind me not to shake your hand ever again."

"Doc says it'll take a few weeks to get a handle on the extra strength and learn to control it. Hey, can you believe the major wanted to have me charged with damaging Republic property?"

"That scat-brained point wouldn't even know where to piss if Kato wasn't constantly holding his hand and running missions for him. It's a good thing we have the captain with us, brother. 'Cause I don't think we'd've survived this long if it had just been the points."

"Thank Oba for small favors."

They followed Sharn for another ten minutes as the Gestori wove through Gangeers, finally pulling into a parking area near the north market district. Sharm and another alien left the car and continued on foot.

Lankin and Sweets stopped. They watched Sharn join a few Gestori and several other aliens who wore masks over their faces.

"That's a Talusar," Lankin said, pointing.

"How can you tell?"

"Build seems about right, and why else would they be covering their faces like that."

Sweets shook his head. "I don't know, Sarge. That's a pretty big stretch even for you."

"Don't you want to know what they're talking about? I think a meeting with a group of masked people that just happen to be the same race as the insurgent group who attacked our positions might be some good intel to bring back to command."

Lankin looked at Sweets, trying to hide his grin.

"No," the leej said, shaking his head. "No, Garo. You're crazy. We have specific orders not to engage. We shouldn't even be here, we should be halfway back to Wolf by now."

The L-comm transmitter buzzed to life. *"Stryker-10 to Command, be advised, we are under attack! I repeat, we are engaging a significant enemy force moving in from the west."*

Lankin exchanged surprised expressions with Sweets.

"What the hell?" Lankin said, picking up the comm.

Blood pounded in Lankin's ears. "Come on, let's go."

I only hope that my actions in battle reflect the values you raised me to hold dear.

15

Sergeant Talon dropped to a knee at the edge of the tree line, struggling to regain control of his breath. His bucket's Battlefield AI had been flashing exertion warnings for the past ten minutes and the increased flow of purified oxygen no longer seemed to help. He dismissed the messages, then blocked any further similar notifications.

The pair of Gestori train crew dropped beside him. Lying on their sides, they gasped for air. The legionnaires practically had to carry the civilians, which slowed their progress considerably. The gray-skinned aliens didn't sweat to stay cool nor did they have the endurance of trained legionnaires.

"Oba, that hurts," Noshey said, favoring his leg. Stoma and Burga set him down gently. He'd taken a blaster bolt to the knee during their retreat, which, despite his armor, had rendered it all but useless.

Noshey held Burga's N-4. The corporal had taken over the SAB and now had the large blaster slung over his back. Burga knelt, inspecting the field dressing he'd applied. "I'm sure it's not up to Lancil's standards, but it's holding up."

Talon's battlefield AI received an update from Noshey's bucket. There was a seventy percent chance the private would lose the leg if they didn't get him to a medical facility soon.

Talon scanned the buildings, his HUD painting red circles on targets up and down the edge of the mining complex ahead. Workers leaned around corners, peering out of windows to see what the commotion was about.

Zeroing in on a tall building two blocks in, Talon tagged it and sent the highlight to the squad's battlenet. He called his team over L-comm, seeking to get them regrouped and together again. "This is the rally point. We need some high ground. Lancil, take your team up to the right, we'll move left."

"Copy that."

Talon turned and pointed at the Gestori. "You, help him." He pointed to Noshey.

Surprisingly, the aliens didn't object. They each draped a legionnaire's arm over their shoulders and lifted him off the ground.

"Burga, you got point."

"Roger that."

"Ah, easy!" Noshey said, adjusting his one-handed grip on the N-4, hopping on his good leg as the Gestori walked him forward.

"You got this, Private?" Talon asked.

The leej nodded. "Feel the thunder, Sarge."

"We are the storm," Talon said.

Keeping low, the men of 1st Platoon crossed the clearing and entered the mining complex proper. Talon stayed a few paces behind Noshey and the Gestori, his N-4 at low ready, eyes scanning for targets. His HUD painted several dots on buildings and in the streets ahead, but the miners weren't the targets Talon was worried about.

Not yet anyway, he thought, crossing an intersection quickly.

Gestori watched them from the roofs of buildings—gray-skinned heads, some still wearing their protective masks from the mines. On the second floor of the building ahead, Talon saw a worker speaking into a small handheld comm. The legionnaire's stomach turned.

"Heads up," he said on the squad's L-comm. "I've got a guy with a comm, second floor, tan building on the right."

"Roger," Burga replied. "Maybe just calling Mom?"

"Not with today's luck."

Burga stopped at the door and waited. The Gestori workers stayed at the edge of the building, allowing Talon and Stoma to pass.

"Breaching," Burga said once Talon and Stoma stacked outside the entryway. He stepped back and booted the door open. Talon followed Burga through, his HUD automatically adjusting to the dimness of the room.

Footsteps pounded on the ceiling.

"Stairs," Burga said. "Northwest corner."

"Move," Talon ordered. "Stoma, hold the floor."

"Roger."

Burga made for the stairs, Talon following on his heels, one hand on the corporal's shoulder. He balanced his N-4 in his hand, keeping it trained on the top of the stairs.

Burga slowed near the top, stopping just short. Talon tapped him on the shoulder and Burga crossed the threshold turning left, clearing the blind corner. Talon held straight, sweeping the right side of the room.

"Get down!" Burga shouted.

"Don't shoot!" a Gestori worker shouted, throwing his hands into the air. The comm clattered across the floor and the alien backed up against the far wall.

Talon stepped around Burga, N-4 trained on the Gestori. "Who were you talking to? Were you relaying our position?"

"No one! I call no one! Please!"

"Looks like an encrypted comm link, Sarge," Burga said, picking the cylindrical comm device up off the floor.

"Who were you talking to?" Talon repeated, leaning close. "Tell me now!"

"My sister, I call my sister." The Gestori bowed his head, keeping his hands above him. "I heard battle and was scared. Please! Don't hurt me!"

Blaster fire echoed in the distance.

"Can you trace it?" Talon asked.

"Negative. Broad spectrum relay, signal could be going anywhere."

"Fix it."

Burga dropped it, then stomped down hard with the heel of his boot, smashing the comm link to pieces.

Talon held his N-4 across his chest, keeping one hand on the grip and pointing with the other. "Don't come out of this house. Don't look for us, don't even think about us. You got it?"

The Gestori looked up, his yellow-gold, slit-eyes meeting Talon's. "Yes, yes, I understand."

Lancil's name flashed on Talon's HUD. "Stryker-10, Stryker-12, we're at the rally point, setting up overwatch. You get lost somewhere?"

"Had to make a detour," Talon said, motioning for Burga to lead them out. "Be advised, I think civilians are relaying our positions to the enemy, how copy?"

"Roger that. Knew those little scat-brained lizards were no good. We've got eyes on a platoon or so, emerging from the tree line due south of our position, Sector-A124, moving into the city."

"We're moving to your position now."

"I've got you on net. You've got five enemy insurgents at your three o'clock, about a half-block south."

Burga turned to Talon for instructions. He'd heard the same information, and Noshey's vitals were still good, but deteriorating.

"Make for the rally point," Talon said. "We'll see how these scum sacks like being ambushed when we turn the tables."

Burga turned and led them north. Talon stayed in the rear, alternating side-stepping and walking backward, keeping a visual on the terrain behind them. He'd learned long ago that legionnaire technology was good and usually gave them a significant advantage over their enemy.

A rocket whistled above them.

Talon looked up just in time to see it slam into one of the refinery towers a block to his left. Impervisteel groaned and support cables snapped with musical twangs as the tower folded in half. Ore and mineral dust from the conveyor belt darkened the sky with black dust.

Ahead, Burga slowed at the final intersection before the rally point. After scanning both directions, he pushed on, keeping his SAB leveled down the street.

Shouts echoed around them, punctuated by blaster fire. A proximity warning flashed on Talon's HUD. Four red circles were parallel to their position.

"Stoma, Noshey, hold up!" Talon said over the L-comm. Immediately the two legionnaires took a step back, then inched closer to the tan brick house to their right. Across the intersection, Burga took a knee at the edge of a similar brick house.

"You see that, Burga?" Talon asked.

"Roger," Burga said, flipping the SAB's bipod down. He proned out behind the heavy blaster and adjusted his optics. "Come out, come out, wherever you are."

A second later, without any further warning, Burga fired. The squad automatic blaster shook as it disgorged seven hundred and fifty blaster bolts a minute, chewing through the street and stitching a line across the building the insurgents were using for cover.

"Move!" Talon yelled, slapping Stoma on the shoulder.

Stoma crossed the street, rounded the corner of a building, then went for the rally point.

Talon waited a beat, then followed. A brown dust cloud curled into the air where Burga's fire ate away at the brick house. "Nice wor—"

Blaster fire slammed into the brick above Burga's bucket, turning up a cloud of dust. The legionnaire shouted a curse, grabbed his SAB, and rolled away from the fire.

Talon jerked his N-4 left. Two figures outlined in red crouched at the edge of an alley to the east, blaster rifles in hand, firing. His finger worked almost before his brain sent the instruction to shoot.

Three quick shots to the chest knocked the first target out, sending the insurgent's blaster rifle flying. Talon adjusted fire and put three rounds into the second target. The final round caught the alien in the shoulder, spinning him around. He landed on top of his companion. Neither moved.

Angry shouts came from Talon's right and a blaster bolt zipped past his bucket. He barely had time to check his HUD for the location when a second bolt slammed into his back, right between the shoulder blades.

Pain flared, despite his armor. The impact sent him stumbling forward, almost losing his balance.

"Sarge!" Burga shouted, getting to his feet and leaping to help. He held the SAB at his waist and opened up on the new targets.

Talon got behind Burga, dropping to a knee, grimacing in pain. His bucket told him the impact wasn't life-threatening. His battle armor had protected him from permanent injury. His AI's assessment of the situation didn't change the fact that it felt like he'd been hit by a truck.

"You okay?" Burga asked, walking backward, sending sporadic fire downrange.

"Fine," Talon said.

"Stryker-10, Stryker-12, you've got multiple enemy targets converging on your position."

"You think?" Talon said. He waved to Stoma. "Keep going. Get to the rally point."

"Roger," Stoma said. He herded the Gestori on while Noshey dragged his wounded leg across the dust-covered street.

Talon stretched, trying to work the pain away. He slapped Burga on the shoulder. "Let's move, Leej!"

I never gave up, not once.

16

Lankin was in Wolf's operation center, his bucket under one arm, listening to the L-comm traffic and cursing Lieutenant Duval under his breath.

At the head of the holo-table, Captain Kato watched Talon's team work their way through the mining complex. The only view on any of the screens was the mining complex, cut out of miles and miles of green jungle.

"Stryker Actual, Stryker-10, request artillery support. Danger close, Sector Alpha-one-seven-two. Insurgent force closing, how copy?"

Duval keyed his L-comm before Kato could respond. "Negative, Stryker-10, artillery request denied. You are too close to priority targets and civilians."

"They aren't civilians, Lieutenant!" Talon shouted, his voice rattling the operations center's speakers. *"They are helping the insurgents!"*

"We have no proof—"

"Stryker-10, Stryker Actual," said Captain Kato. "We are prepping an exfil op as we speak. Hold what you have, I'll have more information to follow, how copy?"

"Stryker-10 copies," Talon said, his tone resigned.

Kato terminated his connection and turned to Duval. "Lieutenant, you will refrain from giving orders, unless those orders are issued by myself or the major. Is that understood?"

Duval went white, then red, finally saying, "Yes, sir."

"Good." The captain keyed a code into the terminal in front of him. A hologram of Major Wyeire appeared above the table.

"Captain Kato, have you put down the disturbance yet?"

Disturbance? Lankin thought, frowning.

"Sir, this is much more than a disturbance," Captain Kato said. "I believe this is a full-scale assault by the insurgent forces. They've forced my men to retreat to the mining complex and are closing on their position as we speak. Request air support and extract."

"It is a *disturbance*, Captain. Nothing more. Instruct your men to engage the enemy and put them down. I will not abide my legionnaires cowering like dogs in the face of ill-equipped and untrained fighters."

"Sir," Kato said, obviously struggling to control his tone. "They have destroyed the transport train and killed civilians. One of my men is KIA and the rest are pinned down. We need the rest of the company down here, Major."

"Captain, I'd advise you to remember your demeanor," Major Wyeire said.

Lieutenant Duval smirked.

The major continued, "Now, I have already begun mobilizing a relief force. However, if it is as hot as you say, I can't risk committing air units in a dangerous LZ. Advise your men—if they want extraction, clear the hostiles first."

"This is ridiculous," Lankin heard himself say before he realized he was going to speak. He put on his bucket and waited the half-second for the internal systems to boot up. HUD populated with data from his suit and he headed for the exit.

"Sergeant Lankin!" Lieutenant Duval called after him.

Lankin ignored him and left, outside into the daylight, heading for the combat sleds.

The lieutenant's name appeared on his HUD. "Sergeant Lankin, stand down."

"I'm not going to let you points put any more lives in danger," Lankin said.

Sweets fell in beside him and he keyed a direct link with his tongue. "Get the squad up."

Sweets nodded and hurried off.

Someone grabbed Lankin by his shoulder and spun him around. Lieutenant Duval, out of breath, eyes filled with fury. "I gave you a direct order, Sergeant. Stand down."

Captain Kato emerged from the operations center behind Duval. He looked from the captain to the lieutenant, then back again without saying a word.

"I gave you an order, Sergeant!" Duval shouted.

The captain nodded to Lankin.

"That's right, you did." Lankin turned and continued on.

"If you don't stop, I'll bring you up on charges! All of you! Insubordination! Disrespect to an officer! You'll hang for this!"

Lankin ignored the barrage of threats and insults that followed. The lieutenant might follow through, but Lankin doubted it. And even if he did, even if he faced a court martial for his actions, even if they threw him in prison or worse, it didn't matter. His duty was to his men, not to anyone else.

A private text from Captain Kato appeared on Lankin's HUD. *KTF.*

By the time Lankin reached the sled, his men were geared up and ready to go. They clustered near the ramp in full jungle battle armor with their buckets on and weapons at the ready.

A handful of marines arrived. Lankin imagined they were part of the QRF force Captain Campbell had organized only to be ordered to stand down by the major. Their uniforms, tactical vests, and ballistic helmets weren't nearly as formidable as the legionnaires' gear, but it was better than nothing. Far better than what most of the galaxy had to offer, including the insurgents. The fact that they'd shown up at all told Lankin what he needed to know. These men were warriors and they were ready to fight.

"The situation is critical, gentlemen," Lankin said. "Alpha squad has encountered a significant hostile force. The train has been destroyed and they're falling back to the mining complex. Requests for air support and artillery have been denied."

Buckets shook back and forth, accompanied by growls of dissatisfaction. Sentiments Lankin echoed.

He nodded. "Our brothers are in trouble out there, and despite orders to the contrary, I do not intend to sit back and hope for a miracle."

Buckets nodded.

"Make no mistake, if you come with me now, you are putting your careers, freedom, and lives on the line. We're going up against a numerically superior force. They are motivated, well equipped, and are entrenched in the terrain. This will not be an easy fight. Are you with me?"

Sweets shouted. "Stryker Company!"

"WE ARE THE STORM!"

"Feel the thunder," Lankin said, nodding. "Mount up."

As his legionnaires trotted up the sled's ramp, Lankin turned to the marines. "This isn't your fight, you know?"

A sergeant, J. VanZant, according to the name tape on his fatigues, spoke for them. "Your fight is our fight, sir. And if you think we're going to let some leejes take all the action, you've got another think coming. Those kelhorned thugs killed some of my friends. We've all got an ax to grind today."

"I won't stand in your way then."

VanZant saluted. "Yes, sir!"

"How's your high-speed driving?"

The sergeant grinned. "I'd tell your men to hang on."

"Roger that." Lankin turned to Sweets. "I want you to find a pilot. Valpasi seemed squared away. Find him and convince him we'll make it worth his while to—"

"Understood," Sweets said. He jogged off in search of the featherhead.

"Let's speed out." Lankin closed the sled doors behind him and took the last open seat in the overcrowded vehicle.

The sled rocketed through the gate, turning hard for the main road. Lankin grinned inside his bucket, holding on tight to the ceiling rail. With a full squad of legionnaires, two drivers, a turret gunner, and marines crammed into the back, the repulsors were working overtime keeping the craft at speed. Loud, incessant thrumming reverberated through the vehicle.

"Heads up, Sarge. Twelve o'clock," Corporal Kessler said over L-comm.

Lankin accessed the sled's external holofeed. Orange smoke billowed into the air from the jungle's tree line, over a hundred meters away.

"They've set the jungle on fire," Lankin said, his stomach twisting. Fighting a battle against overwhelming odds was one thing. Doing it while the world burned down around you? That was something else entirely.

"That smoke is going to play havoc with our targeting sensors," Kessler said.

"Fantastic," Lankin said.

A moment later they left the clearing around FOB Wolf and entered the jungle, their visibility reduced to a few meters in front of them. Sunlight pierced the canopy in tight beams, stretching down to the jungle floor. Bird analogs and other wildlife scattered as the sled screamed down the rudimentary road.

"Stryker-10, Stryker-19, do you copy?" Lankin asked over the company's L-comm.

There was silence for a moment. A long moment, in which Lankin said a silent prayer to Oba that his friend was all right.

Finally, the L-comm buzzed to life. Talon shouted over blaster fire in the background, "Well, it's about time!"

"Didn't think I was going to let you have all the fun, did you?"

"I have to admit..." a pause, followed by several blaster shots, "the thought had crossed my mind."

More shots.

"What's your status, Talon?"

"Well, we've taken control of one of the processing towers, but I'm not sure how long that's going to last. I've got one injured leej and one KIA. We've got about a hundred insurgents advancing on our position, but they've started burning that damned orange smoke. It's fouling up our battlenet."

"Yeah, I saw that. We're en route to your position." Lankin checked the time. "ETA twenty minutes."

Talon laughed. "What, no air?"

Lankin ground his teeth. "No air. Not yet, anyway."

"That scat-brained point."

"Hold tight, we're coming for you."

"I feel safer already."

Lankin cut his connection. He keyed up the battle map, and watched the blue dot representing their sled inching north through the jungle. At least the major hadn't killed their orbital feeds from *Vendetta*.

The sled rocked hard. Lankin grunted, clenching his rail above him. "I said fast, not in pieces."

"Sorry, Sergeant," VanZant said over the sled's internal comm.

"Don't worry about it, just—"

"Oh, sket! Incom—"

The sled lurched sideways as a rocket slammed into the passenger side's front end. The explosion knocked Lankin off his feet, sending him into three leejes sitting on the bench across the aisle.

"Contact right!" someone yelled.

Lankin pushed himself off his men. The sled's twin blaster cannon opened up.

"Out!" Lankin shouted. "Everyone out!"

Someone slapped the emergency hatch release and the rear ramp dropped open, raising a cloud as the sled spun around and rocked to a stop.

Legionnaires scrambled out of the sled, peeling off in opposite directions as they hit the ground. Blaster fire filled the air. Lankin followed his men out. Red dots began populating on his HUD as his squad's battlefield AI marked targets.

Lankin moved up the driver's side of the sled, keeping below the bolts of energy singeing the jungle around him. He yanked open the door and found VanZant slumped over the wheel.

"Sket!" Lankin spat, pulling him out. He set the marine on the ground, propping him against the sled. He lifted the man's head slightly. "Sergeant?"

The marine's eyes opened halfway, dazed. "I—"

"You're okay," Lankin told him. "I'm going to get you out of here."

He ducked, blaster fire tearing into the sled's armor above him.

Someone screamed in pain and the barrage of turret fire ceased. Lankin looked up at a marine slumped over the turret, blood running down his arm.

Lankin keyed his L-comm. "Stryker-1, Stryker-19, we have contact with the enemy in Sector A-1-3!"

Captain Kato replied, "Stryker-19, Stryker-1, break contact and return to Wolf. Orbital scans show a large force advancing on the FOB."

Lankin's HUD told him there were now twenty hostiles closing on his squad.

So many. Where the hell did they all come from?

"Drop two," Kessler advised on the squad's L-comm. "I've got two trucks to the east."

"Cross, Saretti, cover me," Lankin ordered, grabbing VanZant's vest and pulling him to the back of the sled. The marine's eyes fluttered as he struggled to focus on his surroundings. "Medic!"

"You're going to be okay," Lankin told him. He toggled back to the command channel. "Sir, if we can punch through their line and rally with Alpha squad, we might be able to flank the larger force. At the very least, clear an LZ for air support to pick us up at Dirty."

Three more red hostiles vanished from Lankin's HUD.

Finally, Kato said, "All right, Sergeant, it's your call."

Lankin lifted the marine into the sled. "We're joining Alpha Squad, sir."

"Roger that, Sergeant. Good luck."

Lankin killed the connection, ducking as another blaster bolt ricocheted off the sled, slamming into the grass at his feet.

"Stay down," he told VanZant.

Lankin sneaked up along the passenger side, kneeling to inspect the damage at the front. The rocket had hit more earth than vehicle. The fender and armor plating were bent and scarred, but the forward repulsor appeared undamaged.

First bit of luck all day.

He pulled open the passenger door and struggled to catch the body of the dead marine who'd been sitting there. The man's face was a bloody mess, the spiderweb of cracks on the window telling Lankin all he needed to know.

"Alpha squad, on me!" Lankin said, heaving the corpse over his shoulder and trucking it back to the rear of the sled.

Kessler and Saretti reached him first.

"In the back," Lankin ordered, then gently set the marine down on the bed.

Corporal Ralone fired off a long volley into the trees with his SAB as he backed toward the sled. "They're like roaches!"

"Keep 'em occupied," Lankin said.

"Roger that," Ralone answered, laughing. The automatic blaster chewed through the surrounding trees.

"We need to take out their assault truck," Kessler said, pointing to the west. "Somebody get up on the twins!"

"Yeah." Lankin pulled himself onto the back of the sled and ducked next to the armored turret. "Cross, you're driving. Rowan, help me." He pulled the dead marine from the turret and lowered him down to the waiting leej.

A lone blaster bolt hit Private Gemini in the back. The impact sent the legionnaire reeling. He cried out in pain over the open L-comm channel.

"Get him!" Lankin yelled. "Ralone!"

"Get some, you kelhorned dogs!" Ralone swung the SAB back and forth, firing an endless stream of searing blaster bolts.

Lankin swung a leg over the turret and dropped in behind the twin-barreled blaster. He pushed his shoulders into the pads and opened fire.

"Kessler, Saretti, hold on, keep VanZant in the back. The rest of you get ready to move!"

A chorus of acknowledgements flooded the channel as Lankin laid waste to the jungle. Fist-sized bolts of energy raked the foliage, splitting whole trees. Trunks exploded under the onslaught, and trees began tipping and falling into each other, toppling to the jungle floor.

Targeting data on his HUD showed red hostile targets fifty meters west. He adjusted his aim and sent a barrage in their direction. Several of the dots winked out immediately, others scattered.

"All right, flanking maneuver to the southwest, move! Corse, get me to that truck."

The sled lurched forward, rising slightly on its repulsors. Lankin pressed his legs to the sides of the turret to keep himself relatively steady. The vibrations from the blaster cannon and the motion of the sled made it difficult to stay on target, though it was more for effect than anything now.

Blaster bolts twanged off the turret's armor, deflected in random directions. He held the firing stud down, swinging the turret in the direction his HUD told him the fire had come from.

The truck came into view as they topped a hill just to the west of the road. The ancient wheeled vehicle looked identical to the ones he'd seen in town for weeks: a two-seater cab and an open bed in the back. Except this truck had a single-barreled BA74 automatic blaster mounted on a tripod in the bed. A black and green clad figure stood behind it, frantically pulling on the weapon's handle, like he was trying to clear a malfunction.

Bad time to have a busted gun, Lankin said to himself, bringing his cannon to bear.

A group of insurgents, also wearing black and green fatigues, armed with an assortment of blaster rifles and gear, came in from the north, firing at the oncoming sled. Several who'd been near the back of the truck, probably shouting at their friend behind the 74 to hurry, had barely started a frantic retreat when Lankin depressed the firing stud again.

The first volley ripped into the gunner, flipping his body, then Lankin walked his fire down to the fighters trying to escape their fate. He hit several in the back, mid-stride, dropping them to the ground. Another he caught square in the face, leaving nothing but a bloody stump on top of a collapsing body.

Legionnaires on foot engaged the insurgents moving in from the north, calling out target locations over the

L-comm as Lankin continued to focus on the ones near the truck.

"Cross," Lankin said, letting up on the stud. Steam rose from the twin barrels. "Get me clos—"

A blaster bolt whistled through the air and into his shoulder, pushing back against the armored turret. His leg slipped and he dropped through the hatch.

Mom, I don't even know where to start.

17

"*Stryker-19 is hit! Repeat, Sergeant Lankin is down!*"

Talon froze when the report came through the company L-comm. His stomach turned and he dropped to a knee, resting the butt of his N-4 on the ground next to him. He keyed his comm. "Stryker-24, Stryker-10, what's Lankin's status? How bad is it?"

"Not sure yet, Sarge," Corporal Kessler said. "Wait one."

Sket, Talon thought. Thirty more hostile targets had appeared on his HUD in the last several minutes, all converging on their location. He still hadn't figured out where they all came from. It didn't seem possible that a hostile force of this size could slip past Legion detection. Which led him to believe they'd already been on-planet.

Corporal Lancil had finished patching Noshey and was checking Ginn. The private had taken a round to the bucket, denting his helmet and knocking him unconscious. Lancil applied skinpacks to a bloody head wound.

The pair of Gestori workers huddled in a corner by a dumpster. They'd finally stopped crying and whining. They sat there in stunned silence, eyes glazed, completely disassociated from everything around them.

At least they aren't shooting at us, Talon thought.

Behind him, Burga dropped two targets, then backed up to change out charge packs for the SAB. "Running low."

Talon nodded. "I know. Pax, what do you see?"

The squad's sniper had climbed to the roof, using his macros to identify several targets the rest of the team couldn't see. Although with the clouds of orange smoke rolling through the complex, their HUDs were going crazy, significantly reducing their effectiveness. Even with IR filters active, visibility was greatly reduced.

It was comforting to know that the insurgents didn't even have that much. The smoke would likely impact them more than the legionnaires. But insurgencies throughout the galaxy weren't typically known for their tactical acumen.

Pax reported over the squad comm, "Five coming up Main Street to the east, six by compressor two, and three by the loading station. The main force is still up by the barracks. We're going to want to keep heading north."

Talon checked his map and took a deep breath. "They're pushing us north. Lancil, can we move the wounded?"

"Noshey, yes. His knee's pretty messed up, but I've stopped the bleeding and immobilized the leg. Moving him around won't do him any favors, though. Ginn..." The medic shrugged, canting his bucket to the side. "I really wouldn't want to move him far. Not without a medical transport. His head wound is just a minor laceration, looks worse than it is. It's the internal damage I'm worried about."

"Understood."

Several blaster shots rang out from the left. Mazine returned fire and shouted through his external speakers,

"You'd better make nice with your gods, you kelhorned lizards! I'm about to arrange a meeting!"

From overhead came the distinct *krak-bdew* of Pax's N-18 sniper rifle. One of the red dots on his HUD winked out. The sniper had been laying down a steady stream of well-aimed shots for the past ten minutes, which had slowed the insurgent advance considerably. It seemed the enemy wasn't too keen on taking rounds from someone they couldn't see, but still they pressed their attack where they could.

Talon knew they couldn't stay here indefinitely. The insurgents were surely making plans to outflank them. Whatever happened, the sergeant would not allow them to be outmaneuvered.

"Looks like the main bunch is moving again," Pax informed him over the L-comm. "Heading east, through the barracks. I count fifty to sixty."

"Roger," Talon said. "Styker-10 to Stryker elements, we are moving west. Fall back by teams and watch your side streets. Singh, you still have your thermal charges?"

"Affirm."

"Use them."

"Roger that."

Talon could practically see the leej grinning like a kid who'd just put one over on his parents. Like most of the rest of the company, Talon tried to stay as far away from the explosives specialist as he could. After all, bombs weren't typically items you wanted to be around for any length of time—eventually they all explode.

As Singh pushed off to place his charges, Talon keyed the company channel. "Stryker-1, Stryker-10, we have hostile elements encroaching from the south and east, approximately sixty armed insurgents. How copy?"

"Stryker-10, Stryker-1, roger that, sixty armed hostiles," Captain Kato replied.

Talon hesitated, then said, "Request artillery to cover."

"Negative, Actual has deemed the entire area Limited Engagement, no artillery available at this time."

Scat-brained point, Talon thought. Not that he'd expected anything to have changed. All points in the Legion held the ideals of those who appointed them above anything else. After all, if it weren't for the House or Senate, they'd have no shot of serving in the Legion. Not that they would have wanted to in the first place.

"Roger that," Talon finally said through gritted teeth. "What about air support? I have two wounded I need to get out of the combat zone, ASAP."

"According to Actual, the LZ is still too hot," Kato said, making a point to use the major's company designation. It was obvious he disagreed with Wyeire's call and relaying who was making the battlefield decisions was his only recourse, short of disregarding his orders.

As far as Talon was concerned, disobeying orders seemed like the only responsible thing to do. "Sir, without air support, we'll be overrun—it's only a matter of time. We don't have the manpower or resources to hold them off or clear a safe LZ. We need assistance now, not when it's safe!"

"Sergeant Talon," Major Wyeire's voice said before Kato could answer. "You have your orders. You will follow them to the letter or you will face the consequences. I cannot, and will not, risk resources on ill-advised operations. Clear out those rioters. Once I'm satisfied the area is secure, I will authorize the shuttles to pick your team up."

"Rioters?" Talon asked, not bothering to hide the frustration in his voice. "These aren't rioters, Major. These are well-equipped and motivated fighters. They aren't waving around picket signs. They've already destroyed the transport train and injured two of my legionnaires. We are engaged with a hostile force intent on destroying us."

"Sergeant, Command doesn't agree with your assessment of the situation, and I'd caution you to watch your tone. You are treading a fine line, legionnaire."

"Listen here, you ignorant point!" Talon shouted. "This isn't some locals demonstrating their hatred for the Republic. We are all going to die unless you send help."

"Sergeant Talon, stand down immediately or I'll have you up on charges for insubordination!"

"Your charges won't mean sket when they're leveled at my corpse! Our blood will be on your hands, Major. Yours and yours alone."

"You are relieved of your duties, Sergeant Talon! Corporal Lancil, you are now in command of 1st Platoon. Arrest Sergeant Talon immediately!"

Talon looked at the medic, still on one knee beside Ginn. Lancil held both hands out to his side and shrugged.

"Corporal Lancil?" Wyeire repeated.

The major started shouting again and Talon muted him, breathing a heavy sigh of relief when the channel went silent. He toggled back to the squad channel. "Any of you have any problems with that?"

No one responded.

"Then let's go to work." He turned to the Gestori. "One of you help Noshey, the other, carry Ginn. I don't care who. You're no good to us as fighters, but if you expect us to get you out of this alive, you're going to have to help."

Burga and Talon led the squad out of the building and into the maze of alleys, walkways, and roads that made up the Dirty. Lancil and Stoma stayed near the Gestori workers and their injured comrades while Mazine brought up the rear. Pax shadowed them from the rooftops and Singh caught up with them after placing his charges.

They cleared intersection after intersection.

"Hey, Sarge," Pax said over the L-comm. "I've got three targets moving toward you from the west alley, one block ahead on Main Street. Can't identify."

Talon slowed, bringing up his N-4. "Roger."

Burga slipped away from Talon, opening up the space between them. The alley was barely four meters wide. Talon hated the claustrophobic feeling tugging at his mind. Close quarters fighting was something the Legion trained for constantly. And if he was being honest, the ancillary corridors of a destroyer were more cramped than this, but that didn't mean he had to like it.

Talon eyed the map overlaid on the top left corner of his HUD. The Dirty was arranged in a grid of east-west and north-south streets and alleys. Since arriving, the legionnaires had been labeling them and noting landmarks, something the marines should have done as soon as they'd come on station.

"Where they at?" Talon asked, hoping to get some intel beyond the HUD's projected tracker that showed a likely course for the targets to take.

"Twenty meters west and closing. Still no visual."

Talon turned to Burga who nodded understanding.

"Fifteen meters," Pax read aloud from the display on their HUDs. "Ten."

"Now," Talon said, stepping into the street, swinging his N-4 around.

Burga followed, coming up beside Talon, the stock of the SAB pulled tight into his shoulder.

"Stop right there, hands in the air!" Talon shouted over his externals.

Three Gestori dressed in dirty overalls were jogging toward them, all carrying large boxes. At the sight of the two legionnaires, they stutter-stepped to a halt, shouting excitedly in their native tongue. The bucket's translator was having trouble catching their panicked exclamations, and Talon didn't like having to take his eyes off the targets to read the broken Standard scrolling on the display.

"Put 'em down!" Burga shouted, taking a step forward, motioning with the barrel of the SAB.

"Drop the boxes!" Talon ordered.

"No... enemy... no shoot!" the translator scrolled, but Talon couldn't determine which of the workers had said it.

"Put those boxes on the ground and get your hands in the air!"

"Sarge?" Pax asked over the L-comm.

"Wait one," Talon told him. Over his externals, he said, "Drop them now!"

One of the Gestori finally let his crate fall and then twisted, hands moving to something on his back.

"No!" Talon shouted, moving forward, aiming his N-4's barrel right at the alien's face.

The Gestori froze. The other two slowly backed up, still frantically shouting.

Burga came around behind Talon, bringing the SAB up at the two backing away. "You two! Drop the kelhorned boxes! Now!"

"Tell them," Talon told the empty-handed Gestori. "Tell them to do it, now!"

The alien shouted to his companions, motioning for them to drop the crates. The other two shouted back, but threw the crates down and shuffled back.

"Now, stay still," Talon said. "Singh, search them."

The leej quickly patted the aliens down, then moved away. "Nothing."

Talon motioned with his N-4. "Get out of here. Stay off the streets."

The first Gestori nodded and started to shove off. The other two bent over to pick up their crates.

"No," Talon said, shaking his head. "Leave them."

The two aliens made a series of gestures Talon recognized as insults, then joined their companion and were soon jogging away from them. They disappeared into an alley two blocks away.

"What the hell are those?" Talon asked.

Burga bent down, studying one of the crates. "Bucket sensors aren't picking up any sign of explosive. I don't think they're weapons." He clicked a latch on the side of the box and carefully opened the lid. After a moment, he shook his head, laughing. "Greedy scat-brained lizards."

Talon peered over Burga's shoulder. The box was filled with refined ore from the mine. The other two were packed full as well, each of the three boxes worth ten times what Talon made in a year.

Behind them the first of Singh's charges went off. They all turned to see the ball of flame roll above the buildings, sending streamers of smoking debris across the sky. The second charge detonated a block over.

"Two more charges left," Singh said.

The company channel squawked. "Stryker-10, Sabre-1, do you copy, over?"

Talon keyed the channel. "Sabre-1, Stryker-10, I copy. Go with your traffic."

"A little birdie told me you boys needed a lift. We are inbound on your position, ETA five minutes."

Talon laughed. "Sabre-1, that's probably the most amazing news I've heard all day."

"Smoke is playing hell with the sensors," Valpasi said. "Do you have any IR beacons handy?"

"That's affirmative, built into the armor," Talon said and then switched to his squad comm. "Make sure your IR beacons are active."

"Copy, I'll look for it and assume that's where you want a pick up, Sergeant."

Talon checked his map. "We're right on Main, moving north. There's a small loading area about a hundred meters to our northwest, we'll mark that LZ1."

"Roger that, LZ1."

"Move out," Talon said. "Pax, did you copy that?"

"Roger, I'm already moving."

Talon nodded and motioned for Burga to lead the way, leaving three small fortunes lying in the street.

They reached the landing zone and spread out, covering avenues of approach. The space was fifty square meters, filled with empty repulsor bins and push carts used to carry ore down from the mines.

Burga covered the east entrance to the landing zone. The Gestori workers accompanying the legionnaires set Ginn and Noshey down between two bins and stayed close, looking around nervously.

"Okay, Stryker-10, I've got your IR beacons, I am inbound from the east."

Talon searched the sky and finally saw a Republic shuttle dropping out of the clouds.

Talon took a knee, laying his N-4 across his thigh. "Oba, if that's not the most wonderful—"

A rocket streaked out of the distant trees in the distance, trailing smoke, arcing across the blue sky. It bullseyed the belly of the shuttle in a brilliant explosion. The impact slewed the shuttle around leaving its pilot struggling to maintain control.

"No," Talon whispered, heart sinking.

The company channel buzzed. "Sabre-1, we're hit. I'm going to bring the bird down now 'cuz I don't think we'll get another shot. This LZ is too hot!"

You dedicated your entire life to us boys and never once complained about your dishes being broken, or mud in the house, or how messy we left our rooms.

18

Someone was banging an anvil inside Lankin's skull. A high-pitched ringing in his ears reduced everything else to distant, muffled noise. He opened his eyes, trying to blink away the blurriness and the stars that danced in his vision. He was in a combat sled, he knew that much, he was lying on his back, looking up at the ceiling. He could feel the repulsor pads vibrating through the floor.

He'd been in the turret. His hand went to his shoulder, pain flaring and sharpening his returning senses. *Those kelhorned asses shot me.* He inspected his armor. The bolt hadn't penetrated, but he'd have a bruise and he'd be sore as hell for a while.

As he got to a knee, the sled rocked underneath him. He put a hand against one of the benches to steady himself, squeezing his eyes shut, trying to focus.

"Sarge?" someone shouted. It sounded like Kessler. "Sarge, you okay?"

When Lankin opened his eyes again, the jungle was rushing by in a blur outside the open rear hatch—lush trees, colorful flowers, and blue sky. In an instant, everything came back. The Talusar fire teams, the ambush, the dead marines.

"Stryker-22, we are falling back," Cross shouted, his voice echoing in Lankin's L-comm as well as his ear. "Repeat, we are falling back."

"We're pulling away from them," Sevanar shouted down from the turret. Several volleys from the twins reverberated through Lankin's chest armor, then the gun went silent. "If they're still out there, they won't be poking their heads up for a while."

Lankin pulled himself onto the bench, trying to remember what he'd done with his N-18.

No, he thought, *they took that away.* He didn't have his rifle, he'd had an N-4.

"Roger that, Stryker-22," someone responded over the L-comm.

Lankin shook himself, forgetting about his rifle when his gaze landed on Sergeant VanZant. Kessler knelt next to him, wrapping his head in a skinpack. Markyle hovered, helping the squad's medic work on the wounded. Private Gemini was strapped to the opposite bench. Ralone and Rowan hung near the open rear hatch, scanning for hostiles, each with one hand on the overhead rail, the other holding their N-4.

Lankin snagged a loose N-4 from the floor and waited for his bucket's AI to link with the weapon. A second later the power gauge appeared on his HUD: the N-4's charge pack was at half capacity. Good enough for now.

"How are we looking?" Lankin asked, already knowing what the answer was going to be.

"Marine here has a concussion most likely," Kessler said, finishing his treatment. He turned to examine Gemini, who was lying on his chest. "Penetrating wound here."

The leej's back armor was charred and dented from blaster fire, a bolt set on max power by the look of it. The bolt had cracked the armor, burned away his black synthprene, and seared the top layers of skin.

Kessler pulled a narco-pen from his kit and jammed it into the leej's back. Gemini screamed, the muted, agonized cry bleeding from his bucket even without his externals on.

"Dammit, Markyle, help me hold him!" Kessler shouted.

Lankin slid across the floor and pushed down on Gemini's shoulder. Markyle grabbed the leej's legs.

"Stay still, Gem," Kessler said, rifling through his kit. "Can you get his bucket off, Sarge?"

"Yeah," Lankin said. Carefully, he pulled Gemini's helmet off and set it aside.

"All right, Gem, I know you're hurting, but I need to know if you can move your fingers and toes?" Kessler pulled out another narco-pen.

"Think so," Gemini said through gritted teeth.

Kessler pushed the second dose into the legionnaire's back. This time he didn't flinch. "Good. That means your back's not broken."

"Could've fooled me."

The medic produced a tube of quick-seal, pulled the cap off and used both hands to squeeze the yellow gel onto the wound. Gemini grunted as Kessler spread the compound over the wound, making sure it was completely covered. He pulled a large skinpack from the kit and placed it over the wound. Gemini's body relaxed and Lankin let up on him.

In the turret, Sevanar ripped off several more bursts, sending a barrage of blaster bolts chewing through the jungle behind them.

"Sevanar, you still see hostiles?" Lankin asked.

The leej's words were almost drowned out by the cannon as he fired again. "Nobody's sticking their heads up in this mess, Sarge. Just keepin' 'em honest."

"Cease fire then," Lankin said. "Scan for targets. Watch for ambushes. Does anyone know if we got that truck?"

"We got it, Sarge," Cross said. "Lit it up like Unity Day."

Lankin nodded. "Good." His HUD told him they were heading north, following the main road up from Wolf, still on track for the spot where Talon and his team had been ambushed.

"Keep an eye out for additional hostiles. I don't know if the ones we just encountered are the same ones that attacked Talon's team, but I doubt it. There's at least one more insurgent group to the north somewhere, and there's no telling how spread out their line is."

"Roger that, Sarge."

They passed one of the pylons and a moment later drove under the elevated mag-lev track. Another pylon appeared on the opposite side of the road and Lankin's HUD identified it as Pylon 37. Just under twenty more pylons until they reached the ambush point.

"Check your equipment, leejes. I want gear status in one minute." Lankin toggled to a private channel and said, "Stryker-19, Stryker-1."

Captain Kato answered, "Go ahead, Stryker-19. Glad to hear you're okay."

"Relatively, sir. We have broken off contact with the enemy and are continuing north to the Dirty. I have two marines KIA, and one leej injured. I'd say we took out between ten and fifteen hostiles, but I can't be sure."

"The airlift we sent for 1st Squad is pinned down," Kato said. "They reported taking sporadic blaster fire on the way out, and now they're stranded on the ground just outside Dirty. Talon and his men are working their way there right now."

"We should rendezvous with them in about fifteen minutes."

"The major is on his way dirtside. He's bringing two drop shuttles and the rest of the platoon with him to secure Wolf. We've been taking fire from a growing force to the north—our mortar bots have been lobbing volleys for the last five minutes."

Lankin suppressed a curse. "I guess convincing him to send a bird our way is out of the question."

"I'm working on that. Additionally, it sounds like Sabre-1 might have taken damage during the landing."

"Great."

"I'm working through the available options, Sergeant. Limited as they may be. But the major has decided that an extraction at this time would jeopardize our ability to mobilize—if the shuttle didn't make it out of the LZ."

"I understand, sir," Lankin said tersely.

So much for quick extraction. He couldn't blame the captain; he knew all too well where the blame fell. Wyeire wouldn't want to appear panicky or give the impression he had lost control of the situation. A slow, orderly deployment would be exactly his style, no matter the situation on the ground.

On his HUD, status reports from his team began to appear. Within ten seconds, the entire squad had reported in. The team, as a whole, was sitting around ninety percent for charge packs and grenades. *What I wouldn't give for a few AP missiles and a battle tank or two.* But his squad didn't have a heavy like most, thanks to Duval's inability to balance the teams. Tanks... *yeah right.*

"Focus on the fight, Sergeant," Kato said, showing why he held the rank he did. Lankin shouldn't be letting himself get distracted with the whys. That wasn't his job. "I'll work on the rest."

"Copy," Lankin said. "We're about two minutes out from the train crash site, sir. Once we get closer to Dirty, we should be able to coordinate efforts with Alpha."

"Keep me advised, Kato out."

The major's continued refusal of support replayed in Lankin's mind. He fumed at the thought of that arrogant point sitting in orbit, in the safety of the warship, making strategy decisions based on how they would affect his future political career. If there was one thing Lankin hated about the Legion, it was that too many people were allowed to use it as their springboard into the higher echelons of the Republic, not as a chance to serve.

"Son of a—" Cross shouted and slammed on the brakes.

Lankin lurched forward at the abrupt stop. He caught himself before his bucket smacked against the weapon racks at the front of the compartment.

"What the hell, Cross?" Lankin asked, pulling himself upright again.

"Pack of kelhorned hellhounds ran right out in front of me," the driver replied.

Lankin brought up visual and shuddered. Pain flared in his hand. His N-4 clattered to the floor and he pulled his hand close to his chest.

"Sarge, you okay?" Kessler asked.

Lankin barely heard him.

The phantom shriek from the memory of that beast tearing through his hand—ripping tendons, crushing bones, and taking his fingers—filled his mind. The creature's claws grabbed at his shoulder, pulling him toward rows of razor-sharp teeth. He jerked, batting the creature's claws away.

"Whoa!" Kessler said, pulling his arm back. "Sarge, it's okay!"

Lankin shook himself. Warnings flashed on his HUD, his heart rate was elevated. He dismissed the notifications and took a deep breath. "Sorry."

"It's okay," Kessler said. "You all right?"

The last kuruprat disappeared into the jungle and Lankin cursed its existence. "Next time just run them over."

Cross laughed. "You got it, Sarge."

Lankin absently rubbed his three prosthetic fingers.

"You might want to hold on to this, boss," Kessler said, passing him his N-4.

"Thanks," Lankin said, accepting the weapon.

The medic motioned to Lankin's hand. "You in pain?"

"Huh? No, no, not really. I think it's more up here than anything." Lankin tapped a finger against the side of his bucket.

"You sure?"

"Yeah, I'm fine. Really."

"Hey, Sarge," Cross said over the L-comm. "You'd better see this."

Lankin leaned forward, looking at display from the forward-facing cam. "Stop us here." He pounded a fist on the sled's ceiling. "Sevanar, eyes open up there."

"Roger that, Sarge."

The clearing around Pylon 64 was eerily silent. Black smoke poured out of multiple rents along the train. The second engine stuck up from the ground, still connected to a string of passenger cars behind it, one still clinging precariously to the track above.

Disconnected cars in clusters of five or six formed new craters along the route for two hundred meters behind the engine.

The team dismounted and found Gestori workers gathered near the smoking engine, clothes torn, burnt, and stained. They clamored at the legionnaires, begging for help. Bodies had been collected and laid out nearby. His bucket sensors told him a couple were still alive, barely.

Lankin led his team across the clearing, keeping his eyes on the tree line to the east. A large earth berm had been created by construction crews on the far side of the tracks. His HUD remained clear of targets—then it registered the position of a dead legionnaire.

"Stryker-1, Stryker-19."

"Go ahead, 19."

"We found LS-05. He's dead, sir."

Captain Kato sounded more tired than Lankin remembered. "Copy. Bring him home."

The surviving Gestori were gathered around the corpse. His bucket had been removed and most of his armor was missing. They'd taken his N-4, the remaining charge packs, grenades, even his ration kit, leaving nothing behind but his torn and scorched synthprene body glove.

"Stay back!" Saretti shouted over his externals, pointing at the locals. "Get your hands up. Don't move."

The team forced themselves between their fallen comrade and the survivors, keeping their N-4s up and trained.

Lankin dropped down beside the legionnaire.

He recognized him immediately, even without the bucket's having labeled the fallen legionnaire long before he had visuals. Private Bishto, LS-05. By the look of his chewed up base layer and blood seeping through it, Bishto had taken a lot of punishment before he'd fallen. A hero's last stand.

Lankin closed the dead man's eyes, shaking his head.

You were a brave man.

"He held off the attackers as long as he could," one of the workers said. "It was the insurgents who stripped him—not us. They headed off that way." He pointed toward the mines.

"Are you here to help us?" another asked. "We were trapped in one of the cars, couldn't get out like the rest."

Lankin looked up at the Gestori. Blood stained the alien's overalls, his green skin covered by dirt and grime, his short-cropped orange hair matted by blood and sweat.

Standing, Lankin grabbed the closest worker by the collar and pulled him close. He stared into the alien's bright yellow eyes and asked, "Why didn't they kill you?"

The worker stuttered, trying to pull away. Lankin batted away the Gestori's hands as if they were an afterthought. "Tell me! Why did they just leave you out here?"

"We weren't who they were after!" the alien blurted out, voice cracking. "They said to wait here until after the battle was over."

"And who, exactly, were they after?"

"You! They said they were after you, legionnaires! The Republic!"

"Why the hell are the Talusar even here? You have to know something!"

"Please!" the Gestori cried. "Please, I don't know!"

Lankin held the alien's gaze for several seconds, then let him go. The Gestori stumbled back into the protective arms of his companions, who glared at the legionnaires.

"You know they're lying," Saretti said, motioning with his N-4. The survivors cowered at the leej's words. "We should just dust them all right now and be done with it."

"No one is dusting anyone," Lankin said with a calm he didn't feel. He motioned to the injured Gestori workers. "Kessler, see what you can do."

"Roger." The medic stepped through the aliens and started triaging patients.

"Cross, bring the sled up," Lankin ordered. "The rest of you, clear the perimeter."

He backed away from the group as Kessler worked, looked at Bishto's body, then turned away as his mind filled with rage. Lankin moved around the smashed nose of the train, his bucket recording the damage. The engine had chewed a deep gouge out of the earth, leaving a long trench behind it. Pieces of impervisteel frame, machinery, glass, and ore littered the ground.

He didn't even want to guess what this attack would cost the Republic to fix. Hauling off the train would take time, especially in this remote section of jungle, not to mention bringing in new engines and recertifying the mag-lev track.

But why did he care? The Republic had the credits, they just refused to spend them unless it was on some pet project that was certain to bring more political clout, personal favors, or increase the size of their personal accounts. Sure, maybe not all of them, but enough.

Lankin moved around a second car and froze at the sight of a four-wheeled all-terrain vehicle stopped about twenty meters ahead. He ducked behind the train car, bringing up his N-4. His HUD scanned around him but didn't show any hostile targets in the area.

Slowly, he stepped back around the train car, keeping his weapon aimed at the small vehicle. It was empty and looked like the front end had been damaged by an explosion that had left a small crater in the long green grass.

Smoke curled up from underneath its hood. The front axle was broken, and the driver's side wheel rested underneath the frame.

As he neared the ATV, he saw a body lying face down in the crater. A foot lay on the edge of the hole, not attached to the rest of the body. What was left of the insurgent lay in a bloody mess at the center of the small crater, the torso completely shredded by the explosion. He looked down just as he passed what looked like a finger lying in the grass next to his boot.

He knelt to look over the body. It was impossible to determine what race the alien had been, unless he wanted to check out the foot inside the boot, but Lankin decided finding out wasn't *that* important. There weren't any identifying unit tabs, clothing or gear either. Everything was generic, available on any number of—

"Don't move," a gruff voice said behind him.

Lankin froze.

"Drop your weapon."

"Heads up," Lankin said softly into his L-comm, "insurgent behind the second car after the engine. Come in quiet."

"Sket. We're comin'."

Lankin let the N-4 fall to the ground. He turned, looking over his shoulder at his assailant. A mask covered the bottom half of the Talusar's face, the alien's piercing red eyes almost glowing with hate. Black hair hung down in long strands over his orange and black mottled skin. The tactical vest he wore over his long sleeve black shirt was filled with extra charge packs and some ancient-looking frag-grenades. He held a basic blaster rifle, muzzle pointing at Lankin's chest.

"Stand up," the Talusar commanded. "No transmissions. No tricks."

Slowly, Lankin got to his feet, turning to face the insurgent. He slid his hand down to a tactical blade sheathed at the small of his back while simultaneously raising his other hand in surrender.

The Talusar noticed. "Show me your other—"

Lankin lunged forward, pulling the knife and slashing it across the alien's chest. The Talusar stepped back, moving just out of range, but Lankin wasn't finished. He pressed forward, bringing the knife back, dropping his shoulder. He drove his armor into the alien's stomach, knocking him back.

Hands grabbed at the seams in his armor and he felt himself being lifted into the air. The alien was using his own momentum against him. Lankin's feet left the ground and he flipped over the alien's shoulder.

He let out a painful grunt as he landed, stars dancing in his vision. Before he could roll off his back the alien was on him, bringing the butt of his rifle down on Lankin's helmet. He heard the bucket crack and his HUD flickered and went blank, leaving him with a much-restricted view through the physical visor itself. When the Talusar lifted the rifle for a second strike, Lankin thrust his hips up. He grabbed the alien's vest and pulled with everything he had.

The alien cried out as Lankin tossed him to the side, then rolled to continue his attack. His hand came up to stab, but it was empty, the knife was gone. He didn't have time—or field of vision—to find it.

Lankin balled his hand into a fist and drove it into the alien's face. Bones crunched and blood sprayed as his armored hand pounded flesh. He cocked back for another blow, but as he brought his hand down again the alien caught it, stopping it cold.

With an impressive show of strength, the Talusar threw Lankin back. The legionnaire landed on his back, coughing for air. He pushed the pain aside and got to a knee. The alien grabbed the rifle he'd lost in the struggle.

Lankin's hand moved on instinct.

His blaster pistol was drawn in an eye blink, sight picture locked, and he pulled the trigger. The pistol fired and a red-hot blaster bolt slammed home, knocking the Talusar fighter back. Lankin transitioned smoothly to a two-handed grip and squeezed the trigger again. This time the weapon barely moved as he fired. He put five more bolts into the alien's chest as he fell, dropping his rifle.

Lankin stood, keeping the sights leveled, watching for any sign of life. After several moments, he was satisfied and stepped closer. The Talusar was dead. Blood seeped through his dark clothing and stained the grass underneath his body.

Lankin pulled off his helmet and visually scanned for other targets but found none. He holstered the pistol and put the helmet back on, slapping a palm against its side. The HUD flickered back to life, fuzzed, then vanished again.

"Great," he said, pulling off the helmet again.

Kessler and Saretti appeared around the smoking train cars, N-4s pointed toward the leej and his foe.

"You all right, Sarge?" Saretti asked.

"Fine," Lankin said, retrieving his N-4. "Going to have to get this thing repaired, though."

"Let me have a look at it, Sarge." Saretti held out a hand.

Lankin hesitated, raising an eyebrow at the private.

Saretti shrugged. "I got a thing for electronics."

Relenting, Lankin held it out. "How are the Gestori wounded?"

"A couple are critical," Kessler said. "If they aren't seen soon..."

"I know."

"What are we going to do with them?" Saretti asked, turning the helmet upside down and examining the internals. "They ain't going to all fit in the sled."

Lankin didn't like the idea of leaving them behind, but where they were going, the extra bodies would only get in the way and slow them down. "We leave them."

Kessler grimaced, leaning in close. "Sarge, I—"

Lankin held up a hand. "There isn't anything we can do. We can't take them with us and we're not going back to Wolf. Talon's team need us there ten minutes ago. They know the way."

"Bird reported taking fire on the way out to Dirty," Kessler reminded him. "Means there's more Talusar in the jungle between here and Wolf."

"They aren't coming," Lankin said.

A shadow played across the ground, followed by the deep reverberating thumping of repulsor engines as a

Legion assault shuttle dropped out of the sky. It kicked up a gust of wind as it flared for landing, its rear cargo ramp already folding down. Landing pistons hissed as the shuttle settled on to the ground and 2nd Platoon's commander Lieutenant Fox strode down the ramp.

"You boys need a ride?"

Your love made me feel like there were no other children in the world and that I was your entire life's mission.

19

"No, absolutely not." Lieutenant Fox turned away from Lankin and pointed from his men to the wounded Gestori workers. "Get them loaded up."

Lankin started after him. "Just hear me out, LT. If the major's orders were to retrieve us and bring us back to Wolf to backfill the marines, don't you think he'd want as many leejes as he can get?"

"I'm not having this discussion, Sergeant."

Lankin gave Kessler and Saretti an exasperated look, but both leejes still had their buckets on. He had no way of knowing if they shared his expression. "Sir, if we don't do something now, Talon's squad is going to get overrun. Now, I can take the sled and maybe make it there in time; you'll be in the clear and be safe back at Wolf in the Major's good graces. But if we take her," Lankin used his broken helmet to point at the assault shuttle, "we *can* get there in time and save some legionnaire lives."

"You think I *want* to leave Talon out there?" Fox said, hands out to either side. "I have my orders."

"Your orders are wrong, sir, and you damn well know it."

Several members from 2nd Platoon stopped what they were doing to watch the exchange, some still holding litters loaded with Gestori workers. Lankin felt his face flush, knowing what it looked like, knowing what they were thinking. He didn't have any love for Duval at all, but if anyone outside his platoon had ever gone against Captain Kato like he was doing now, there'd be hell to pay.

"I know Talon is your friend and I sympathize, but the major was very clear. Retrieve you and the civilians and return to Wolf. Nothing else."

"Captain said the major wasn't sending out any birds at all after what happened with Sabre-1," Kessler said. "What changed his mind?"

Fox hesitated for a moment, canting his bucket slightly toward the Gestori workers. He didn't linger long, but it was long enough. Lankin knew exactly why the lieutenant had been authorized to make the trip all the way out here, and it wasn't to pick him and his team up.

"He sent you out here for the civilians." It was a statement, not a question. Lankin knew the answer before he'd even finished speaking.

Fox nodded. "That's right."

"I cranking knew it," Kessler said, throwing up his hands. "Scat-brained little self-absorbed piece of—"

"You better watch yourself, Corporal," Fox said, pointing. "You're walking a dangerous line. Captain Kato is already engaging the enemy at Wolf. We don't have time for this."

Lankin motioned for Kessler to stand down. "Fine. Forget the bird, we'll take the sled. Can't leave it out here anyway. Let's get VanZant and the others transferred over. Hopefully we won't run into any other patrols on the way there." He nodded to his two leejes. "Get it done."

Kessler and Saretti hesitated for a moment, then both said, "Roger that," and moved off.

Fox watched Lankin's legionnaires from the back of the sled. Lankin kept his eyes locked on the lieutenant, his mind racing through engagement plans. There had to be a way to change his mind. Fox wasn't a point like Lieutenant Duval or the major, and even though he had half the time in service as Captain Kato, Lankin could see that he would be a good officer. It was obvious the man was conflicted, but Lankin didn't think the internal argument was over whether or not the decision would make him look good in the major's eyes.

"Here, Sarge." Saretti held out Lankin's helmet. "One of your display circuits got bumped. Should be okay now."

"Thanks." Lankin took his bucket back, turning it over in his hands. His eyes flicked from the helmet up to Fox. "Not that I'll need it any time soon."

They were halfway through loading the wounded when Fox said, "For Oba's sake. Stop!"

The leejes of 2nd Platoon froze in their tracks. Blood pounded in Lankin's ears as a pit of anticipation grew in his stomach. Fox turned, facing him, dipping his chin. "You're right."

"Sir?"

"Talon won't last up there if we don't go help him."

Lankin couldn't help the smile that crept across his face.

Fox pointed at him. "If I go down, you're going down with me, Sergeant." He turned to his men, lined up in front of the shuttle. "Transfer the wounded to the sled. Partlow, you're driving and don't give me any sket, I don't want to hear it."

Kessler appeared next to Lankin, putting a hand on his shoulder. "You certainly do have a way with people, Sarge."

"We're not screwing around up there, Sergeant," Fox said. "In and out, you got me?"

Still smiling, Lankin said, "Yes, sir. Take names and kick ass."

Kessler laughed. "Feel the thunder. Right, Sarge?"

Lankin slid his bucket down over his head. The HUD came to life and he toggled his externals. "Feel the damn thunder."

Thank you for loving me so much.

20

"Movement right," Pax announced over the L-comm.

Talon dropped to a knee and peered around the corner, holding his N-4 back to keep the barrel from flagging him. Two target icons appeared on his HUD, moving up to flank them on ground level, one block over. He was sure there were more, but if Pax couldn't see them...

"Roger," he said, checking the power level on his N-4's charge pack. Thirty percent. He'd toggled blast power of the weapon down to just over stun. His shots might not kill an armored foe, but they'd put the enemy on their back and extended the life of the pack by twofold. Still, he would run out eventually and so would the rest of his team.

"Sabre-1 to in-bound Stryker elements, where the hell are you guys?"

"We're coming!" Talon replied, ducking as a blaster bolt zipped through the air above him.

"We've got the LZ secured, but I'm not sure how long that'll last. You need to expedite, Sergeant."

"Understood."

They were stalled among a lot containing large eight-wheeled vehicles with enormous dump-bins in the back. They were arranged in haphazard rows. Some looked like they hadn't been driven in months, others had obviously been parted out. Cables, bolts, lugs, and larger parts lay strewn around the duracrete.

The plan had been to commandeer one of the vehicles and hightail it to the shuttle. But so far no one had been able to get one of the big hulks fired up, and hotwiring them while under heavy enemy fire was proving more than a little difficult.

Something exploded several blocks away, followed by a volley of blaster fire.

"They just took out the power relay station," Pax said. "Looks like another group of ten or so moving in from the west."

Talon stepped out from the corner, N-4 leveled down the alley. He took several small steps forward, watching the target icons slide closer to the edge of the building to his right. He held his breath as the first one reached the corner, finger already pressing on the trigger.

A Gestori woman ran into the alley and screamed at the sight of the legionnaire. A second worker appeared, almost running into the first. He threw his hands up and screamed for the legionnaires not to shoot.

"Down!" Talon yelled, heart pounding. "On the ground now!"

The woman screamed again, dropping to her knees as the man stepped in front of her with his hands up, waving. "No! No! No!"

"Get down!"

"What the hell are they doing out there?" Singh rushed past, pushing his N-4 behind him to pat them all down. "They're clear."

Blaster fire zipped through the air, chewing into one of buildings across from them. Dust and debris sprayed out from the duracrete walls.

The woman screamed again as the man pulled her to her feet.

"Get them back!" Talon shouted, grabbing them both and pulling them out of the middle of the road.

He moved to the corner and fired a volley blind. Return blaster fire filled the air, raking the street and walls.

"You've got a mounted 74 approaching your position, Sarge!" Pax advised over L-comm. "Plus five hostile targets."

Singh and Mazine moved up beside Talon. "What you need, boss?"

Talon shook his head. "We don't have time for this. If we can't get one of those trucks running, we're going to have to move out on foot. That shuttle crew doesn't have the luxury of waiting for us to show up and they damn sure can't take off in all this. Toss out a couple frags. Singh, set what anti-personnel charges you have left, and let's get moving."

"Roger," both men said together.

The two legionnaires stepped around Talon and heaved fist-sized grenades down the street. They went off in quick succession, their dual *whoomp whoomp* reverberating through the building at Talon's back, shaking his insides.

"How much farther to the landing site, Pax?" Talon asked.

"Couple hundred meters to the edge of the complex, it's right there. Straight through that lot of ore haulers. Looks like two groups of Talusar are moving on it, though—oh, sket!"

An explosion sounded in the distance, and a column of smoke curled into the air where the shuttle was parked.

"Sabre-1, Stryker-10, are you okay?"

"Kelhorned orange-skinned, sket-brains just blew out my portside nacelle! We're not going anywhere fast."

"Doesn't look good, Sarge," Pax confirmed. A second later the N-18's distinctive *krak-bdew* pierced the air, followed by another, and the sniper's voice came over the L-comm. "Target down."

Blaster fire streaked into the black steel framework around one of the hauler's buckets. Sparks rained on Talon's armor. He spun, dropped to a knee, and fired.

His shots struck his attacker in the hip and chest, spinning him sideways. As his first target fell, his eyes shifted to a second. A three-round burst put him down.

"We need to get to the bird now!" Talon shouted.

Another Talusar emerged, holding a large shoulder-fired rocket in both hands. He brought the weapon up. Talon was halfway through his targeting transition when he heard the *krak-bdew*!

The attacker's head disintegrated into a mist of blood and gore. The rocket launcher thumped to the ground, but the insurgent's body stayed upright, as if it was still processing what had happened. A moment later the body fell, sending up a puff of dust.

"Nice shot, Pax!"

"They're bringing up another technical," Burga shouted over the L-comm. He fired off a volley, then took cover behind the front of one of the haulers. "Sket, I'm out. Mazine, I need another pack for the SAB!"

Talon moved around Burga, firing random shots down the street as Mazine unslung his pack. Burga let the spent pack drop, then slipped the new one over his shoulders. Mazine helped reconnect the charge cables, and Burga went back to work.

"Pax," Talon said, coming back to exchange his own pack. "We need to stop that technical."

"I don't have a good shot on it, Sarge. I'm running out of room up here."

"Sket. Rally up, Pax. We're moving out."

"Roger that."

The team reached the end of the lot and stopped behind a retaining wall. Pax dropped down from a single-level garage, his sniper rifle slung across his back. He drew his pistol and sent six bolts down the alley, then trotted over to join the rest of the team.

"Twenty meters," he said. "There's a handful of hostiles closing in. The technical had to make a detour, not sure where they went. Shuttle's just on the other side of this clearing."

Talon looked over his legionnaires, lingering on the two injured men. The Gestori hunkered close to the wall, flinching at the incoming blaster fire. Talon wondered how long they'd stick around. To this point at least, there must not have been anywhere else for them to go.

On Talon's HUD, a mass of target icons was growing to the west, joining another cluster of dots from the south.

The shuttle sat in the middle of the clearing, a bevy of blaster fire flashing off its hull, smoke rising from a gaping hole in the fuselage. A small group of insurgents were clustered around a corpse wearing a marine flight suit.

"Sket, we're too late!" Talon shouted.

"Burga, Lancil, hold here. Pax, Mazine, Stoma, you're with me."

Talon sprinted into the clearing without waiting for his team to acknowledge, firing at the assembled fighters. The aliens spread out, but Talon's fire took several down. He changed his angle of approach when two of the attackers returned fire.

Stoma came in from Talon's left, catching two insurgents on the run. Plumes of dirt sprayed up from his volley. A round caught the first in the leg, sending him sprawling. The second slowed to help his companion and took a blaster in the back. He fell over the first and Stoma gave them another long burst from his N-4.

Talon's HUD flashed, warning a projectile explosive had been thrown in his direction. The ground several meters to Talon's right exploded, sending a geyser of soil into the air. Screams flooded the squad's L-comm channel. Talon caught a glimpse of a legionnaire pinwheeling through the air.

"Mazine!" Talon shouted, searching for the attacker who'd thrown the fragger. One of them darted out from behind the smoking shuttle engines and Talon dropped him with a three-round burst.

His HUD told him Mazine's vitals were critical, but he was still alive. "Lancil, up! Cover!"

He darted to Mazine's side. The bottom half of his legs were gone, severed at the knees by the explosion. The synthprene under suit began to constrict, stopping the blood pouring from the wounds, soaking the grass.

Talon let his N-4 hang, slipped his arms under the leej's armpits, and pulled him toward the shuttle. Lancil and Singh appeared, covering Talon, laying down suppressive fire. Talon didn't stop until his back hit the shuttle's chassis. Carefully, he laid Mazine down. Lancil knelt next to the wounds, already rifling through his kit.

"Go," Lancil said, slamming a narco-pen into one leg, then another. Mazine screamed, trying to sit up, grasping as his severed legs. The medic ignored the leej's protests, tossing the pen. "Go, I've got this. Secure the shuttle."

Pax rushed by, jumping over a broken shard of hull. "We've got incoming on the backside!"

"Stoma!" Talon shouted.

"Roger that," the leej yelled back, following the sniper.

The shuttle was scorched with blaster marks. Talon let his N-4 hang from its sling, pushing it behind him, then drew his blaster pistol and ducked through the hole. He switched his ultrabeam on as he stepped into the darkened interior, more to blind anyone inside than for himself. His bucket's night vision adjusted to the bright beam of light. A broken panel sparked, illuminating the shuttle's bay in flashes of orange light.

Something moved to his right. He raised the pistol just as a figure in black stood up near the front of the compartment.

A Talusar in a stocking cap with a black scarf around his neck shouted something, bringing his own weapon up. Talon fired twice. His shots punched into the alien's chest. The Talusar bounced off the wall, stumbled forward, and tripped over something.

Talon's eyes flicked to what the alien had tripped over. His stomach turned.

Sweets's helmet had been removed, as well as most of his armor. Blood covered his face but had stopped flowing. His short brown hair was matted and caked with the stuff.

Talon knelt beside him, pushing the man's eyes closed. "Rest, my friend. May Oba guard your soul."

In the cockpit, one of the pilots was dead, slumped over, still strapped into his seat. The crew chief lay in a pool of blood at the rear of the compartment, his flight suit filled with blaster holes.

Talon slammed a fist into the bulkhead and screamed in frustration. He ignored the pain. Anger flared inside him as he turned back to his fallen friend, knowing the deaths could've been prevented. He suppressed another out-burst— his bucket told him his blood pressure and heart rate were critical, logging the levels for review.

Log what you want, you scat-brained AI, he thought, stepping back through the blast hole, leaving the relatively serene interior, returning to the chaotic battle.

We're going to die out here. He ducked the sparks spraying from the craft.

Lancil was still working on Mazine's legs. The wounded legionnaire wasn't moving.

Across the clearing, Burga's SAB was spitting an almost constant barrage of blaster fire, punctuated by bursts from Noshey's N-4. A steady staccato cracked from an N-18 on the other side of the shuttle as Pax worked through targets. The sniper was deadlier and more accurate than anyone Talon knew.

The SAB fire ceased and Burga's voice came over the L-comm. "Shifting fire! Shifting fire! They're moving to flank us from the north. I think that 74's back!"

The corporal lugged the large weapon to the near side of a parking overhang, then dropped behind it and began dousing the approaches with blaster fire. The SAB shook as it spat out its deadly hailstorm of super-heated energy projectiles. Dust plumed up from the ground as the blaster unloaded, obscuring the leej from view.

"Rifle's black," Pax called out. With the N-18 out of charge packs, all that was left to the sniper was his blaster pistol.

Back across the clearing, the Gestori workers were pulling Ginn to the other side of the wall. Beside them, Noshey propped himself up against the edge so he could lean on his good leg and fire back. He had to readjust after every burst so he wouldn't lose control of his N-4. Burga dropped down from the overhang opposite Noshey, laying down a wall of fire with the SAB.

Pax appeared from behind the shuttle, changing charge packs out of his pistol. "Burga, look out, that truck's—"

DAT-DAT-DAT-DAT-DAT-DAT-DAT

The ground in front of Burga erupted under a maelstrom of heavy fire from the insurgents' vehicle-mounted automatic blaster. The line of fire chewed through the wall the legionnaire lay behind, spraying bits of brick and smoke into the air. Burga rolled, leaving the SAB. The 74's high energy bolts turned it into so much slag.

"We need suppressive fire on that truck now!" Talon shouted, wishing his heavy had packed more A-P missiles.

Stoma and Pax raced back across the clearing to help their pinned down comrades. Stoma pulled Burga to his feet. Pax tossed a fragger down the street toward the technical.

The detonation was answered by a volley from the 74. Hundreds of high energy blaster bolts streaked by, ripping into the ground and chewing through the wall concealing the legionnaires.

Talon centered his N-4 and fired, catching the truck's gunner in the leg, just below the mounted weapon's blast shield. The Talusar dropped, still holding the 74's firing handles, yanking the barrel straight up and sending arcs of red and orange bolts into the sky. Four more insurgents appeared behind the truck. Two grabbed their companion and pulled him from the bed, another hopped over the side and started working the gun.

Talon fired again and missed. Still more insurgents added their blaster rifles to the chaos. The legionnaire ducked behind the shuttle's wing as bolts stitched across the fuselage above him. Even as he hit the ground, Talon knew he was going to die. In another second, the 74 would open up and shred him and his team to pieces.

"Get—"

Talon's warning was interrupted by a rapid *thrrrrrrp* drowning out all the blaster fire around him. Something exploded and he felt warm air blast him from above. His bucket's sound dampeners kicked in against a devastating boom. A powerful thrumming reverberated through his chest, shaking the ground underneath him.

But he wasn't dead.

"Stryker-10, be advised, hostile heavy weapon platform neutralized. What's your status, over?"

Talon looked over the shuttle's wing and saw fire and smoke pouring out of the weapons truck. A Republic assault shuttle flew out of the pillar of smoke. Strapped to the fuselage, a leej at the top of the open rear hatch sprayed the ground with blaster fire from a door-mounted heavy blaster cannon.

The mass of insurgents fled, spreading out in all directions as hundreds of blaster bolts rained down. Screams of pain and fear filled the street as the soldiers were cut down from above. Bolts stitched across the ground, throwing up plumes of earth and grass, plowing through the enemy.

"I love the navy!" Talon shouted, getting to his feet and adding his own fire to the assault. Multiple dots vanished from his HUD every second, but still more targets moved up from the west.

Pax shouted over the L-comm. "Rocket!"

You raised me to stand up for myself.

21

Lankin raked the ground with blaster fire from his place next to the heavy crew gunner on the assault shuttle, mowing down a pack of insurgents with an SAB, even as they turned to flee the cannon fire. His HUD flashed—movement to his left, an insurgent hefting the HE-45 launcher onto his shoulder.

"Rocket! Contact left!" Lankin shouted, adjusting fire even though he knew he wouldn't reach the target in time.

Immediately the shuttle banked to take evasive action.

He saw the launcher flash, but the assault shuttle's engines drowned out the blast noise. Alarms wailed inside the shuttle as it banked away from the incoming rocket, barely avoiding it. The rocket shot passed the shuttle's aft section, leaving a trail of smoke in its wake.

Gritting his teeth against the shuttle's inertia, Lankin brought the SAB on target and squeezed the trigger. The automatic blaster shook in his hands. The air around him sizzled, making it nearly impossible to see his targets on the ground without his HUD's visual aids. After several seconds he let up on the trigger, pausing to better inspect his work.

A tangled mass of insurgents, as if they'd all wanted to run the same direction, littered the ground. The HE-45 launcher lay next to one of the shredded corpses. Lankin centered his optics on the weapon and put another burst of fire into it, making sure nobody else could use it.

All the while the heavy gun bellowed its fire, pushing insurgents farther back. Plumes of soil and duracrete sprayed as the gunner tracked the scattering Talusar, fleeing through rows of hauler trucks and ore containers. Lankin sent several random bursts in the direction of the hostile targets, encouraging the enemy to continue to run.

"Put us on the ground," Lieutenant Fox ordered over L-comm.

"Roger that," the pilot responded.

The shuttle banked slightly as it turned and descended to the clearing between the downed shuttle and the edge of the mining complex. Lankin and the rest of Bravo squad and 2nd Platoon hit the ground running.

"Secure the area," Lankin said, leaving the legionnaires from 2nd platoon.

His men responded with a chorus of affirmatives and moved out to take up overwatch positions around the downed shuttle.

Lankin's HUD identified Talon. His battle armor had taken a beating, but the man was still standing.

"You're one crazy idiot, did you know that?" he said.

"I believe the term is reckless." Lankin held out a hand. "Always knew I'd have to save your ass one day."

"Yeah, you, the navy, and the rest of the platoon," Talon said. "Sure did take you long enough. I damn near had to kill all of them, my—"

Something smacked into Talon's bucket, knocking the leej off his feet. Lankin dropped next to his friend, shielding him.

"Sniper!" Lankin shouted over the L-comm. "Kessler, on me!"

At the edge of the clearing, a leej from 2nd platoon sent a barrage of SAB fire downrange.

Saretti joined him, effectively covering the entire area. Rowan and Markyle helped Noshey and Mazine up the ramp while Singh and Corse covered them.

Kessler and Lancil appeared at Lankin's side. Both medics went to work, pulling the legionnaire behind the cover of the downed shuttle. The sniper round had impacted behind Talon's right ear, denting the leej's helmet. The lack of scorch marks suggested it had been a solid projectile, not a blaster bolt.

"Looks like they're regrouping to the northwest," Burga advised over L-comm.

"We need to get him on the shuttle," Kessler said, running a gloved hand over the dent in Talon's helmet.

Lankin's HUD painted almost forty targets converging on the landing zone. Now that the assault shuttle was no longer spewing out hate and death from above, the Talusar seemed determined to continue the fight.

"Fire everything you've got!" Lankin shouted. "Burn it to the ground!"

A rocket streaked away from the shuttle's ramp, where another 2nd platoon leej stood with an aero-precision launcher over his shoulder. The rocket slammed into the red brick facade of a two-story maintenance garage and exploded. The fireball filled the street with smoke.

"Frag out!" Singh yelled, lobbing his grenade over the wall between them and the hauler lot. A second later the *whoomp whoomp* shook the wall.

As Kessler and Lancil hauled Talon onto the shuttle, Lankin keyed his company channel. "All Stryker elements, fall back to the shuttle! All Stryker elements, on me! We are leaving!"

One by one, Lankin's legionnaires disengaged and re-treated, followed by 2nd platoon. The insurgents rallied, sending blaster bolts downrange, chewing through the ground and into the assault shuttle's shields.

Seconds before Private Stoma reached the ramp, he took a blaster bolt. He landed hard, face down on the ramp and was immediately grabbed by two leejes and pulled the rest of the way ahead of incoming fire.

The leej with the aero-precision launcher dropped it and transitioned to his N-4 when insurgents started firing from behind the still smoking technical truck. He let loose with a volley of fire, taking three down before an enemy bolt hit him in the side. He bent, one hand holding his wound, the other keeping his weapon up and firing.

"Fall back!" Lankin shouted, running to help.

The injured legionnaire took two more hostiles down before several rounds hit him in the chest. The impacts pushed him back but didn't knock him down. His externals came to life and his voice roared with fury and hatred. He completed a lightning-fast pack change, then pressed on, advancing and firing on the enemy.

Lankin found a target and dropped it. He heard the voice of 2nd Platoon's lieutenant. "Legionnaires, we are leaving!"

"Screw these kelhorned bast—aaaah!"

A bolt struck the leej's leg, spinning him off-balance. He put out a hand, stopping his fall, then brought his weapon back up and continued to fire until his charge pack was depleted. He cursed, ejecting the spent charge pack, and reached for another.

His head snapped back with a sickening *whack,* sparks erupting from the green armor. The N-4 fell from his hands and he dropped like a rock, bucket bouncing off the ground.

"No!" Lankin shouted, depleting his own charge pack.

Lankin tossed his N-4 aside and heaved the private over one shoulder. His robotic hand clamped down on the armor. He drew his blaster, firing in a wild spray as he sprinted for the shuttle.

Markyle and Rowan ran down the ramp, adding their own fire to Lankin's barrage. He felt hands on him, pushing him up the ramp and into the shuttle's bay.

"We're all in," Lancil advised over L-comm. "Get us the hell out of here!"

The heavy crew gun wreaked destruction on any insurgents foolish enough to be in the line of sight now that the legionnaires were clear. The shuttle's repulsors whined and the deck vibrated under Lankin's feet. He lowered the injured legionnaire to the deck.

"I've got him, Sarge," Kessler said, already working on pulling the leej's armor off.

The legionnaires from 2nd gathered around their fallen comrade. One of them pulled the man's bucket off. Blood trickled from the side of his mouth, running down his cheek. He coughed, eyes meeting Lankin's and raised a hand.

Lankin took the offered hand. "You're going to be okay."

"Did we... did we show them the... thunder?" The kid's voice was barely a whisper.

Lankin worked his jaw, feeling his rage boil inside his chest. "They felt it. They felt the sketting thunder."

To protect those who couldn't protect themselves.

22

"Awful lot of contacts still out there, Sarge," Burga said.

"There are," Lankin agreed, watching the hostile dots increase on his HUD. The shuttle shot toward Wolf, crew guns blazing until they were safely out of range. So far, over a hundred contacts had been confirmed by the legionnaire's battlenet, another thirty to fifty suspected.

Within minutes, they were descending toward Wolf. The shuttle slowed, making a sweep over the base before turning around to land beside two drop shuttles arranged near the east side of the base. Charlie and Delta squads spread out to support the marine elements guarding the walls. Several heavy weapon emplacements had been erected in the guard towers and the remaining combat sleds had been moved in front of the gates.

Lankin was first down the ramp to meet Captain Kato and Major Wyeire. Lieutenant Duval jogged up behind the two officers.

Lankin saluted. "Major, Captain."

"How's your team, Sergeant?" Kato asked, nodding to the legionnaires filing out of the shuttle. A team of Repub marines ran over with repulsor stretchers and helped load up the dead and wounded. Kessler gave instructions to the marines with Talon and they headed off for the medical tent.

"Three KIA: a kid from 2nd, Sweets, and Bishto. Several injured. We need to get Sergeant Talon up to *Vendetta*, ASAP."

"We'll get a shuttle back up as soon as we have these—"

A rocket streaked overhead. It spun and looped around, obviously confused by Wolf's ECM generator, then zipped off to the north, exploding in an empty field.

Lankin tapped his bucket. "Saw about a hundred and fifty contacts on the way in, Captain."

Kato nodded. "That's our count as well."

Major Wyeire crossed his arms. "It'll be a good fight."

"Sir, with all due respect, some of my men don't have time for a good fight. We need to get Talon to *Vendetta* now. Sir, I'm pleading with you: Ask *Vendetta*'s skipper to send down a bombing run, sir."

Wyeire laughed. "Sergeant, I understand you and your men have been through an ordeal down here, but I think something of that magnitude is overkill in this situation. We're not talking about a superior force here. They may have more troops, but we are more than a match for their numbers."

"An ordeal?" Lankin couldn't believe what he was hearing. Was the man that blind, or just willfully ignorant? He turned to Kato. "Captain, I—"

An explosion ripped through one of the overwatch towers in a gout of flame and debris. The blast sent three legionnaires spinning wildly through the air. Lankin's

HUD identified them as members of Charlie squad, their bio-readouts negative. Marines pulled the dead legionnaires away from the burning rubble and spreading flames.

Missiles corkscrewed overhead. Blaster fire sizzled the air and the L-comm squawked with combat chatter.

"Major, sir," Lankin said, his tone probably more forceful than it should have been. "We need to—"

"Stand down, Sergeant," Lieutenant Duval snapped. "You heard the major's orders. Sir, this legionnaire has been nothing but insubordinate, and I have the holorecordings to prove it. Our forces are better equipped and better trained than the enemy. We'll push the hostiles back and—"

"It's not about pushing them back, Lieutenant!" Lankin shouted, any composure he had left, gone. "It's about killing them first. It doesn't matter how. If we continue this fight, we will lose a hell of a lot more than just six men. Those troops out there are motivated and have no reservations about going up against a full company of legionnaires. They will not stop. Our only option is to KTF!"

The major's face turned into a raging scowl. "I will not be spoken to like this by some damn sergeant. I want that man thrown in the brig immediately!"

"Styker-11, Command, enemy forces are breaking off to the south," Burga announced over L-comm. "They're going to flank us."

Two marines took fire atop the walls, dropping to the ground, motionless. A legionnaire from Delta squad took their place, firing his N-4 indiscriminately into the enemy.

Lankin ducked at the sound of an N-18 firing and glanced back to see Pax prone on top of the assault shuttle they'd landed in just moments before. He fired again, then again and again.

Grenades detonated outside the walls to the west. On the wall, Burga opened up with his SAB, raking it back and forth, chewing through an enemy Lankin couldn't see. Singh joined him a second later, then Corse and Saretti. All four legionnaires operated as one, firing, reloading, covering, and firing again.

A rocket struck the base of the southwest tower, punching through the wall below and snapping the tower supports, sending marines jumping for safety. The tower toppled, crashing through the wall, opening a large gap in the base's perimeter.

"Get that bird back up in the air," Kato ordered. "I want its guns in this fight and I want the twins on those combat sleds doing some damage. *Now.*"

"Sir!" Lankin shouted, grabbing the major by the arm.

Duval forced himself between the two men. "Stand down, Sergeant! You heard the major! Someone arrest this man!"

Lankin stepped back and rammed a fist straight into the lieutenant's bucket, sending him sprawling. The major gasped, standing open-mouthed, glancing back and forth between Duval and Lankin.

He turned to Kato. "Captain..."

Kato held up a hand. "*Vendetta*, this is Stryker-1, do you copy?"

Commander O'Donnel, *Vendetta's* executive officer came over the comm. "Stryker-1, *Vendetta*, go ahead."

"Captain, what are you doing?" Major Wyeire asked. He pointed at Lankin. "I said arrest this man!"

Kato ignored the major. "Request bomber and fighter support, half a klick west of my position, danger close. Grid Section 8-Bravo-3."

There was a brief silence, then the commander replied, "Affirmative. Fighters have been scrambled and are inbound. Time on target, two minutes."

"Roger that, *Vendetta*. Stryker-1 to all Stryker elements, be advised, we have incoming fighters, two minutes!"

The ground vibrated under Lankin's feet as a row of mortar bots fired, sending a hail of rounds over the wall. Even under the awesome blanket of firepower they unleashed, the Talusar continued to charge Wolf, undeterred.

Wyeire glared at the Captain. "*Vendetta*, this is Major Wyeire, belay that fire mission. Captain Kato is not in command down here, I am."

From all fours, Duval said, "I'll have you sent to the mines on Herbeer, Lankin, you piece of sket."

"*Vendetta*, this is Captain Kato, Wolf is under heavy assault by a large hostile force. If you do not launch that fighter mission, we *will* be overrun. Do you copy? Continue with mission!"

"Captain, you are hereby relieved of duty!" Wyeire shouted, hopping with outrage. "*Vendetta*, break off the attack."

Another barrage of rockets screamed down into the barracks. The explosions ripped the building apart, sending marines flying and tossing a sled on its side. A large impervisteel crossbeam whipped through the air into the two drop shuttles, slicing through their hulls, grounding them in place.

"Incoming!" someone shouted over L-comm.

A second later, two explosions ripped through the remains of the southwest tower, tearing through the barricades on either side of the tower's base.

"Hostile targets, two hundred fifty meters out and closing!" someone else advised.

On Lankin's HUD, multiple clusters of dots appeared, converging on the destroyed watchtower. "If they make it through the walls, we won't be able to hold them off."

"Bravo and Charlie teams shift fire to the northwest," Kato ordered. "Keep those kelhorned bastards back! Major Wyeire, I understand you don't want to look weak here, sir, but if you don't order that strike, it won't be a matter of weak or strong. We'll all be dead."

"Commanding a failed operation in which all his legionnaires were killed is how they will remember you, Major," Lankin said, hoping to push the point into his brain. "Is that how you want to be remembered?"

"Back off, Sergeant!" Duval shouted, unholstering his sidearm. "You're both dangerously close to mutiny, never mind the outright insubordination. You'll both be—"

Lankin brought his N-4 to low ready, his eyes locked on the lieutenant's hand. "You're going to want to put that away, Lieutenant."

"Is that a threat? I am well within my rights to preserve the chain of command by any means necessary,

Sergeant. And mutiny in the face of the enemy is punishable by death."

Lankin flicked the N-4's safety off with his thumb. "I don't think you want to try that. I guarantee you, you'll lose that race."

"Major, please," Captain Kato said. "You have to see this is a dire situation."

Wyeire regarded his legionnaires for a moment, flinching as another rocket exploded behind them. "Stand down, Lieutenant."

"Sir?"

"I said stand down." He keyed his L-comm. "*Vendetta*, Stryker Actual, proceed with fighter mission. Repeat, proceed with fighter mission."

"Roger that, Actual. Fighters inbound."

An instant later, the sky thrummed with tri-fighters and tri-bombers, appearing well before they should have if *Vendetta* had actually called off the assault. The fighters roared over base, their guided missiles and heavy blaster bolts chewing up the Talusar ranks. On their heels, the bombers swept over the field, thousands of microbombs pouring from their open bays.

A chest rattling *whoomp* rolled across the base and the ground vibrated under Lankin's feet. A plume of earth and rock blossomed. A moment later, a second bomb hit, then a third, chewing a wide path of destruction through the assaulting forces. Three more slammed home and six enormous clouds of dirt and debris climbed high above the treetops, filling the sky.

The cacophony of blaster fire died away and an eerie silence fell over Wolf.

"All units, report contact to Command," Captain Kato ordered.

A series of reports came back, advising their contacts were destroyed or retreating. Of the hundred and fifty hostiles that had filled Lankin's HUD, only thirty or so remained. His bucket's AI logged the rest as KIA or wounded.

"Vendetta Flight Lead, Stryker-1, positive mission, hostile targets neutralized."

"Roger that, Stryker-1."

"Lieutenant Fox," Kato said over L-Comm, directing 2nd platoon's OIC. "Take Charlie and Delta Squads and clean up the rest. I don't want any of those bastards thinking a second attack is in their best interests."

"Roger that, Captain."

Already the assault shuttle was circling back, descending toward Wolf's medical tent to load the wounded and return to *Vendetta*. Within minutes the shuttle was full and lifting off, with more wounded waiting for transport.

Kato turned to Lankin. "Sergeant, the shuttle's full and some of our guys didn't make the cut. I want you to organize a convoy to get the remaining wounded to the spaceport. We can get them up from there as fast as waiting for a return trip and we need to make sure the port is secure from any insurgent attacks."

"Yes, sir."

There are some bad people in the galaxy, and
sometimes they need to be taught a lesson.

"Sket, that hurts!" Talon gritted his teeth, hand pressed against his skull.

"Don't touch," Kessler said, pulling Talon's hand away from the skinpack. "And try not to move around too much. You've got a pretty bad concussion, Sarge."

"You're telling me. Those meds you gave me aren't helping."

"You have to give them time to work through your system," the medic said, adjusting the repulsor stretcher's position in the back of the Gestori truck. "Be glad you regained consciousness. I am."

A convoy of two sleds and three Gestori trucks waited in a line just inside Camp Wolf's main gate, loaded down with a combination of Repub marines and legionnaires, some wounded, some ready to secure the spaceport. Every legionnaire that could still fight would remain on-planet until the rest of the 71st could be sent from their destroyer, *Swift*.

And who knows how long that'll take, Talon thought.

Pax, Burga, Lancil, and Singh appeared at the back of the truck to see their team leader off. The sniper pulled off his bucket and smiled. "You look like hell, Sarge."

"Didn't know this was a beauty competition," Talon said.

"You're lucky you were wearing your bucket." Lancil nodded at the sergeant's bandaged head.

"Yeah, well, that's why we have 'em." Talon grimaced. "And I'm not sure if lucky is the way I'd describe it. Where're the rest of the guys?"

Burga motioned to the truck ahead of them in line. "Up there. Noshey's not looking too good, but he didn't make it on the shuttle out of here."

"Lot of guys had it worse during the attack on Wolf," Kessler said.

"What are we waiting on?" Talon asked.

Lankin joined Talon's men. "Marines are loading up the last of their wounded now." He pulled himself into the bed of the truck and took a knee next to Talon's stretcher. "Let's go!"

Talon grimaced and suppressed a cough. "What are you doing?"

"Leading the convoy trip to the spaceport. Captain's orders."

Private Ginn's voice came over the L-comm. "All right, we're loaded up and ready to go. Moving out in sixty seconds."

"Good luck, Sarge," Burga said, extending a hand. "We'll hold it down until you get back."

Talon smiled and shook his friend's hand. "Thanks."

Lankin steadied himself on the side of the truck as the convoy sped out of Camp Wolf. It bounced and swayed down the road. "Bumpy ride compared to the sleds. And here I thought rank had its privileges."

"Not when you're at the bottom of the medical priority list," Talon said. "Sorry to hear about Sweets."

"Me too."

Ten minutes later they were driving through Gangeers. The streets were mostly deserted, save for the occasional pedestrian crossing hastily after the convey had gone by. It seemed even the city's bots were missing in action.

"Wonder how long it'll be quiet like this?" Lankin asked, watching the tops of the buildings slide by. The crystal blue sky painted above the red brick buildings almost made him forget the carnage they'd left behind at Camp Wolf. "I'm actually surprised there aren't a bunch of demonstrators out, protesting the airstrikes."

"I heard you decked the lieutenant," Talon said.

"Yeah. Probably shouldn't have done that."

"He deserved it. Damn point. But no, that was stupid. You might get thrown out of the Legion. Or worse. What's Wyeire going to do about it?"

Lankin shrugged. "No time to say, not while there's wounded to evac and a spaceport to secure. I doubt anything'll happen until this is completely over. He's already trying to contact the locals and debrief them, trying to cut down the negative public fallout from the battle."

"Sket, it wasn't our fault. In fact, had we not been here, those kelhorned insurgents would've overrun this town without a second thought."

"I know that, and you know that—the entire company knows that. Hell, I'm sure there are some locals who know that. Will that make any difference? Probably not. It's not just about protecting Republic property and assets, it's about capturing the hearts and minds of the people. Watch, the House of Reason will latch onto this as a huge failure by the Legion and use it to gain more control over our operations. It's not going to end well, I can tell you that."

Talon rested his head on the stretcher. "I'm glad I'm going to be out of sight for that nonsense. Looking forward to retiring and leaving the outfit. Go retire on some backwater planet on galaxy's edge and farm algae or something."

"I can't picture you as a farmer."

"Neither can I." Talon nodded at Lankin's exposed prosthetic. "How's the hand?"

Lankin flexed the mechanical fingers. "It's going to take some getting used to. It's a lot more powerful than I expected, I really have to concentrate when I'm using them so I don't break things. Not to mention trigger control. It's going to be awhile before I feel comfortable behind an N-18 again."

"Going to have to go through sniper school again? I mean, assuming you're not in prison."

"Hell, no. You couldn't pay me enough to go through that ag—"

A high-pitched whistle cut through their conversation. A split second later, something exploded in front of their truck. Talon could see the tendrils of smoke and fire.

"Contact right!" Lankin leaped from the truck and fired at an enemy Talon couldn't see.

Talon pushed himself up on his elbows, looking over the side. Several wounded legionnaires piled out of the trucks in front and behind, engaging targets on both sides of the convoy. He pulled his sidearm and swept the road behind as a handful of marines streamed out of the rear sled. Blaster fire filled the street. Several marines dropped as soon as their feet hit ground. He could hear the screams of the dying as he struggled to push himself up.

"Stryker-1, this is Stryker-19," Lankin said over the L-comm. "Gangeers is contested. Heavy contact with more insurgents. Requesting air support!"

"Copy. The assault bird just finished dropping off her load, I'll redirect her to your position."

Unspoken was the fact that not even Captain Kato could convince the major to bomb such a densely populated civilian center. This was going to be a slog of a fight on the ground.

His skull throbbed, blurring his vision. He swung his legs over the tailgate, cautiously searching for the street before planting his feet, fearful of simply falling out. Two more marines dropped in front of him.

"They're everywhere!"

"Three to the north!"

"I'm hit!"

To Talon's left, three masked Gestori emerged from a gap between buildings, rushing toward him. "Garo!" He raised his pistol and dropped one of them before they reached him. The two remaining tackled him into the back of the truck. One slammed a fist into his nose. Pain flashed as cartilage snapped. Warm blood poured from his nose, running into his mouth. The other wrenched the pistol from his hand, breaking two of his fingers in the process. They were shouting to their wounded comrade, who appeared with something in his hand. Talon struggled against their hold but couldn't break free. The third Gestori hopped into the bed. He opened a black canvas bag and pulled it over the legionnaire's head.

Everything went dark.

The Legion teaches that lesson well.

24

"Garo!"

Lankin had already disembarked, found cover, and dropped a masked attacker with a blaster bolt to the chest before he spun around at the sound of his name being called. He saw Talon shoot one of three attackers. Two Gestori fell on the wounded sergeant, throwing a barrage of punches to the legionnaire's face.

Lankin ducked as another bolt zipped past. He dropped to a knee, swinging his N-4 up, searching for the shooter. A masked Gestori male in dark brown robes stepped out from behind an open door, blaster rifle pointed in Lankin's direction.

He launched himself away, rolling under the Gestori fire. The street behind him erupted with blaster bolts that missed their mark. He came up and immediately dropped a target of opportunity—another Gestori who'd been exchanging fire with a pair of marines. Keeping low, he moved up the far side of the lead sled, which absorbed blaster fire while its twin guns chewed away at any attacker its gunner could sight.

The Gestori shooter continued to send long, undisciplined bursts of blaster fire near the place Lankin had last occupied, oblivious to the fact that the legionnaire had moved. Lankin popped up above the hood and fired twice. The Gestori's head exploded in a mass of gore, spraying blood on the brick wall beside him.

Two marines appeared next to Lankin, sharing identical confused and scared expressions.

"What the hell is going on, Sergeant?" one asked.

Lankin swapped out charge packs. "I don't know. Spaceport's gonna be tougher to reach than we hoped. Watch the north, don't let anyone flank us."

A lone bolt sparked off the sled's armor above their heads. The marine Lankin answered screamed and dropped to the ground, covering his head. The second marine turned and fired blindly, burning through a quarter charge pack before letting up.

"Hold this position," Lankin said.

He moved back down the line of trucks under blaster fire streaking overhead. "Stryker elements, report."

"At the rear of the column, Sarge," Mazine replied. "Got a group of about six advancing on our position."

"I'm coming to you."

"Get off me!" a muffled voice shouted.

Lankin spun and saw two masked Gestori pulling one of the wounded marines out of the back of a truck. He struggled, kicking out but hitting nothing but air. They'd thrown a hood over his face. A third Gestori came from the alley behind them, trying to grab the marine's flailing legs.

Lankin shot the third one in the back just as it wrapped an arm around the marine's feet. The alien fell forward, almost knocking his companions over. The one on the right drew and fired a projectile rifle. The bullet slammed into Lankin's left arm, right above the elbow, finding a gap in the armor.

At the same moment, the marine kicked out hard and jerked himself free. He dropped and rolled away from the alien still holding on, trying to break loose. He tripped the Gestori who'd shot Lankin, knocking him to his rear.

Ignoring the searing pain, Lankin tried to bring his blaster rifle up, but his wounded arm was sluggish to respond, almost limp. He gritted his teeth and brought the N-4 up with his good arm. His mechanical fingers weren't nearly as dexterous as his human ones, but they weren't affected by stress or exhaustion or injury. They worked the same, every time. He held the rifle out and fired. The bolt struck home right between the Gestori's yellow eyes, snapping the alien's head back. Without slowing, he found the third Gestori and gave him an identical shot.

The marine pulled the hood off his head and threw it aside, kicking one of the alien corpses. "Kelhorned lizards!"

Lankin reached out a hand. "Come on—"

Movement flashed in his peripheral before someone tackled him from the right, knocking him into one of the trucks. The impact jarred his N-4 loose, sending it clattering. Fists began thumping against his armor. Lankin grabbed for the attacker, managing only to get hold of the Gestori's mask and pulling it clear of his face.

The alien stumbled back and recognition hit Lankin like a transport shuttle. "You!"

It took a minute for Lankin to remember the name… Sharn, the worker's rep from the townhall meeting, Doctor

Pendisa's father. The Gestori's face contorted with rage and he charged again.

Lankin blocked a punch, then drove his fist into the alien's gut. Sharn let out a gasp of pain and went to his knees. Lankin held onto the alien's robes, keeping him from falling all the way down.

"Why are you doing this?" Lankin demanded, lifting him up.

The Gestori spat on Lankin's faceplate. "Republic scum!"

Another masked Gestori appeared from a building to Lankin's right. The legionnaire drew his blaster pistol and fired off three shots.

Something exploded near the back of the convoy, filling the street with smoke and flames. The twin guns of the combat sled sent blaster bolts through the billowing smoke, racking storefronts and sparking off their vehicles.

"Stop this!" Lankin said, leveling his pistol at Sharn's head. "Stop this now."

"Go to hell, legionnaire!"

Lankin pressed the barrel of his pistol into the alien's scaly, gray skin. "Call them off, or I swear to Oba, I'll end you right here and now and you'll never see your daughter again!"

"Pendisa is a true believer! She will understand my sacrifice!"

Engines roared above them as a shuttle appeared over the buildings, hovering over the remains of the convoy. The door gunner opened up on the street at the rear of their column as the craft steadied itself. Several legionnaires jumped from the open ramp, taking positions on the roofs of the buildings on the far side of the street. Within seconds they were engaging the enemy.

"Come on!" Lankin shouted, pulling Sharn along with him. He stopped at the back of Talon's truck; it was empty. He shoved the Gestori against the side of the bed. "Where'd they take him?"

Sharn spat at him, hitting his visor. Lankin slammed his bucket into the alien's face. Blood spurted from Sharn's mouth. He started to sag and Lankin held him firm.

"Where is he?" Lankin roared.

The Gestori's yellow eyes glared back at the legionnaire, brimming with loathing.

"Target's clear!" came a status update over L-comm.

Lankin gripped the alien's clothes tighter, Sharn's blood running over his hand. "You're going to tell me."

"Your friend is as good as dead."

"He dies, you die," Lankin told him. It wasn't a threat, it was the truth. He activated his comm. "Sound off, they've taken hostages. Who's missing?"

The reports started coming in over L-comm. Five were missing, namely Talon, Mazine, and three marines.

"We got some more KIA by the lead sled," a marine reported. "Pair of marines and a legionnaire."

The reports continued to roll in. Three more marines had been killed by blaster fire and Gemini was critical.

Lankin keyed his squad channel. "Kessler!"

"Already on it," the medic replied. "Let me work!"

Another combat sled pulled up at the rear of the convoy, disgorging a handful of marines. Captain Kato was the last out and jogged up to Lankin.

"You're shot," Kato said.

"It's nothing," Lankin told him. "I'm fine."

"What's this?" Kato asked, nodding to Sharn.

"This little kelhorned lizard knows where Talon is and he's not talking."

Kato studied the Gestori for a moment. "You're the Gestori Workers League representative. What is the meaning of this attack? We're here protecting your sorry asses!"

Sharn laughed. "Protecting? You steal our life's work, and you call that protecting? Only a Republic lackey could think what you're doing here is anything but downright theft. You people come here under the guise of aiding a needy people, but you never stopped to ask yourselves if we actually needed help."

"We didn't ask for this assignment—your government asked for our assistance and we came."

"Did they?" Sharn shook his head.

Lankin lifted him up again, slamming him back the truck. "We don't have time for this. Where did you take our men?"

But the Gestori was too fixated on other things. "We pleaded with your government to stay away. Tried to convince them our world wasn't safe for outsiders. Did they listen? No."

"The explosion that killed the envoy team," Kato said. "That wasn't an accident."

It dawned on Lankin that his captain was pursuing this dialogue—rather than just breaking bones—in the hopes that Sharn might give him something he could use to find Talon and the others.

"We should have made the message a little clearer," Sharn said. "We blamed it on malcontents and rebels, hoping the civil unrest here wouldn't be worth the trouble."

"You don't know the House of Reason very well," Kato said.

"House of Reason," Sharn spat. "They just sent in more troops and started taking whatever they wanted. We should've seen it coming. Slavers of the known galaxy, that's what you are. You come and take, without any concern for anyone but your precious Republic."

"What do you want?" Lankin asked.

"We want you to leave."

"Tell us where to find our missing and maybe we will."

Sharn laughed. "It's too late. I told you they would die and so they have."

Lankin raised a fist but Kato pulled his arm back down.

"I'm getting something," Kato said, raising a hand to his bucket. "Scrambled message from a masked transponder."

The captain was silent for a minute, obviously listening to the transmission. It must have been coming through the command net, a channel Lankin didn't have access to.

"Sket," Kato said, finally.

"What is it, sir?"

"Demands from his buddies." Kato motioned to Sharn. "They're demanding all Republic forces leave the planet or they'll start killing hostages. Major wants us back at Wolf ASAP."

Sharn laughed hysterically. "This is far better. Leave now, coward dogs of the Republic."

Lankin jerked Sharn hard. "You son of a bitch! If any of those hostages are killed—"

"Then what?" Sharn demanded. "You'll kill me? I've dedicated my life to the liberation of my people. If that means I must martyr myself in order for them to be free, I consider that a price well worth paying."

Burga, Cross, Pax, and Kessler appeared behind the captain.

"We've got the wounded loaded back up, sir," Burga said.

"Roger that." Kato turned for the sled. "Bring him with us."

"Oh sket, Sarge," Kessler said, looking at Lankin's wound.

"It's nothing."

"Like hell it's nothing." The medic pulled off Lankin's armor, then started cutting away the synthprene.

Lankin gritted his teeth against the pain as Kessler worked. "You're not thinking about negotiating with these people, are you, Captain?"

"That's not my call, Sergeant. Sounds like Major Wyeire is already in talks with them."

"That's a load of sket, Captain, and you know it! Ouch!"

"Hold still." Kessler prodded the open wound.

"These scumbags don't have any intention of returning our people alive," Lankin said.

"What do you want me to do about it, Sergeant? Not everything in life can be solved by punching your superior officers and storming off! Now we—" Captain Kato calmed himself and continued. "We can't do anything about it now. We don't know where our people are, and I seriously doubt your friend here is going to talk. We still have critically wounded men that need evac and direct orders to return to Wolf."

"They can't be far," Lankin said. "They're here somewhere."

"You'll never find them!" Sharn shouted. "And you will die trying! Do not risk their lives! Leave this planet!"

"Get him out of here," Kato said to Burga and Cross. The leejes hauled the Gestori off, kicking and shouting.

"The bullet didn't hit anything major," Kessler said. "I can put on a skinpack for now, but you'll need to have surgery to remove it and repair some of the muscle damage."

Lankin shook his head. "Story of my life."

Captain Kato motioned for Lankin to board the nearest sled.

Lankin didn't move.

"Look, Garo, I know Chase is your friend, but—"

"I'm going to find him, Captain." Determination burned inside Lankin, squeezing out whatever fatigue or pain he might have otherwise felt. "I'm going to find him and bring him back. He'd do the same for me. For any of us."

"I'm not authorizing what few legionnaires I have left to start kicking down doors and tearing through homes. We're spread too thin as it is and besides that, we don't have any idea where to start."

"Wrong, sir," Lankin said. "I have a pretty good idea."

I might have finally met my match, but I don't want you to be sad.

25

It took five minutes of negotiating the back streets and alleys of Gangeers to reach the clinic. The five-man legionnaire team was stacked at the rear entrance, listening for any sign of the enemy. Officially, they were MIA, a concession Captain Kato made before taking the rest of the wounded back to Wolf.

This whole operation has been one giant concession, Lankin thought.

"Where'd they all disappear to?" Burga asked from his position at the head of the stack. "No way we dusted 'em all."

"Off licking their wounds maybe," Cross offered.

"With the ass kickings we've been handing out, I'd bet they aren't too keen on engaging any time soon," Burga said.

"I wouldn't count them out so quickly," Lankin said, eyeing the rooftops. "They're out there somewhere. These kinds of people never seem to get the message."

Pax checked his N-4's charge pack. "Sounds to me like we need to talk a little louder."

The legionnaires nodded agreement.

"We're looking for the female doctor," Lankin said. "Pendisa."

"And she's going to know where our guys are?" Burga asked.

"If she doesn't, she'll know where to start."

"Engagement protocol?" Pax asked.

"If a lizard is armed, you shoot," Lankin said. "We're not taking any more chances."

"Roger that."

"Looks like the door's locked," Burga said, testing the handle.

"Don't worry, I've got a key." Lankin squared himself on the door, took a half-step back, then rammed his boot into it.

Burga led the team into a long hallway lit by a single flickering light strip on the ceiling. Lankin followed him, then Cross and Kessler, letting Pax hold the rear.

It only took a few seconds to reach the clinic proper.

"Don't move!" Burga shouted.

He went right, Lankin held straight, leveling his N-4 at three Gestori men sitting on a bed. "Get your hands up! Don't move!"

Whether or not they actually understood what he was saying, the three aliens threw their hands into the air, yelling something back at Lankin he didn't understand.

Kessler and Cross filed in behind him, both heading off to deal with similar groups of locals confined to hospital beds. Panicked screams and angry shouts followed the legionnaires' sweep. A nurse dropped a tray of tools as she stumbled into a patient sitting behind her. Both toppled onto the floor, knocking over a cart and spilling its contents.

Lankin hovered on the three for a second longer, then seeing no threat, kept moving. "Doctor Pendisa!"

To his left, Burga shoved a Talusar against the wall, shouting at him to sit down. The orange-skinned alien roared at the leej, shoving him back. Burga rammed the butt of his N-4 into the side of the alien's head, knocking him out cold.

"No one move!" Lankin shouted. "We're here for the Doc—"

Halfway down a row, a Gestori male sprang from his bed, lunging for Lankin with arms spread. Lankin side-stepped, pushing his N-4 behind him on its sling and grabbing the alien with both arms. He used their momentum to pull the Gestori off-balance, sticking out a foot and tripping him. The alien cried out in surprise as he fell, then slammed down hard, grunting in pain. Lankin stepped back, reaching for his N-4.

Pax appeared at the Gestori's head and carefully set his pistol against the alien's skull. "I wouldn't do that if I were you."

Something clinked against the tile floor and a second later the Gestori's hands appeared, fingers spread. A primitive metal scalpel lay on the floor next to him, a reminder of the backward and dated medicine practiced in this clinic. Pax kicked it away, then slammed the butt of his pistol down on the alien's skull with a wet crack and the Gestori collapsed.

"That's *enough*!" a female voice cried above the chaos.

Lankin turned to see Pendisa, hands outstretched.

"Don't move, lady," Cross shouted.

"It's okay," Lankin said.

Pendisa stopped, never taking her yellow eyes off Lankin. "What is the meaning of this, Sergeant?"

"I think you know already, Doctor. You're a smart woman."

"Yes," Pendisa said, lowering her hands. "And so what would you have me do?"

"I'll be honest with you, Doc. I'm having a hard time picturing you as a terrorist. Doesn't really line up with the whole 'do no harm' thing."

"No harm?" Pendisa scoffed. "And what is it you think you are doing here? A good thing? A *just* thing?"

"I'm here for my men."

"Wrong, Sergeant Lankin! You call me a terrorist, but you are the ones who are stealing from my people. You think because you wear that uniform, that makes you better than us? Or that it excuses you from your part in *enforcing* this oppression against the will of my species? Is your cause somehow more righteous than ours, because we don't wear armor?"

"This is not a debate."

"If someone came into your house and started taking all of your things, then set up armed guards in your living room for *your* security, would you fight back?"

"I said I'm not here to have a political debate. I don't care about you or how righteous your Oba-damned cause is. I'm here for my men, plain and simple."

"And you thought they'd be here?"

"I know you know where they are, Doctor. You're going to tell me."

Pendisa cocked her head. "Am I?"

"If you ever want to see your father again, you will."

The doctor opened her mouth to respond, but hesitated.

"We have him, Pendisa. Caught attacking our medical convoy not ten minutes ago. You know what the House of Reason does to terrorists out here on the edge? Legion rules. Meaning our CO decides his fate. And he's not in a forgiving mood today."

"I don't believe you."

"Believe him," Burga said.

"He's not lying," Cross added.

"Now, I'm not making any promises," Lankin said, doing his best to sound sympathetic, to sound like he cared about the Gestori doctor's feelings. "I expect that no matter what happens right here and now, your father will be tried. He made his choices and I can't help that. But I can tell you without a doubt, that unless you give me something right now, his verdict will be quick, guilty, and the sentence harsher than you can imagine."

"Kelhorned Republic scum," Pendisa spat.

"Clock's ticking."

"Tell them nothing!" a Gestori male shouted.

Cross turned, pointing his weapon at the alien. "Shut up! Nobody else speaks!"

"Don't betray the cause, Pendisa!" another Gestori added.

Cross slammed the barrel of his N-4 into the alien's stomach, sending him to the floor.

"I don't know!" Pendisa shouted.

"Then I'll send you a vid of your father's last words," Lankin said. He turned and sketched a circle over his head with a cybernetic finger. "Let's move out and follow the other intel trail."

"Wait!" Pendisa exclaimed, hand outstretched.

Pax leveled his pistol at her head. "Don't, lady!"

Lankin turned, motioning for Pax to lower his weapon. "Something you want to say, Doc?"

"Please... I wasn't included in this operation," Pendisa said, moving close enough to Lankin that she could reach out and touch him. "But I doubt they'd stay in town any longer than they have to. They're probably on their way to the caves."

"The caves?"

"Traitor!" an angry Gestori roared.

"Shut it!" yelled Burga.

Pendisa nodded. "There's a waterfall in the foothills to the east of the mountains. It's where the main group of Talusar—Freedom Raiders—have been staying."

"Freedom Raiders," Lankin said, shaking his head at the name. "Okay. How do I get there?"

"There's a map," Pendisa told him, shoulders slumping. "In the basement. No electronic records are kept of anything, in order to circumvent Republic intelligence algorithms."

"*Oosa!*" the Gestori Burga had hit shouted from his knees before adding in Standard, "You're a traitor to your people, Pendisa!"

Burga kicked the Gestori square in the jaw. He sprawled to the floor, unconscious.

Lankin leaned forward. "If you're lying..."

"Please, don't let them kill my father."

"If I get my men back in one piece, I'll see what I can do."

"Then hurry. I saved your life once and now I've given my life on this planet for you to save your friend and my father. Do not waste it."

After herding the patients into a back room and locking them in, Lankin and his team followed the doctor down a flight of stairs to a locked door. She tapped a code into the panel on the wall and the lock clicked open. Pax pulled her away.

Inside, tables lined three sides; pictures and operational charts, diagrams of Gangeers and the mining complex plastered the walls. One entire wall was covered with a topographical map showing an area at least twenty kilometers around the city. The main road and mag-lev track connecting all three locations was marked in blue and every so often the pillars were marked with red thumbtacks. Several secondary roads that hadn't been on the intelligence provided to the marines showed at least seven different routes through the jungle.

"Oba," Lankin mumbled, shaking his head in disbelief. "How did we miss this?"

"Too trusting," Pax said. "Shoulda KTF'd and assumed everyone was hostile. Because they were, man."

A small lake at the top left corner of the map was marked with a green flag. A blue line coming out of the mountains to the north ended at the top of the lake.

"The caves?" Lankin asked Pendisa, pointing.

She nodded.

"They've got rosters with all our information here, Sarge." Burga ran a finger down one of the papers pinned to the wall. "Squad info, weapon assignments, shift schedules... the works."

"And check this out," Pax said, rifling through stacks of paper on one of the tables. "Looks like shipping manifests and transport logs. Looks like they've been skimming, changing weights and counts and keeping some back for themselves."

Pendisa laughed. "Skimming? You say that like *we're* the ones in the wrong? That is our ore. It's ours, not yours!"

"Not how the Republic sees it," Pax said, without looking up. "Your people made a deal. Hey, looks like they've been contacting someone in the edge, setting up deliveries off-world to something called Scarpia. Don't see any financials, though. No paid invoices."

"What do you say to that, Doctor?" Lankin asked, unable to resist, given the treasure trove they just uncovered. "That's a sket-ton of ore to be just giving away. Getting it off the planet alone would cost a fortune. Whoever's on the receiving end is getting one hell of a deal."

"Our agreement was to help you find your missing comrades in exchange for my father's life," Pendisa hissed. "And you're wasting time."

"Intel is going to have a field day with this place," Cross said.

Lankin nodded. "Let them. Doc's right. We've got other priorities right now." He keyed a secure channel to Captain Kato.

"Go for Kato."

"I've got a lead on our men, but we've stumbled across some intel I know we're going to need later. Can you send a squad of marines with some leejes to the clinic?"

"Might be a minute until the major lets anyone else off-base. What have you found about our MIAs?"

"Have a possible location for them. Supposed to be the base of operations of the insurgency as well."

"Listen, Garo, your team can't handle that alone."

"No, sir. I agree with you. But we need to move quickly. The Gestori will wipe out this intel if we leave, I know it."

Kato sighed. "I'll make something happen. I think I can get Lieutenant Fox and men from 2nd Platoon to your position to 'pick up some MIAs' without causing too much turmoil."

"Copy that," Lankin said, a grin plastered to his face. "We'll double-time it back to Wolf once they help us clear this room out."

"Copy."

"And sir, if you can get the assault bird on standby, I think we'll have some flying to do."

*I stood with my brothers against evil and
fought for those who couldn't.*

26

"I said hold him," marine corpsman Beem said, pushing a fellow captured marine back down as he writhed in agony on the cold cave floor. The third captured marine and Mazine adjusted their positions on either side of the wounded man Beem worked over, struggling to hold him.

Pain pulsed inside Talon's skull as he shifted position to get a better look at the marine's wounds. He'd taken a projectile round in the shoulder during the battle for Camp Wolf and a second round just above the left leg during the convoy ambush. Beem pulled away more blood-soaked clothing, wiping the glistening red liquid as it flowed from the marine's pelvis.

"I don't see an exit wound," Beem said. "Bullet's still in there somewhere."

The young marine groaned, arching his back in obvious agony.

Talon turned to the Gestori guarding them. "You're just going to let him bleed out? He needs medical attention."

The guard sat on the edge of a wooden table ten meters away, one foot propped up on a chair, his old slug thrower draped across his chest. "So he dies. What do I care? He shouldn't've been here in the first place."

"He won't be much good to your bosses if he dies," Talon growled, fighting to keep himself upright. "Might even blame you."

Talon eyed the stack of legionnaire armor on the table just behind the alien. They'd stripped it off him and Mazine as soon as they'd loaded them into the trucks back in Gangeers, leaving them only their black synthprene bodysuits to wear. The thought of making a grab for his stolen armor crossed his mind, but he immediately rejected the idea. Even if he managed to get there before the guard could shoot, the armor would likely only prolong his eventual death. The cave was a dark maze, and Talon had counted at least thirty armed insurgents while he was led to the holding area.

The guard seemed to consider Talon's words, then fished a small field kit out of a pocket and tossed it over. Talon caught it, pulled it open, and found several skinpacks.

He held the kit out to Beem. "Here."

"That's a start," the corpsman replied, "but it's going to take a lot more than this."

Talon continued his assessment of their situation as the corpsman worked over his wounded brother. They were about fifty meters from the mouth. The cave opened behind a waterfall that spanned almost the entire thirty-meter mouth. Daylight filtered in through the curtain of water, giving some light but not enough that Talon could make out any of the terrain beyond.

The cave was damp and the constant roar of the waterfall echoed through the expansive space. Several generators thrummed, powering the light strips hanging from the rock ceiling in what Talon thought of as the main cave. A few lighting strips led off around curving natural tubes.

In the main space, tables made from repurposed doors set on old shipping crates lined every wall, stacked with weapons, food, and other equipment. Several Gestori and Talusar were shouting at each other near what looked like the command station, partitioned off with wooden walls, almost like an office hab separator. One of the Gestori kicked over a table, sending its contents flying. Another Gestori shoved him for the offense, shouting in their native language. A third stepped between them, pushing them apart.

"They aren't happy about something," Mazine said.

"Nope," agreed Talon. "Something's happened."

"You thinking escape and evade?" Mazine asked.

Talon shook his head. "Wouldn't make it very far without leaving the wounded. And besides, we don't have any idea where we are. How long were we in those trucks—ten, fifteen minutes?"

"At least."

"We could be anywhere. They know the terrain—we'd never have a chance."

"That marine isn't going to last very long," Mazine said so only Talon could hear.

"I know."

Talon pressed the heel of his hand into his temple, trying to alleviate the pounding. He squeezed his eyes shut and mentally willed the pain to go away. It didn't. He opened them and grimaced as another wave of pain turned his stomach.

"You okay, Sarge?"

"Fine. It's just a headache."

Next to them, Beem sat back, wiping bloodstained hands on his drab olive uniform pants, shaking his head. "That's about all I can do for him."

Talon didn't bother to ask if the marine was going to make it or not. The kid's sweat-drenched, pale face told the legionnaire everything he needed to know. Beem had done a fine job bandaging him up, but he'd already lost too much blood. Nothing short of being transported to the *Venedetta*'s trauma center would save the man now, and the Gestori were unlikely to help them make the trip.

"Heads up," Mazine said.

Talon looked up and the leej nodded at three Gestori thugs walking toward them. The lizards had pulled their masks down, wearing them as loose scarves around their necks. Their green scales glistened in the damp air, almost like they were sweating. The lead Gestori, dressed in black and armed with two rusty slug-thrower pistols holstered to each thigh, pointed at Mazine and said something Talon didn't understand.

The second alien had a red cloth wrapped around his head and wasn't wearing a shirt. His olive-colored scales faded to pearl, the edges of each individual scale trimmed in black. A matching patch of pearly scales covered one side of his face.

The third was dressed in the same black uniform as the first and had Talon's tactical belt draped around one shoulder. Somehow, he'd managed to strap on one of the legionnaire's shoulder plates and had several random pieces of equipment hanging from clips on his vest.

Mazine pushed himself up to his knees as the two Gestori approached while their leader looked on, hands on hips. "What the hell do you want? Don't... get off!"

"Hey!" Talon yelled as they jerked the legionnaire to his feet.

"Back!" the first Gestori shouted, pointing at Talon.

Mazine struggled against his two captors, trying to pull free. He managed to get one hand loose and spin back away from one alien, but the other held tight, keeping the leej from getting very far. The Gestori shouted and rammed a fist into his side. Mazine groaned in pain and tried pulling farther away.

"What are you doing with him?" Talon demanded, pushing himself to his feet, forcing the throbbing pain behind his eyes away. "If you're looking for intel, you're not going to get any. He doesn't know anything. Take me!"

The shirtless Gestori, Eye Patch, punched Mazine again. The legionnaire doubled over, almost knocking Shoulder Plate off his feet. Shoulder Plate yanked on Mazine's arm so hard Talon was sure he'd pull it right out of the socket. Eye Patch managed to get hands on him again and wrenched the legionnaire's arm around behind him, giving Mazine no option but to go with them, or have his limbs pulled from their sockets.

The leader shoved Talon back. He tripped over the dying marine and fell, landing hard on his back. Pain shot through him like lightning, almost masking the throbbing in his skull.

"Hey, easy!" Beem shouted, helping Talon off the ground and then checking his patient.

The Gestori hauled Mazine off without another word, half-dragging, half-carrying him deeper into the cave. They disappeared behind the command post walls, and the shouting resumed.

"You all right, Sergeant Talon?" Beem asked, satisfied that no further harm was done to the marine Talon had tripped over.

"Fine," Talon said, getting to his feet.

"Get down." The guard motioned with his rifle.

"Go screw yourself," Talon told him. "I want to know what they're doing with my leej!"

From the darkness of the cave came a loud *crack*.

Talon flinched at the gunshot, then rage took him. "You bastards!"

He charged the guard, reaching for the rifle. The sudden movement caused the pain behind his eyes to flare, turning his stomach and blurring his vision. The Gestori easily sidestepped and brought the butt around, smacking it into the back of Talon's skull, knocking him down and amplifying the pain in his skull. Talon bounced against the wet rock, the air knocked from his lungs.

Angry shouts accompanied the slapping of feet against the floor. Soon several pairs of hands lifted him up. Talon struggled against his captors but couldn't break free. Talon was convinced he was next, that they would drag him off and shoot him. But they simply tossed him down again, returning him to the prisoners.

Beem helped him sit. "Let me look you over, Sergeant. Another blow to the head is not good given your—"

"Do not worry, Legionnaire," the Gestori leader said. "You will get your chance to die for your people. But not until I say."

Talon pulled away from Beem, the rage burning inside him, screaming at him to attack. But the blinding pain in his head made his vision spotty; the room spun and his nausea churned.

A hand grabbed his shoulder, holding him steady almost as much as pulling him back. "Sarge, don't. Now's not the time."

Talon glared at the Gestori, letting his hatred flow free. "I will kill you. Count on it."

He found that he was crying and didn't know why. The concussion. It had to be.

The alien grunted, then went back to the command post with a laugh, leaving the prisoners to themselves. His two lieutenants arrived a minute later, dragging Mazine's body. They dropped it unceremoniously into a corner where they all could see it.

"Oba-damned bastards." Rage flared again at the sight of the leej's body. Talon suddenly vomited.

The corpsman got clear of the mess. "Sergeant Talon..."

"We need to start working on escape plans," Talon said, ignoring the marine. "I'm sure the company will be..."

"Sergeant!"

The marine's harsh tone broke his train of thought and Talon turned. "What?"

Beem nodded, indicating the wounded marine on the floor between them. The kid's eyes were open, but it was obvious there was no life in them.

"Ah, dammit," Talon said, beginning to cry again. He felt as though he had no control of himself. "We're going to kill all of them."

Beem ran his fingers across the dead marine's face, closing his eyes. "This was his first assignment. Hasn't been out of boot three weeks."

"He was a good marine," Talon said, wiping away his tears, in control once more. "He'll be remembered. We won't let his sacrifice go unanswered, trust me."

Several minutes later, more insurgents arrived at the cave, calling others to them and shouting commands. Soon they were packing up equipment, consolidating supplies and tearing down anything not attached to the walls.

"They're leaving," Cantarus said. "Are they leaving? Does that mean it's over, Sarge?"

Talon was fighting the urge to just lay down and sleep. His head was killing him. "I doubt it."

Someone shouted at the mouth of the cave, then someone else. A Gestori appeared, pointing behind him through the waterfall, and shouted again. Immediately, the insurgents stopped what they were doing, grabbed their weapons, and began to form up.

"What's happening?" Cantarus asked.

Talon straightened, ignoring the pain. "The..." He tried to remember the name of who he was talking about. It started with an 'L' but everything was swimming. Nothing was as it should be in his mind. "... the good guys are here."

I only hope I made you proud.

27

"Thirty seconds!" the pilot advised over the L-comm.

"Remember," Lankin told the legionnaires packed into the shuttle's bay, "there are friendlies down there. Watch your backgrounds and take good shots."

"Where do you want us to collect the Gestori prisoners?" Private Cross asked.

"There aren't going to be any prisoners," Lankin said.

The remaining members of Alpha and Bravo squad nodded understanding. If the men with them from 2nd platoon had a problem with what Lankin's orders, they didn't show it.

The shuttle flew through a cloud of mist. The lake the waterfall emptied into appeared below them, surrounded by grass banks and trees. The water masked the cavern from satellite imagery, but as the shuttle banked, their target was obvious.

Several Gestori were in the process of loading crates into a line of trucks along the northern bank. Wide camouflaged netting had been erected over the convoy, concealing it from above. A group near the back of the formation looked up, pointing and shouting as the shuttle descended.

Water sprayed up around the ramp as the shuttle leveled off, hovering over the water.

The door guns blazed, ripping the trucks and any Gestori near them to pieces.

"Go! Go! Go!" Lankin shouted.

The sergeant followed his team out, dropping into the shallow water. He forced down the pain in his arm, brought his pistol up with his good hand, and fired at a Gestori coming from behind one of the trucks untouched by the assault shuttle's barrage, his rifle already leveled.

"Contact front!" Lankin shouted.

Behind Lankin, the shuttle's engines whined as it lifted back into the air. The guns continued spraying the area with blaster fire. The crew gunner worked the weapon back and forth across the line of trucks.

The legionnaires spread out along the bank and in the shallows, dropping targets as they appeared. A grenade landed in the water a foot away from Singh and exploded a moment later. The explosion hurled the legionnaire into the air with a plume of water.

Lankin, Cross, and Burga reached the first smoking truck, immediately putting their backs to the engine block for cover. Lankin counted fifteen hostile targets emerging from the cave on the near side of the falls and another three on the far side.

"Cover me!" Sevanar shouted, diving to help Singh. Kessler and Saretti advanced to cover as the leej recovered their fallen comrade. Sevanar threw Singh over his shoulder and all three ran for the protection of the trucks.

"Push! Keep pushing!" Lankin called out.

The Gestori fell back as the legionnaires pressed on, violently seeking to keep the advantage they'd won. Sevanar caught a bullet in the back, knocking him forward, off his feet. He dropped Singh and landed hard on his chest. The ground around them erupted with gunfire.

"Contact right!" Lankin shouted.

Pax fired his N-18, taking down the target across the water. The other two Gestori scrambled to find cover. The N-18 barked again. And again.

"Clear!" Pax announced.

"Keep pushing!" Kessler dropped an empty charge pack from his N-4 and slapped in another. "They're going to pin us down if we stay here!"

Rowan and Saretti moved between two of the trucks, flanking a group of Gestori coming down a path from the cave entrance.

Lankin sent a burst of suppressive fire at the Gestori. "Kessler, regroup with Rowan and Saretti—keep those lizards honest!"

"Roger that!"

"Come on," Lankin said, moving to the cab of an undamaged but abandoned truck in the caravan.

Burga, Lancil, and Cross followed.

Lankin climbed in, found the ignition and the truck roared to life. "Get in!"

Lancil climbed into the passenger seat, Burga and Cross jumped in the back. "You sure you don't want me to drive?" asked Burga. "You only got one good arm, Sarge."

Lankin put the truck in gear and jammed the accelerator. "I've got this."

The tires spun on the damp grass. Lankin jerked the wheel hard with one hand, spinning the truck around. The rear end slewed into a pile of crates. He straightened out and headed up the path.

Beside him, Lancil fired his N-4 through the windshield, hitting several Gestori coming out from behind cover to fight back. Blaster fire from Burga and Cross in the back stitched through another group. A bullet smashed through the windshield in front of Lankin, slamming into the padded headrest just behind his right ear.

He flinched, but kept his boot pressed against the pedal. Another Gestori tried to run across the road in front of them. Lankin gripped the wheel tighter and angled the truck so he wouldn't miss. "Bump," he said and launched the alien into a boneless tumble then swerved to run over him.

The truck bounced, knocking Lancil and Lankin around. Something crashed in the bed and Lankin risked a look over his shoulder. "You all right back there?"

"You drive worse than my grandma, Sarge!" Burga said, pushing himself up off the bed.

"Hold on!"

The waterfall hit hard, caving the shot-up windshield in, pouring into the cab. Lankin's HUD automatically adjusted for the low-light conditions in the cave, switching to infrared. A group of insurgents scattered, diving for cover as the truck careened through the waterfall.

The wheel shook in Lankin's hand as he angled for another roadkill. "Beep, beep, mother—"

"Look out!" Lancil pointed.

"Oh, crap!" Lankin jerked the wheel to the left, trying to steer the truck away from a large stack of crates in the center of the path. He slammed his foot down on the brake, but it wasn't enough. The truck crashed through the pile, sending dozens of large metal crates flying.

Lankin bounced forward, slamming into the steering wheel, knocking the wind from his lungs. Pain flared in his chest and he knew he'd broken some ribs. Lancil shot through the open windshield. Burga and Cross slammed into the back of the cab, denting the sheet metal before spilling over the side.

Lankin shouldered his way through the door and dropped to the damp stone floor, his breath ragged and wheezing. He tasted the metallic tang of blood in his mouth. Shouting and gunfire echoed around him. Sparks erupted off the side of the truck. Burga and Cross struggled to pick themselves up and join the sergeant.

The Gestori he'd tried to mow down came out from behind the truck, coordinating their advance in native shouts. Lankin raised his pistol and fired twice, hitting two Gestori, dropping them in their tracks.

"Where's Lancil?" Cross shouted, dropping another one.

Lankin jerked his head toward the front of the truck and coughed. "Went out the windshield."

"I'm good," Lancil said over the L-comm, though he sounded anything but. "I see Talon and the marines. Thirty meters in on the left."

"Let's go," Burga said, weaving through stacks of crates.

The legionnaire hugged the left wall. Blaster fire flashed and bolts zipped past, erupting in showers of sparks against the rock as those defending the cave closed in on the intruders. Without stopping, Burga shot two Gestori at almost point-blank range.

Lancil joined them as they wove through several more stacks. They kept low, blaster and other small arms fire ricocheting around them. A round caught Cross in the arm, but Lancil managed to grab him before he fell.

"Keep moving!" Lankin shouted, firing. He turned and used one of the crates as a brace to steady his hand. He dropped two more before the pistol's charge pack beeped empty.

"Reloading," Lankin shouted, ducking behind the crate.

Cross dropped to a knee behind the sergeant, sending a barrage of bolts over the top of the crate.

"Grenade!" Burga shouted.

The explosion rocked the ground and the blast knocked Burga off his feet, sending him crashing into the cave wall.

***

Talon pushed himself off his chest, looking where the grenade had gone off. The explosion had thrown a leej into the cave wall and two more had appeared to help him. A fourth, armed only with a pistol, covered them.

In the darkness, and without his bucket's vision aids, he couldn't tell who they were. But it didn't matter. He got to his knees, forcing himself to ignore the pounding in his skull and the queasiness in his stomach. It was getting worse and he was having trouble seeing straight.

A bunch of Gestori ran past, taking cover behind a row of supply crates. Two began setting up a crew-served repeating blaster, unfolding its stand and pulling a connecting cable from a charge case. A third insurgent took a knee and fired his slug thrower at the leejes by the wall.

The pistol-wielding leej took a round. He dropped to a knee, brought his pistol around, and returned fire. Sparks erupted from the crates and stacked equipment as blaster bolts raked past. The Gestori ducked away from the blaster fire, then sprang back up and shot again, hitting the leej in the leg.

If they get that machine gun set up, those guys won't have a chance, Talon thought, forcing himself to his feet despite the wave of nausea washing over him.

The Gestori, Shoulder Plate, slapped the charge connector into the weapon's receiver as Eye Patch locked the weapon into its mount, shouting at his partner to hurry. Shoulder Plate closed the cover, and they began lifting the weapon onto one of the crates.

Talon lunged, almost falling as he stumbled across the damp stone floor, roaring as he threw himself into the insurgents, knocking the machine gun off the crate. Stars danced in his vision as he tackled Shoulder Plate to the ground. He could barely see, but he pressed the attack regardless, slamming his fists into the back of the alien's head.

Eye Patch rolled away, got to a knee and lunged forward, knocking Talon off Shoulder Plate. Talon grunted as his back slapped against the stone floor. Eye Patch came on, pulling a knife from a scabbard on his belt. Talon swung a foot up, hitting the Gestori's hand and knocking the blade free.

Beem appeared at the corner of Talon's vision and charged into Eye Patch. The two toppled over the supply crates.

Shoulder Plate roared, coming back for more. Talon's eyes found the knife Eye Patch had dropped. The leej rolled away from a foot stomp that would've crushed his skull and wrapped his fingers around the hilt.

Shoulder Plate was reaching for him. Talon reversed his roll and brought the knife down hard. The blade bit into the alien's forearm, slicing through to the other side, spraying blood. The Gestori screamed and recoiled, jerking Talon off the ground. He held tight, letting his momentum carry him on top of the lizard. The Gestori slipped on his own blood and he crashed to the ground.

Talon pulled the blade free and crawled on top of the alien. Cantarus appeared at the Gestori's head, punching. The lizard rolled on his chest, almost throwing Talon off, but the leej plunged the knife into the alien's back.

Shoulder Plate roared and struggled to push himself off the cave floor. "For Gestor!"

***

Lankin clutched his knee and limped. The impact of the projectile against his armor left what must be a bruise all the way through to the bone.

"Almost empty," Cross announced as he swapped out charge packs in his N-4.

"Here," Lankin said, gritting his teeth and pulling his last charge pack from a pouch. "Do you still see Talon?"

"Yeah, he's got his hands full with a—"

An explosion ripped through the cave. The blast wave knocked Lancil to the ground. A cloud of dust rolled over them as bits of rock clinked off his armor.

"What the hell was that?" Lankin shouted, a new laceration trickling blood down his exposed cheek.

Lancil coughed, picking himself up. "Too big for a fragger."

Cross fired a burst from his N-4. "Some kind of bomb?"

"Sergeant Lankin," Kessler said over L-comm. "You guys all right in there?"

"Fine." Lankin grimaced, using a supply crate to pull himself up. To his left, a Gestori was picking himself up next to a marine who lay facedown. Bracing himself on the crate with one hand, Lankin fired three rounds, dropping the alien on the spot.

Blaster fire echoed from somewhere.

"HUD shows one hostile left near the back of the cavern," Lancil called.

"Cross!" Lankin shouted, pointing.

"On it, Sarge."

The legionnaire took off at a jog and a minute later Lankin heard Cross's N-4.

"Clear!" Cross announced over the L-comm.

Lankin straightened and took a long breath. "Where's Talon?"

Smoke curled up from the large crater in the center of the cavern, accompanied by dozens of small fires where what must have been a bomb had gone off. Lankin coughed from the smoke and bits of debris still hanging in the air.

Fragments of equipment, weapons, supply crates, and wooden furniture were strewn across the cave along with the remains of several bodies. He could see a Gestori foot in a pool of blood, an arm draped over a destroyed machine blaster and a torso wearing a legionnaire tactical belt on the edge of the crater.

Lankin's breath caught in his throat when his eyes fell on a human corpse in the crater, almost completely obliterated by the explosion. The face was burned and disfigured. A piece of shrapnel protruded from his cheek, just under his right eye. The blast had ripped apart his chest, leaving a hole big enough to fit a legionnaire helmet through.

He collapsed, his stomach turning as a knot of agony, both physical and mental, overcame him. He doubled over, retching.

Cross appeared beside him, putting a hand on Lankin's shoulder.

"Kelhorned lizard blew himself up just to kill one of us?"

Lankin licked flecks of spittle from his lips and pushed himself to his feet. He stared at Talon's body, mind reeling. Rage swelled inside him even as a crushing anguish filled him. "I'm sorry."

The rest of his team filed in around them, at the edge of the crater.

"Outside perimeter secure, Sarge," Kessler said. "Command's asking for an update, sir."

Lankin nodded, taking a long, deep breath. He saw the machine blaster lying on its side and replayed what had happened in his mind. *He saved us.*

He opened his mouth to say something but closed it again when nothing came. There wasn't anything to say. His friend had paid the ultimate price. Sacrificed himself to save all of them. How do you thank someone for that?

After several quiet moments, Lankin said, "Advise Command. Mission accomplished."

Let Garo know his friendship meant the
galaxy to me.

28

"Do you need anything else?" the nurse asked, picking Lankin's dinner tray off the table next to his bed.

"No, thanks. I appreciate it."

"I'll be here 'til morning. Just give me a ring if you need something, okay?"

Lankin nodded. "Thanks."

The nurse pulled the glass partition shut behind her, leaving him alone in his room. He laid his head back on the pillow, then turned to admire the setting sun outside.

It'd been three days since Republic Task Force 37 had relieved *Vendetta* on Gestor, allowing the cruiser to return with her battered legionnaires for treatment and resupply. Seven companies of Republic army soldiers had landed in force and quickly secured the city, declaring martial law and imposing strict limitations on travel through Gangeers and the mining complex.

A brief investigation led to the arrest of sixty-three more Gestori insurgent fighters and sympathizers, thanks in large part to the intel cache found beneath the clinic. All of those captured were already en route to a Court of Reason for trial and possibly execution. The House of

Reason was speaking harshly about the need for a swift and unambiguous response to the situation to show other allied worlds that treason within the Republic would not be tolerated.

That didn't bode well for leniency, no matter what Lankin might have promised Pendisa.

He'd watched the marines escort the doctor and the rest of the town's leadership across *Vendetta*'s flight deck to the holding pens set up to house the insurgents for the trip back. He still couldn't figure out why she'd done so much to help him, while at the same time planning the operation that would kill so many of his friends.

One of those moral compromises people make just to get through life.

The glass partition slid open, bringing Lankin out of his thoughts.

"You look like sket," Captain Kato said, smiling. Instead of his legionnaire armor, the man wore a well-worn, black leather jacket, tan cargo pants, and shirt.

Lankin laughed, nodding. "What is this? Bring your civilian to work day?"

"Mandatory leave," Kato explained. "Major Wyeire ordered the company to take a few days to recuperate before starting the rest of the debrief. You ask me, he just wants most of us away when he files the after-action report. Good news is that he and Duval are willing to let things against you drop, provided that no one makes a scene about what went down. How you holding up?"

"I'm okay," Lankin lied. "Room service here beats anything else the Republic has to offer."

"Yeah, well, don't get used to it. Soon enough they'll remember you're just a lowly leej and send you back to general like everyone else."

"Until then, I'm taking all the advantage I can."

"You mind?" Kato asked, nodding to the foot of the bed.

"Go for it."

The captain pulled the sheet back, cocking his head to admire the work.

"Before too long I'll be more machine than man," Lankin said, wiggling his mechanical toes. The movement was slightly jerky, something the doctors assured him would improve over time.

Kato shook his head. "Half-man, half-bot, huh?"

"Pretty much. Doc said I was lucky the bullet missed the armor seam. Packed enough of a punch to destroy the tendons and bones but left everything else. They were actually trying to convince me to take a medical yesterday, can you believe that?"

"That's surprising."

"You're telling me. I told them where they could put their medical. I've got another week in here, then some physical therapy, then I'll be back on line."

Captain Kato smiled, but Lankin knew the truth. He was done being a legionnaire.

"Take your time," Kato said, gently clapping his hands.

"Heard anything about why the Gestori were stealing from themselves?"

"Best guess is they were trying to disrupt the operation enough that the House of Reason would deem it too dangerous and unprofitable and give up on control of the ore."

"They don't know the House very well, do they?"

"Better than you might think. A few delegates had already delivered speeches on the faults of the Legion—and its 'oversized budget'—before things were finally brought to heel."

Lankin turned his head on the pillow, looking at a holopainting from an artist he recognized but whose name he couldn't recall. "Nice."

"Not all bad. We managed to pull some interesting intel out of that safe house you found under the doctor's office, though. They'd been working with a group of Mid-Core Rebels to smuggle the ore off-world in exchange for arms and supplies. All the estimates we've seen so far indicate they managed to smuggle off upwards of several billion credits worth before we arrived."

"That's a lot of money."

Kato nodded. "Hell, you could practically buy your own destroyer for that."

"Were they able to track down that Scarpia place?"

"Apparently, Scarpia is a person, not a place. I tried to look him up, but his file is restricted, ultra-high classification. Not even my buddy in Dark Ops could tell me anything about it."

"Go figure."

Kato tapped a finger on Lankin's mechanical foot. "You know, they're recommending you for the Order of the Centurion. Talon too. The Legion, I mean. House of Reason doesn't want any part of this show. Too many questions."

A lump formed at the back of Lankin's throat. "I heard. Think we'll get the full treatment on Utopion?"

"Probably not."

Lankin nodded. "Good. If we could've gone in full strength, I wouldn't have these, and Chase and a lot of other good men would still be here. It should've been me back in that cave. I should've saved him. Instead, I got him killed."

"Those kelhorned lizards killed Chase. Not you or anyone else. They did. Don't ever think otherwise. He fought bravely and his leadership saved lives right up to his last seconds, as did yours. It might be just a medal, but it does mean something to the people who really matter. True legionnaires know what it means to earn it, what it means to wear it. Sergeant Talon was a hero and no one can take that away from him."

Lankin turned his face and stared out the window. "He deserved better."

"They all did. Here."

Kato tossed a small blue case onto Lankin's chest. Lankin opened it and chuckled. "That was quick."

"Ha. Not what you think. Open it."

Lankin flipped open the lid. A small silver pin of a round targeting reticle centered on a horizontal N-18 rifle glinted from its velvet pad.

"General Davis instructed me to inform you that you are now an accredited sniper. The official paperwork will be completed in a few weeks, but the general wanted you to have that ASAP. He sends his compliments."

"I almost forgot about that," Lankin said, pulling the pin signifying a sniper's first kill from the box and turning it over in his fingers. "Doesn't seem like such a big thing after everything else that happened."

"It was a bad situation all around. But everyone stepped up to the challenge and did their duty."

Lankin clenched a fist around the pin. "Some more than others."

Kato nodded. "Services are in four days. I tried to push them back, to give your injuries more time to heal, but..."

"I'll be there."

"You need to heal, Sergeant. I have a feeling things aren't going to be slowing down anytime soon and I'm going to need my team leader back. Word is, they're already sending us replacements, most fresh from boot."

"Captain, unless you give me a direct order not to attend the funeral, I'm going. If I have to crawl on my hands and knees, I'm going."

Kato smiled, then nodded. "I knew you would say that."

"Thank you, sir."

"I'm going to insist, however, that you take leave after. Command's already approved it."

"And then I'll join back up with Stryker?"

The captain's smile faded. "Garo..."

Lankin gave a resigned sigh. "I know. Just... hoping, ya know?"

Captain Kato nodded. "It's a shame but there's truly nothing I can do about it. This isn't a House of Reason or point issue, this has been Legion practice since the Savage Wars."

"I know." Lankin looked away. "What's next for everybody else?"

"Rumor is the House of Reason is stepping up the Legion's foreign affairs operations, which I would call a fancy way of saying social engineering backwater worlds at galaxy's edge to make sure they're falling in line with the official party line."

"Since when did we become politicians?"

Kato laughed. "We've always been in politics, Sergeant. Only now we're doing it with sleight of hand and crooked smiles instead of blaster rifles and tanks. Unless I miss my guess, the Legion is getting ready to go through some major changes over the next few years, and most of them we're not going to like."

Lankin laughed. "Maybe the cybernetic decommission isn't so bad."

"Nice try, but I don't believe that for a minute, Garo. But to that end, once the bureaucrats and brass start forgetting who and what we are, the only thing we're going to have is ourselves. So what I'm saying is, don't let your aim get rusty, wherever you wind up."

"Roger that, sir. I'll be ready."

I love both of you and will miss you dearly.
Your Son,
Chase

Lankin didn't know what was bothering him more, the throbbing in his leg, or the incessant rambling of Lieutenant Colonel Wyeire. The fact that Stryker Company's commander had received a promotion only days after returning from Gestor didn't help either. It seemed the House of Reason and Senate couldn't move points up the command chain fast enough.

"...and had it not been for all the courageous and self-less acts of heroism exhibited by these legionnaires, the Gestori mission would not have been won. Victory came at a high price, and these men will never be forgotten. They showed true loyalty to their fellow legionnaires and true dedication and commitment to the Republic."

The hundreds of officers, politicians, and family members arrayed in front of the stage clapped when Wyeire finished. Lankin had to resist the urge to shake his head at the audacity of these people. Didn't they realize they were cheering the deaths of his friends, his brothers, his family? Looking out over their faces, Lankin felt an overwhelming disgust for those assembled.

After the clapping died down, the lieutenant colonel continued, "The heroic actions taken by every single member of Stryker Company stand as a testament to the Legion's continued strength and resolve. As a unit they performed to the highest standards of excellence and all contributed to the success of the mission.

"In keeping with the best traditions of the Legion, the names of the fallen have been recorded at the Legionnaire Memorial on Utopion and have been awarded the Distinguished Service Cross for their extraordinary heroism in the face of the enemy.

"Staff Sergeant Chase Talon, who sacrificed himself to save the lives of his brothers, will be receiving the Legion's highest commendation, the Order of the Centurion, and will be honored at the Hall of Honor at the Legionnaire Training Grounds."

The lieutenant colonel had to pause again to let the clapping die down.

"And now we come to our final presentation. Sergeant Garo Lankin, step forward, please."

Lankin stood, gritting his teeth at the soreness in his leg. The doctors assured him the discomfort was simply phantom pain, but it sure as hell felt real to him. He stepped up to the marked spot on the stage next to the podium and came to attention.

Captain Kato appeared at Lankin's side as the lieutenant colonel said, "Attention to orders."

The assembled military members, Legion or otherwise, stood in unison, their movements echoing across the expansive chamber.

"For conspicuous gallantry and intrepidity, at the risk of his life, above and beyond the call of duty while serving with Stryker Company, Alpha Team, 71st Legion, on Gestori Prime. Sergeant Lankin, while on an overwatch position, protected members of his unit by killing an armed insurgent attempting to smuggle high-powered weapons into the Area of Operation. Despite being injured, Sergeant Lankin took the initiative and charged into the fight as Sergeant Talon's team came under attack while on escort. He received several minor injuries during the beginning stages of the battle, and after a marine was killed, Sergeant Lankin took his position in the turret and pressed the attack, breaking through enemy lines to rescue several Republic marines and Gestori civilians.

"Moreover, he put himself in harm's way to rescue fellow members of his unit who had been pinned down and were taking heavy fire from the enemy. When the medical convoy he was with came under fire from Gestori insurgent forces, Sergeant Lankin was wounded, taking a bullet to his left arm, and despite that injury, he pressed the attack and fought off the insurgents, capturing one high value target. These actions were critical in locating the enemy stronghold where they'd taken several hostages during that same raid, including Sergeant Talon. Once again, Sergeant Lankin disregarded his own injuries and led an attack on that stronghold, dispatching many enemy combatants and destroying their ability to continue operations.

"Sergeant Lankin's daring initiative and bold fighting spirit through the battle significantly disrupted the enemy and inspired the members of his unit to fight on. His unwavering courage and steadfast devotion to his legionnaire and marine comrades in the face of almost certain death reflected great credit upon himself and upheld the highest traditions of the Legion and the Republic. Captain Kato."

Lankin turned to face the captain and saluted. Kato returned the salute.

Speaking to Lankin, though his voice was amplified for the benefit of those gathered, Kato said, "The Order of the Centurion is the highest award that can be bestowed upon an individual serving in, or with, the Legion. When such an individual displays exceptional valor in action against an enemy force, and uncommon loyalty and devotion to the Legion and its legionnaires, refusing to abandon post, mission, or brothers, even unto death, the Legion duly recognizes such courage with this award."

The captain placed the medallion over Lankin's head and saluted again.

"Well done, Sergeant."

"Thank you, sir."

The audience clapped and cheered as Lankin returned the captain's salute. As the commotion died down, Wyeire brought the ceremony to a close and dismissed them.

Kato smiled at Lankin, extending his hand. "Now it's time for that leave, eh?"

"No," Lankin said. "There's one more thing I need to do."

He found who he was looking for at the end of the front row. He took off his peaked hat and tucked it under one arm. "Mister and Mrs. Talon?"

The older couple turned, their eyes red and faces streaked with tears. Talon's father nodded and extended a hand. "Sergeant Lankin. Congratulations on your award. Chase always had good things to say about you in his letters. Thank you for your service, son."

"Of course, sir. I'm very sorry for your loss. Chase was a great friend and an even better soldier. He won't be forgotten."

Talon's mother sniffed, wiping away fresh tears. "Were you with him... at the end?"

Lankin hesitated. "Yes. I was."

"Did... did it..."

He swallowed. "He died bravely, ma'am. It was fast. There was no pain."

She broke into sobs and pressed her face into her husband's chest. He kissed the top of her head and smiled at Lankin. "Thank you, son."

"I have something for you, sir." Lankin produced the chip Talon had given him and held it out. "Chase wanted you to have this."

Talon's father accepted the chip with quivering fingers. "What is it?"

"A letter, sir," Lankin said. "His last."

THE END

Dear Mom and Dad,

If you're reading this, I'm not coming home. I'm sorry about that. I love you very much and I miss you already.

I want you to know that it isn't anyone's fault. We all fought hard, I guess it was just my time to go. When Oba calls you home, you don't get to ignore him. If you get nothing else from this letter, know this: I died for a reason. I died fighting alongside my brothers and I wouldn't have wanted it any other way. You may not want to believe that now, but I hope someday you will.

The Legion is a calling and the day I signed up, I gave my life to that calling.

I want you to know just how important both of you are to me. I could not ask for a more caring set of parents. Take heart in the knowledge that you raised a smart, caring, and courageous young man, and everything I am today, I am because of you two.

Although it might seem like my life was cut short, I believe I have lived a life that most can only dream of.

Dad, my friend, my teacher, my idol. You taught me to be brave. You taught me to not ever take sket from anyone. I remember what you told me when I signed up: you'll come home a hero, or you'll come home in a box.

Guess I figured the hero part was pretty much locked up.

I only hope that my actions in battle reflect the values you raised me to hold dear. I never gave up, not once.

Mom, I don't even know where to start. You dedicated your entire life to us boys and never once complained about your dishes being broken, or mud in the house, or how messy we left our rooms. Your love made me feel like there were no other children in the world and that I was your entire life's mission. Thank you for loving me so much. You raised me to stand up for myself. To protect those who couldn't protect themselves.

There are some bad people in the galaxy, and sometimes they need to be taught a lesson. The Legion teaches that lesson well.

I might have finally met my match, but I don't want you to be sad. I stood with my brothers against evil and fought for those who couldn't.

I only hope that I made you proud.

Let Garo know that his friendship meant the galaxy to me. I love both of you and will miss you dearly.

Your Son,
Chase

JOIN THE LEGION

You can find art, t-shirts, signed books and other merchandise on our website.

We also have a fantastic Facebook group called the Galaxy's Edge Fan Club that was created for readers and listeners of *Galaxy's Edge* to get together and share their lives, discuss the series, and have an avenue to talk directly with Jason Anspach and Nick Cole. Please check it out and say hello once you get there!

For updates about new releases, exclusive promotions, and sales, visit inthelegion.com and sign up for our VIP mailing list. Grab a spot in the nearest combat sled and get over there to receive your free copy of "Tin Man," a Galaxy's Edge short story available only to mailing list subscribers.

INTHELEGION.COM

GALAXYS EDGE
TIN MAN

ANSPACH   COLE

GET A FREE, EXCLUSIVE SHORT STORY

THE GALAXY
IS A DUMPSTER
FIRE...

HONOR ROLL

We would like to give our most sincere thanks and recognition to those who supported the creation of *Stryker's War* by subscribing as a Galaxy's Edge Insider at GalacticOutlaws.com

Guido Abreu
Elias Aguilar
Bill Allen
Tony Alvarez
Galen Anderson
Robert Anspach
Jonathan Auerbach
Fritz Ausman
Sean Averill
Marvin Bailey
Matthew Ballard
John Barber
Russell Barker
Logan Barker
John Baudoin
Steven Beaulieu
Randall Beem
Matt Beers
John Bell
Daniel Bendele
Trevor Blasius
WJ Blood
Rodney Bonner
Thomas Seth Bouchard
Alex Bowling
Ernest Brant

Geoff Brisco
Aaron Brooks
Marion Buehring
Daniel Cadwell
Van Cammack
Zachary Cantwell
Steven Carrizales
Brian Cave
Shawn Cavitt
Kris (Joryl) Chambers
Cole Chapman
David Chor
Tyrone Chow
Jonathan Clews
Beau Clifton
Alex Collins-Gauweiler
Garrett Comerford
Steve Condrey
Michael Conn
James Connolly
James Conyers
Jonathan Copley
Robert Cosler
Andrew Craig
Adam Craig
Phil Culpepper

Ben Curcio
Thomas Cutler
Alister Davidson
Peter Davies
Nathan Davis
Ivy Davis
Ron Deage
Tod Delaricheliere
Ryan Denniston
Aaron Dewitt
Christopher DiNote
Matthew Dippel
Ellis Dobbins
Cami Dutton
Virgil Dwyer
William Ely
Stephane Escrig
Steve Forrester
Skyla Forster
Timothy Foster
Mark Franceschini
Richard Gallo
Christopher Gallo
Kyle Gannon
Michael Gardner
Nick Gerlach
John Giorgis
Justin Godfrey
Luis Gomez
Thomas Graham
Gerald Granada
Don Grantham
Gordon Green
Tim Green
Shawn Greene
Jose Enrique Guzman

Erik Hansen
Greg Hanson
Jason Harris
Jordan Harris
Adam Hartswick
Ronald Haulman
Joshua Hayes
Adam Hazen
Jason Henderson
Jason Henderson
Kyle Hetzer
Aaron Holden
Tyson Hopkins
Joshua Hopkins
Christopher Hopper
Curtis Horton
Ian House
Ken Houseal
Nathan Housley
Jeff Howard
Mike Hull
Bradley Huntoon
Wendy Jacobson
Paul Jarman
James Jeffers
Tedman Jess
James Johnson
Randolph Johnson
Tyler Jones
John Josendale
Wyatt Justice
Ron Karroll
Cody Keaton
Noah Kelly
Caleb Kenner
Daniel Kimm

Zachary Kinsman
Matthew Kinstle
Rhet Klaahsen
Jesse Klein
Travis Knight
Evan Kowalski
Byl Kravetz
Clay Lambert
Grant Lambert
Jeremy Lambert
Brian Lambert
Lacy Laughlin
Dave Lawrence
Alexander Le
Paul Lizer
Richard Long
Oliver Longchamps
Sean Lopez
Brooke Lyons
John M
Richard Maier
Brian Mansur
Robet Marchi
Deven Marincovich
Cory Marko
Pawel Martin
Lucas Martin
Trevor Martin
Tao Mason
Mark Maurice
Simon Mayeski
Kyle McCarley
Quinn McCusker
Matthew McDaniel
Alan McDonald
Hans McIlveen

Rachel McIntosh
Joshua McMaster
Christopher Menkhaus
Jim Mern
Pete Micale
Mike Mieszcak
Brandon Mikula
Ted Milker
Mitchell Moore
William Morris
Alex Morstadt
Nicholas Mukanos
Vinesh Narayan
Andrew Niesent
Greg Nugent
Christina Nymeyer
Colin O'neill
Ryan O'neill
James Owens
David Parker
Eric Pastorek
Carl Patrick
Trevor Pattillo
Dupres Pina
Pete Plum
Paul Polanski
Matthew Pommerening
Jeremiah Popp
Chancey Porter
Brian Potts
Chris Pourteau
Joshua Purvis
Nick Quinn
Eric Ritenour
Walt Robillard
Daniel Robitaille

Joyce Roth
Andrew Sebastian Sanchez
David Sanford
Jaysn Schaener
Landon Schaule
Shayne Schettler
Brian Schmidt
Andrew Schmidt
Alex Schwarz
William Schweisthal
Aaron Seaman
Phillip Seek
Christopher Shaw
Ryan Shaw
Brett Shilton
Vernetta Shipley
Glenn Shotton
Joshua Sipin
Scott Sloan
Daniel Smith
Tyler Smith
Michael Smith
Sharroll Smith
John Spears
Peter Spitzer
Dustin Sprick
Graham Stanton
Maggie Stewart-Grant
John Stockley
William Strickler
Shayla Striffler
Kevin Summers
Ernest Sumner
Shayne Sweetland
Travis TadeWaldt
Daniel Tanner

Lawrence Tate
Tim Taylor
Mark Teets
Steven Thompson
William Joseph Thorpe
Beverly Tierney
Matthew Titus
Jameson Trauger
Scott Tucker
Eric Turnbull
Brandon Turton
John Tuttle
Jalen Underwood
Paul Van Dop
Paden VanBuskirk
Paul Volcy
Anthony Wagnon
Scott Wakeman
Christopher Walker
David Wall
Scot Washam
James Wells
Kiley Wetmore
Ben Wheeler
Theron Whittle
Scott Winters
Gary Woodard
Brandt Zeeh
Nathan Zoss

DEAR READER

Amazon won't automatically tell you when the next Order of the Centurion Stand-alone (or Savage Wars, or Wraith Trilogy, or Galaxy's Edge Season 02) releases, but there are several ways you can stay informed.

1. Enlist in our fan-run Facebook group, the Galaxy's Edge Fan Club, and say hello. It's a great place to hang out with other KTF-lovin' legionnaires who like to talk about sci-fi and are up for a good laugh.
2. Follow us directly on Amazon. This one is easy. Just go to the store page for this book on Amazon and click the "follow" button beneath our pictures. That will prompt Amazon to email you automatically whenever we release a new title.
3. Join the Galaxy's Edge Newsletter (inthelegion.com). You'll get emails directly from us—along with the short story "Tin Man," available only to newsletter subscribers.

Doing just one of these (although doing all three is your best bet!) will ensure you find out when the next Galaxy's Edge book releases. Please take a moment to do one of these so you can find yourself on patrol with the next group of brave legionnaires and experience with them their next gritty firefight!

ORDER OF THE CENTURION CONTINUES...

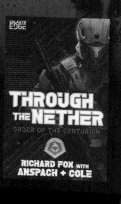

Josh Hayes grew up a military brat, affording him the opportunity to meet several different types of people, in multiple states and foreign countries. After graduating high school, he joined the United States Air Force and served for six years, before leaving military life to work in law enforcement. His experiences in both his military life and police life have given him a unique glimpse into the lives of people around him and it shows through in the characters he creates.

Jason Anspach is a best selling author living in Tacoma, Washington with his wife and their own legionnaire squad of seven (not a typo) children. In addition to science fiction, Jason is the author of the hit comedy-paranormal-historical-detective series, *'til Death*. Jason loves his family as well as hiking and camping throughout the beautiful Pacific Northwest. And Star Wars. He named as many of his kids after Obi Wan as possible, and knows that Han shot first.

Nick Cole is a Dragon Award winning author best known for *The Old Man and the Wasteland, CTRL ALT Revolt!*, and the Wyrd Saga. After serving in the United States Army, Nick moved to Hollywood to pursue a career in acting and writing. (Mostly) retired from the stage and screen, he resides with his wife, a professional opera singer, in Los Angeles, California.

Printed in Great Britain
by Amazon